How To Find Your Way Home

Also by Katy Regan

One Thing Led to Another
The One Before the One
How We Met
The Story of You
Little Big Love

KATY REGAN

How To Find Your Way Home

MANTLE

First published 2022 by Mantle
an imprint of Pan Macmillan
The Smithson, 6 Briset Street, London EC1M 5NR
EU representative: Macmillan Publishers Ireland Ltd, 1st Floor,
The Liffey Trust Centre, 117–126 Sheriff Street Upper,
Dublin 1, D01 YC43
Associated companies throughout the world
www.panmacmillan.com

ISBN 978-1-5290-2034-2

1 3 5 7 9 8 6 4 2

A CIP catalogue record for this book is available from the British Library.

Typeset by Palimpsest Book Production Limited, Falkirk, Stirlingshire
Printed and bound by CPI Group (UK) Ltd, Croydon, CR0 4YY

To Lizzy Kremer, with love and thanks

There's me, standing at the open bathroom window again, the ladder up against it, so close I can touch it. A figure is halfway up it, climbing steadily higher. There's a storm brewing. I can feel the wind picking up, the air growing cooler; I can sense it rolling in from the estuary, across the marsh edgelands before me, which lie under a blanket of leaden sky, the dark clouds contrasting with the grass, making it seem a brighter green, like a football pitch under floodlights. And now the swifts . . . I can hear their screams from far away, but getting nearer. They are just black dots at first, but then their scythe-shaped wings come into focus, and soon they're so close I can make out their individual feathers. They come thick and fast, a black cloud, flying past the ladder and into the bathroom, as if fleeing from the storm. The wind is making the ladder shudder, the glass of the open window shake. 'Stop!' scream the swifts. 'You're going to kill him.' Then the ladder falls backwards, in slow motion. An almighty thud as something hits the ground. The figure at the bottom now, blood seeping from a wound I can't see. I watch it, spilling outwards, spreading over the marshes, turning the hay russet like the fur of a wounded animal, creeping like a trickling brook, out towards the sea.

'Stork'

Canvey Island, Essex, 1987

Whoosh! Stephen woke to the sound of his bedroom curtains being pulled open.

'Well, Stevie, you've got a new sister,' Dad said. 'Emily Adele Nelson – born three hours ago. She's absolutely perfect.'

Stephen pulled himself up on his pillows, his legs jiggling already, his belly feeling as if something was trying to get out, he was so excited.

Outside, the sky was gold and pink over Canvey Marshes, and there was a beam of sun across his duvet cover. The birds were singing too, but extra loud, as if it was a special hello to the baby: *Welcome to your first day in the world!*

Four days later, Stephen stood at the front room window with Grandma Paradiso, waiting for Mum and his new baby sister to arrive back from hospital.

'When will they be here, Grandma?'

'Any time now, Stephen, just be patient. Jiggling your legs like that won't make her come any faster.'

While they waited, Grandma explained how a stork had brought his new sister; how babies' souls about to be born lay in the marshes where storks made their nests, and waited patiently until a stork came, picked them up and delivered them to their new family.

Stephen wondered if the stork would still be there now, with Mummy and Emily – that's if they ever arrived.

Less than ten minutes later an ambulance came trundling around the corner. Not with a blue light or a nee-naw, but calmly like an ice cream van. It had to go slow because it was carrying precious treasure. Grandma Paradiso came with Stephen outside. There was a man in a green uniform opening the back doors of the ambulance. He asked Stephen if he'd like to come and look inside and Stephen looked up at his grandma, who smiled and said, 'It's all right, love,' and gave him a gentle push. 'Off you go.'

The inside of the ambulance looked how he imagined a spaceship might look, with tubes and pumps and switches everywhere. There was a bed on wheels with a green blanket over it that looked itchy and, at the back, a big blue chair, where Mummy was sitting, holding the baby, beaming. She was wearing no lipstick, her hair was unbrushed and Stephen had never seen her look happier or more beautiful.

'Hello, sweetheart,' she said, quietly. 'Come and meet your new sister.'

The baby was wrapped up like a caterpillar cocoon, and she was crying, like a kitten. Daddy helped Mummy and the baby out of the ambulance and inside. Mummy sat down on the couch, holding Emily; Stephen sat beside them. He couldn't stop looking at this precious present the stork had brought. Grandma Paradiso was saying, 'Aah, aw,' and Daddy was going back and forth, bringing cups of tea, saying 'Hee-hee!' to himself and rubbing his hands together. He put down steaming cups for Mummy and Grandma, then all of a sudden grabbed Stephen and hugged him so tight, it was hard to breathe, but Stephen didn't care; he'd never felt happiness like it.

'Stephen, do you want to hold her?' he said and Stephen wanted to, badly, but looked at Mummy who said, 'I'm not sure that's a good idea, sweetheart. Maybe in a few days when she's a bit bigger.' So, Stephen had to make do with just stroking her head instead, which wasn't hard like his, but squishy on top like the blow-up mattress he slept on at Grandma and Grandad Paradiso's house, which was called 'El Paradiso', hence the name he'd assigned to his maternal grandparents.

Grandma Paradiso slapped her knees. 'Oh, Alicia, come on. It's not every day he gets to meet his little sister, is it? As long as he's careful. Maybe with cushions on the couch?'

And so, Daddy helped him get propped up on the cushions. He had to sit really straight and still, with his back against the couch.

'Oh Stephen, look at that, the moment of truth!' said Grandma. Then Mummy passed the baby to him, as carefully as if she were Jesus. She was much lighter than he expected – as light as putting a teddy on his knee – and she made funny, squirmy faces, and when she yawned, the bright red inside of her mouth reminded him of a picture in one of his nature books that he loved so much, of a baby thrush, waiting to be fed. All these things together made him giggle with delight and look up to his mother who drew in a breath. 'Be careful, Stevie, she's not a doll, you know. If you drop her . . .'

'I won't drop her,' he said, never more certain of anything in his life. He was the big brother now, after all, and it was his job to love and protect his little sister, to keep her safe forever.

Chapter One

Emily

London, March 2018

If you'd looked through the window that Saturday evening in early March, what would you have seen? A warmly lit open-plan space for living and dining. In the foreground, a soft, vintage leather sofa, a sixties floor lamp emanating a cosy orange glow. Further back, a dining table, tastefully laid with Moroccan-inspired eclectic crockery and flickering with tea lights.

Finally, at the very back, the kitchen area; bijou but chic with its metro tiles and aluminium pendant lights over the kitchen island and hob, on which there is a Le Creuset dish bubbling and, beside it, a man: tall, boyishly chiselled and bequiffed, the sleeves of his navy-blue shirt rolled up to reveal toned forearms, stoning fresh lychees, a cocktail shaker at the ready.

Does he live alone? you might wonder. Perhaps too many feminine touches for this to be a bachelor pad. And you'd be right. Although you wouldn't have seen me, owner and sole official inhabitant of this two-bedroomed, two-storey maisonette, chief orchestrator of this picture of aspirational living – thirty-something urbanites preparing to entertain. That's because I am upstairs, up the slatted staircase at the end of the short entrance hall, still in a towel after my shower, hair in a turban, sitting on my bed in the light of my laptop. I've got Facebook open, my heart up somewhere near my throat, where it seems to live permanently these days, as I type the name into the search box:

Stephen Nelson

I haven't done this for a while, but it's my birthday next week, another year further from that June day when he was taken from me. Almost twenty years ago now. And the gravitational pull towards the search for him becomes inescapable around this time. I always step it up.

I click on 'show all' and press my palms together, fingertips to my lips in an unconscious praying action. Facebook reveals sixty-one of them. I scroll down to where I left off yesterday: ten Stephen Nelsons down, fifty-one to go. Why couldn't he have been called Xavier or, I dunno, Piers? This would all have been so much easier.

Stephen Nelson number eleven is a Man United supporter (that's him out, then) and appears to have met

Barry Manilow several times (that's *definitely* him out). Number twelve went to Preston Poly but has somehow found himself living in Kazakhstan – moving on. Number thirteen, though? 'Artist', it says, avatar of an eagle – my stomach seems to float. I click on it, my pulse drumming, but this Stephen Nelson must be seventy if he's a day, and so I close my laptop with a defeated sigh just as my boyfriend James – the handsome lychee peeler with the nice forearms, I'm sure you guessed that – pops his head around the bedroom door, face full of affection and, I know it, lust. We've only been together five months and are very much still in *that* stage. The stage I don't ever seem able to get beyond, before things fizzle out, for reasons that currently baffle me.

'Hi,' I smile.

'Hi,' he says. 'I brought you a little livener.' And he puts a martini, complete with lychee pinned to the glass rim, on the bedside table. I thank him. He tips his head to the side and smiles at me – he has very sexy dimples. Then he frowns. 'You on Facebook again?' he says. 'Em, you know it makes you feel crap and anyway, shouldn't you be getting ready, sweetheart? They'll be here in twenty minutes . . . In fact, just enough time . . .'

And he hops onto the bed.

'Just enough?' I tease. 'You'll be lucky to last half that.'

'Right!' And with that he burrows and growls into my

neck, pretending to eat it as I squeal with laughter, pulling my towel tighter. 'Get off! I'm joking! We do not have enough time!'

So, he flounces off in a mock-huff and the smile drops from my face as I put my laptop on the floor, my chest tight because I know that's it until tomorrow now, and I set about getting ready quickly. I leave my hair to dry naturally wavy, put on mascara, lipstick and the outfit I chose a week ago: a grey-marl pleated skirt and hot-orange scoop-back T-shirt with the slogan 'Happy Days' across the middle. Silver hoops. Bare feet. It's an ensemble I hope hits just the right note on the effort scale, that says I'm totally at ease in my own skin, my own home.

Ten seconds later, the doorbell rings and I go downstairs to find James is already greeting Dan and Vanessa, who are ebullient, excited to have been invited for dinner at their best friend's new girlfriend's flat at last, laden with gifts of orchids and botanical gins. This will be the third time we've met and also marks one of the last evenings I remember of my old life. The life I had constructed around me like the tough, prickled outer shell of a horse chestnut, before it was cracked open and the truth of my life was laid bare, as frighteningly untouched and uncharted as that shiny conker hidden inside.

*

'Hey, big fella!' I can hear the man-slap Dan gives James from the kitchen, where Vanessa and I are doing the female greeting equivalent, which is complimenting each other on our outfits. (I am dismayed to see she is as groomed as Meghan Markle, whereas my hair's still damp and I haven't even got shoes on.) I'm glad of that livener martini and thankful to get stuck into more, to get everyone relaxed and having fun. *You never know*, I think, wryly, *maybe even you* . . . I bring out the canapes I've made.

'Oh my God.' Vanessa reaches enthusiastically for a smoked salmon blini with her impeccably manicured hand. 'You got a takeaway curry when you came to ours. I feel awful! You've gone to so much effort.'

'Don't be daft. I have not,' I say, ignoring the look on James's face, and the fact that his eyebrows have shot up somewhere by his hairline. He got up at 2 a.m. this morning to find I was still awake, poring over my cook-books and the weekend food supplements I rip out for inspiration.

'Darling, you do know it's just my mates coming, don't you?' he'd said. 'Not Marco Pierre White.'

Dan is James's best friend from university and works as a property developer. I'm a housing officer in the council's homeless department, so you could say we work on opposite sides of the same coin. James is an architect. That's how we met, at a residents' campaign meeting about an estate that was up for demolition. He seemed as passionate as me about people being kicked out of their homes, funnily enough.

Dan, on the other hand, operates refreshingly shamelessly from the dark side. He's not conventionally attractive, but what he lacks in looks he makes up for in charisma and flamboyant shirts – tonight, a gecko-covered Hawaiian number even though it's still very much winter, and pouring with rain outside. Vanessa, his wife, is the kind of woman so confident in her own skin she doesn't need an Adonis on her arm to make her feel good anyway.

She looks around. 'This flat is gorgeous. You have such good taste.'

'It is a super flat,' adds Dan.

'Oh God,' I say. 'It was dirt cheap and an eyesore when I bought it. I had *no* furniture. Luckily, I love rummaging in charity shops. I'll take any old crap from a skip and upcycle it.'

Vanessa looks perplexed at my total inability to take a compliment. 'Well, it's beautiful,' she says, simply.

'Yeah, she's got great taste, haven't you, babe?' says James. 'Especially in men.'

'I'd say it's questionable at best.' Dan chuckles and I laugh along, simultaneously feeling he's hit a nerve. As I've said, I don't have a great track record in that department – no one seems to stick. *Please God, let this be different*, I think, enjoying the warm feeling the alcohol is giving me, looking over at James. He's certainly handsome and he's kind. Too kind sometimes; it makes me nervous. Makes me feel like I don't deserve it.

'So, our news,' says Dan over dinner, 'is that we're moving to the country!'

'Bloody hell, people,' laughs James. 'Four beds not enough for you?'

'I know, we're just disgusting,' says Vanessa, unapologetically. (That, I realise, is exactly what they are – unapologetic. It's kind of refreshing.) 'But we want more space. I want to try for another baby soon, and, as everyone knows, I want at least one more after that.'

Dan rolls his eyes affectionately. 'Only if I can have my Porsche Cayenne, honey, that was the arrangement!'

'Oh shush – he is joking, by the way,' says Vanessa, slapping him playfully. 'What I'm saying is that we want it to be our forever home . . .' She stops, and pulls an endearingly genuine face of horror. 'Jesus, did I just say that?'

Pavlova demolished and more wine poured, the music is turned up, as well as our voices.

James shouts to Dan, 'So what's the latest *grand projet*, Danny boy?'

And Dan's eyes light up, like he thought nobody would ever ask. 'Well, we've got some beautiful resi schemes down by the wharf in Wapping: two and three-bed luxury apartments. They're selling like hot cakes off plan, most of them to foreigners . . .'

'And what do they start at, those?'

'The luxury ones? Well over a mil, I have to confess,' says Dan and, with a naughty twitch of his lips, 'but damn, they're lush . . .' And he continues to wax lyrical, Vanessa joining in, and I half listen, watching the rain, which has been going on for days now, drumming against the window – when will it stop? I realise I'm mesmerised by these people's brazenness, the ease with which they occupy their privileged place in the world. And I am struck by how I inhabit two opposing worlds: the haves and the have-nots, the social climbers and the socially sunk, and how there really is no justice as to which one you end up in. How the angels end up in hell far too often. Angels like my brother.

'Also, can I just point out' – Dan's voice, getting more exuberant as the night goes on, breaks my train of thought – 'we've got some beautiful affordable ones starting at half what the luxury ones are going for, so, yeah . . .' He rubs his hands together. 'See, I am doing my bit, Em. Houses *are* being built!'

'Hardly *affordable* ones,' I say, licking my spoon.

Dan's not fazed.

'I mean, come on, in what world is half a million pounds *affordable*?' I continue. 'And affordable to whom? How many of these houses are bought by people who then actually live in them?'

James puts an arm around me and pulls me into him. 'Don't get her started, you'll never win,' he says proudly.

'And she is more than entitled to her own opinion,' says Dan.

'Why, thank you,' I say, sarcastic but not offended. I can more than handle the likes of Dan. 'Not that it's an opinion – it's a fact.'

'What can I say?' Dan shrugs. 'Supply and demand. I just sell what the market will pay.'

'Yeah . . .' says James. 'And Emily just mops up the mess you make.'

'Oh, all right!' Dan throws down his napkin in a mock tantrum. 'She is, of course, a much better person than me. Most people are.'

Everyone laughs, including me, but it's as if I can see myself from the outside suddenly, as if I'm standing in the rain, and I can see my laugh is forced, my face rigid; and the more I think about this, the more self-conscious I become, convinced that everyone can tell. A memory is ignited, a kind of déjà vu: me, watching my mother through a window as a child. She's in the midst of one of the dinner parties she was always throwing for the upwardly mobile of Canvey Island. She looks glamorous with her hair up and her diamanté earrings that sparkle in the candlelight. She's laughing, throwing her head back, chatting and gesticulating. Then she stops, even though everybody else continues. She's still smiling with her mouth but it's gone from her eyes, and I think she is wearing the same expression as I am right now; she is wearing a mask.

That's what you'd see, if you'd looked through the window: four thirty-something friends, 'upwardly mobile' themselves, I suppose, having dinner, chatting, having fun on a Saturday night, me in the middle in my orange top that says 'Happy Days' on it. But I'm not happy, not in my soul, and I know already that James and I won't be going the long haul; that he'll somehow slip through my fingers. I can't do life, you see, everything feels wrong; I can't make plans or commit to anything; I can't love or be loved. Not while there's this piece of me missing, this giant hole in my heart.

Chapter Two

Stephen

London, two weeks later

Just DON'T GET WET. It's rule number one. If you get wet, you'll never be able to get warm. Then the bone-ache will set in, the uncontrollable shivers. Man, the shivers. Once you're in the grip of those, you're done for, basically. Once you are that cold, you won't be able to think of anything else, won't be able to keep your wits about you – and if there's one thing you need to survive on the streets, it's your wits.

So that's rule number one: stay out of the rain – and Stephen had broken it. To be fair, it had been impossible not to. London had seen almost two weeks straight of rain – 'the wettest March on record,' said the news-stands. It had gone from light drizzle to biblical downpours and right back through the spectrum again, so that now, at 7.30 a.m., London resembled a concrete bog. It was as if a great, dirty wave had reared up off the Thames, crashed down on the city, then retreated, leaving everything dank and dripping.

Water ran in rivulets down roads and into gutters; dripped off trees and bushes that he and others like him used for shelter; gathered in pools on benches he might ordinarily have lain on. It had even, somehow, driven itself inside Stephen's 'spot', an unused doorway between a McDonald's and a launderette in Camberwell in the south-east of the city. Unless it was warm – in which case he always found some awesome pocket of urban wild in which to sleep unsheltered, his face to the sky – this spot was where Stephen sat with his sketchbook and drew his birds.

It never stopped amazing him, the information you could glean from sitting at street level, in the same place, at the same time, every single day: in his last stint in this spot, Stephen had seen people lose and gain weight, friends and partners. He'd seen people get new jobs, hairstyles, cars and dogs. He could read the faces of those who passed every day like he could read the weather; he knew when they were troubled and when things were looking up. He knew the minutiae of their lives, when they probably hadn't even noticed he existed.

He sat up in his makeshift bedroom. It consisted of bits of cardboard and carpet cut-offs he'd found in a skip (he'd been chuffed with that particular find), a mattress, a sleeping bag and a blow-up travel pillow. His mate Jimmy had given him the travel pillow. Jimmy was a diamond guy; many of them were. There were a few bad apples you steered clear of, those who'd rob your organs if they could, but in general, if there was one thing Stephen had learnt in his fifteen years on and off the streets, it was that the less you had, the more you gave; the more you'd suffered, the more you were attuned to others' suffering. The more resilient. Mind you, this was all beginning to feel like a test of that resilience. Twenty minutes ago, he'd woken aching and damp, knowing he had to act, fast. His travel pillow was soaked, along with everything he owned (apart from his binoculars, which remained around his neck, sacred as a locket): his bedding and mattress; his sketchbook and pencil case; the clothes on his back. Like a reflex, he'd gone straight to the side pocket of his rucksack and unzipped it to find, thank God, that his birding notebook was still there, still dry.

Most importantly, the 'Top Five' list, in its A4 plastic sheet tucked inside, was dry too. As he'd done a thousand times before, he unfolded it, read it.

1. Spot TWO rare birds in twenty-four hours
2. Go on a night birding woodland walk
3. See an owl in flight
4. See a seabird colony
5. Watch the swifts' migration from the Spurn Peninsula

The other consolation was that he'd had the foresight to wrap what clean, dry clothes he had in a plastic bag. His main concern now then, if he was going to achieve anything today, was to get out of these soggy clothes and into dry ones.

He began rolling up his bedding and packing the rucksack. He was so tired, he felt drunk. He wasn't drunk, though, and for that, he was grateful, because while it was always tempting, he'd learnt the hard way that your problems were still there when you sobered up, only with a bad head to contend with too. He was thirty-five years old, and it was hard to know how he'd got here sometimes. Life, especially on the streets, became like one of those papier mâché bowls you used to make at school: comprised of so many layers, all becoming grubbier and more frayed over time, harder and harder to differentiate from each other.

His plan right now, to be presentable for his mission today, was to go to Starbucks, where hopefully the accessible toilet would be free so he'd have space to have a wash and get changed in peace. He rolled a cigarette then stood up, hauled his rucksack on his back, something that was as natural and unconscious to him as blinking, and set off.

It was only a five-minute walk up the high street but it took much longer, since his back was wrecked from sleeping on the damp concrete, and his legs felt like sacks of wet sand. A full bus heaved past, creating a mini tsunami, which drenched the whole of Stephen's lower left leg. The blast of warm air when he finally opened the door to Starbucks, the smell of fresh coffee and pastries, of normal, functioning lives, was such a comfort that it brought a lump to his throat. The place was packed even though it was still early: commuters getting their flat white to take on the tube, yummy mummies with children not yet old enough to be at school. He could feel their eyes on him as he made his way to the back where the toilets were. He could see, but tried not to notice, how they placed their hands protectively on their children's shoulders and ushered them out of his way.

'Sorry, sorry,' he mumbled, edging past with his huge rucksack from which various paraphernalia hung. 'Sorry, can I just . . . ?' He avoided meeting anybody's eyes, knowing that it made people feel uncomfortable. He couldn't help meeting one woman's, though: dark glossy hair in a ponytail; pretty, the image of rude health. He smiled at her, but she looked quickly away again, as though if she were to hold his gaze, smile back at him or, God forbid, talk to him, she might catch something, might feel something she didn't want to feel, might have to do something. And Stephen wanted to say to her, *It's all right, you don't have to do anything, you don't have to give me money* (although money helped, you couldn't deny it), *but just meet my eyes, please? Smile, start some banter about this apocalyptic weather or the size of my ludicrous rucksack, which you'd do if it wasn't me carrying it, I can tell. I can tell you're the type of friendly girl to strike up conversation with strangers – just not strangers like me.*

Victory! The accessible toilet was free, the door wide open, and so he quickly bundled himself and his rucksack inside, locked the door and leant against it, savouring the sweet rapture of being alone in a safe, warm environment, simply having privacy. Then he put the plug in the sink, turned on the hot tap, allowing the room to fill with steam as he peeled off soggy layers: a fleece, a jumper, a long-sleeved top and T-shirt. In the harsh overhead light, the stains on his clothes were all too obvious, and the humidity in the room intensified the smell, so that even though he was alone, he felt hot shame rise from his cheeks to the tips of his ears.

When he was a kid he'd loved his baths; they were his sanctuary. He used to take the latest edition of *Young Ornithologist* – going straight to the back page and 'Peter Trussell's Top Five' to see what was featured in that issue – and lock the door and lie there until his skin was shrivelled and someone inevitably shouted up the stairs at him to get out. This particular stint on the streets had been six weeks – six weeks of winter without a place at a hostel where he'd not be pushed drugs or booze, a temptation he could not afford, and in that time, he'd managed to procure only one set of clean, dry clothes that he rotated, washing the other set at the Salvation Army drop-in centre when he could organise himself. When you were hungry, cold and dead on your feet, it was an ongoing battle to stay on top of that stuff; personal hygiene just didn't rate highly on your list of priorities. That's not to say Stephen didn't try when he got the chance, and now that he had, the hot water on his skin, mottled from the cold, was – oh! It was heaven.

He pumped some soap from the dispenser into his hands, and working up a lather, stood bare-chested as he shaved, then washed. The fragrance of the soap evoked a memory: the blossoming magnolia tree in the back garden of Mum and Dad's Merlin Drive house on Canvey Island; the scent of spring and all the thrilling promise that held for him as a nature-mad kid.

Stephen could see himself now – six years old or thereabouts – standing at the sink in the avocado bathroom, having a wash before bedtime, his baby sister already tucked up in her cot. The bathroom window is open; Stephen can see the magnolia tree, can smell its perfume on the breeze.

In this memory, as in so many, he is transfixed by the birds, the bullfinches and chaffinches, flitting from one branch to another. He is entranced by how free they seem. They appear to want nothing from him and this makes him want to give them everything. He loves their jerky movements and their colours: a magpie is never just black and white, it has tails of sapphire and shots of emerald; a blackbird's eye is rimmed with the colour of egg yolk; and sparrows wear grey hats, that fasten under their chins.

Bending over the sink now, Stephen splashed the last of the suds from his face and chest, then, pulling paper towels from the dispenser, patted himself dry, wincing at the roughness on his weather-worn skin. His face sore but clean at least, he made a start on his bottom half, pulling off the damp trainers, then the socks that were wringing wet and – he couldn't lie – stank like a fish-monger's bin. He took off his tracksuit bottoms, heavy with moisture. Naked now, he dunked wet wipes into hot water and cleaned himself as best he could. He put fresh pants on, and the clean shirt – the only shirt he owned – because he wanted to be smart today. He put on a jumper, and then stood, all six foot two of him, on the toilet, careful not to bang his head, from where he was able to dunk one foot then the other into the sink to wash them. The steaming water on his chilblains was agony, but the trick was to persevere, grit your teeth, because the rewards of clean, dry feet were sweet, especially if you had in your possession, as he did, a pair of clean, dry socks to put on afterwards – truly, the golden ticket.

He was just submerging his right foot, when there was a knock at the door, making him jump. He swore, loudly.

'Excuse me?' More knocking. 'Is that you, Mr Nelson, in there?' Shit, it was Hussein, the manager. Stephen recognised his voice but didn't answer, although what he thought he was going to achieve by not answering, he didn't know. It wasn't as if he could climb through the minuscule window or disappear in a puff of smoke. That was the problem with being homeless: you were invisible most of the time, except when you wanted to be, at which point you seemed to stick out like a fucking great beacon. 'If that's you, Mr Nelson, you need to come out and leave the premises as soon as possible, or else I shall have to call security.' Stephen surveyed the scene inside the toilet: him, still in pants, a pile of dirty clothes on the floor, one foot in a sinkful of filthy water.

He looked at the toilet ceiling as if for divine strength. 'Give me ten seconds, okay? I'll be right with you.'

Five seconds later, there was another series of knocks, louder and more impatient than previously. 'I said I won't be a second. Jesus . . .' He hurriedly pulled on clean jeans, picking up the discarded clothes and shoving them in his rucksack. There was the officious sound of keys jangling, the lock being turned. 'Hey, hang on . . .' Stephen raised his hands, slowly, in disbelief and exasperation, but the door opened and he was met by what felt like a sea of faces, their blank expressions like a wall between him and, well, the rest of society.

Hussein reached his hand out towards him, as if coaxing a wilful child. 'Come,' he beckoned.

'I'm coming. I'm just putting my rucksack on.'

'Out,' ordered Hussein, as if Stephen was now not just a wilful child, but a disobedient dog. 'Now. We've told you before that the toilets are for customers only.'

Stephen finished putting his rucksack on, hung his binoculars around his neck before being ushered out, Hussein's hand on his shoulder, steering him towards the door of the cafe.

'Mummy, what's that man done?' he heard a child say, as he passed.

'I don't know, darling,' answered her mother. 'I think he's just a naughty man.'

Ejected from Starbucks, Stephen stood on the glossy, wet street and took out his tobacco tin. *Naughty*, he thought, with a rueful smile. *A handful, trouble.* These were labels he remembered from his childhood, and yet it was kind of baffling, because he'd never set out to be any of those things.

'Swift'

May 1991

'Milly,' Stephen said to Emily, who had plonked herself cross-legged in the middle of the couch. (That extra E was still too much for his attention span, or so everyone said.) 'Get off, 'cause I'm going to jump and I don't want to land on you.' Milly, four years old with tangled blonde hair and juicy cheeks, dutifully slithered off, turning around to look up at him.

He needed to ace this. To jump from one arm to the next, then over his dad's chair and back again, without any slips, otherwise he'd have failed at the 'Kamikaze couch challenge'.

He jumped.

'Tony!!' Unfortunately, his launch coincided with the moment Mum passed the open lounge door with the hoover. 'He's still using the furniture as a climbing frame. Please take him out, will you? Get him to run off some of that energy, for crying out loud.'

Mum seemed to talk about 'crying out loud' a lot recently.

The trouble was, the kamikaze couch challenge was addictive. Once you started, you had to keep going until you got it right all the way through. Any slipping and you'd have to start again. So, Stephen jumped, but tripped over the belt of the karate kit he was wearing from his lesson earlier and went flying into the standard lamp, which fell onto a side table and knocked over – just his luck – a full glass of Vimto. There was an almighty crash.

'Stephen!!' His mother turned the hoover off. 'For the love of God.' And she marched into the lounge, where there was now a violent Vimto splatter all over the sofa. 'My suite! My new suite. For crying out loud.' And this time, she *did* cry out loud, which Stephen couldn't help but think was a bit of an overreaction. 'Stephen Anthony Nelson, you're like a bull in a china shop. Take him out, Tony, will you?'

Dad walked in. 'How many times do I have to tell you not to jump around on the furniture?' He was still in his butcher's apron, and Stephen could detect the metallic stink of blood. 'Come on, let's get out of here.' As well as a smile playing on his lips. 'Your mother needs some peace. Get your wellies on, grab your binoculars, we'll go to the marshes.'

Stephen's house backed onto the marshes, although wherever you were on Canvey Island, you were never far from them, severed as it was from the rest of England by the Thames Estuary on three sides, and a labyrinth of muddy waterways on the other, which bled into the land to form the marshes. Grandad Paradiso once described them as Essex's answer to the Mississippi Delta.

Stephen didn't need any encouragement. He leapt up, fetched his binoculars, which were never far away, and began to pull on his wellies in the front porch. Milly, standing next to him, begged to come along too.

'I want to go with Deeby!' she said – Deeby because she couldn't say Stevie – rose-bud mouth pursed in a theatrical pout.

'Not over my dead body,' said Mum. 'You're four, you're going to bed.'

'I go with Deeby!' Emily protested again, wrapping her arms around her brother's hips, then sliding down to his ankles.

Stephen smoothed her hair from her forehead, which was damp from her bath. 'Soon, okay? You'll be old enough soon.'

At eight years old, Stephen wasn't allowed to venture to the marshes alone, and only Dad would go with him. The rest of the time he had to be satisfied with gazing out at them from his box-room window. But he was always aware of their presence, the fact they were out there, alive, even when under the blanket of night. And he craved them constantly: the boggy, beautiful, wildness of them.

It was gone 6.30 p.m. by the time Stephen and his dad left the house and made their way towards the alleyway that led to the marshes. Being early May, midge-hatching season was underway, and the air was humming and cloudy with them. Stephen ran ahead, as he always did, dodging the clumps of dock leaves, big as cabbages.

'Steve, don't run too far ahead,' shouted Tony as Stephen vaulted over the kissing gate, the green-brown edgelands now spread out before him. Stephen did as he was told, although it was against his every instinct to stop. He wanted to run till his thighs burnt, through the reeds that towered over him, over the saltwater pools with the still-blue sky reflected in them; the bogs he knew were teeming with life. In the distance, to his left, stood pylons and, behind those, a row of oil rigs wedged into the sea. To his right there was a cluster of red-roofed houses. His other life, his other world, the ordinary one of school and rules, wasn't far away but if anything its closeness made this space all the more exotic to him, all the more special. At the same time, coming here felt to him like coming home.

They followed the wooden signs for the bird hide, as they always did, Stephen skipping alongside Dad, his arm outstretched, so he could feel the reeds tickle his skin. Stephen loved the sounds as much as he loved the space out here: the wind, creeping through the grasses, that reminded Stephen of rain, when it first, softly, begins to fall; the hum of traffic coming from the A130; and the occasional train, slicing through the countryside with its ghostly sigh. Stephen liked these reminders that the town was nearby. It was as if England and all it had to offer was right here, at the edgelands – a world within a world. And it had been rolled out like a map, for him to run free over.

He and Dad sat next to one another on the bench in the bird hide, which overlooked a lagoon, gold with the setting sun. Tony had the binoculars but Stephen didn't mind. This was how they'd worked it since they'd started birdwatching together: Tony had the binoculars first, got the focus as sharp as he could, then, once he'd found something worth seeing, passed them over to Stephen.

Stephen took the small ring-binder notebook and pen that he always carried out of his cagoule pocket, took a moment to scour the lagoon's silky surface and wrote down his findings:

- common egret (2)
- snipe (1)
- greylag goose (4)
- tern (4)
- black-tailed godwit (6)

They left the hide just as the sun's edges were beginning to melt. Their voices were muffled, buffered by the long rushes at either side of them, but the bird chatter was rising with the closeness of dusk, and, laced along the telephone wires, the starlings had gathered for their sunset conflab.

It was quite by accident they made it as far as Benfleet Creek. They'd been chatting and watching as a marsh harrier circled above, eventually swooping down on its dinner, not noticing how far they'd walked. Then they were there, at the thick, clay-packed banks of it, and the sun was so low by then, it shimmered like liquid mercury, spilt across the dark peat.

Stephen and Dad stood passing the binoculars between them; the odd squawk and the sound of beating wings against water were the only things breaking the quiet. Then, so suddenly it made them both jump, a high-pitched screaming sound came from nowhere, and the sky was filled with what looked like hundreds of fragments of charred black paper, fluttering frenetically in all directions.

'Bats!' said Stephen, excited.

'No, they're swifts,' said Dad, grinning up at the sky.

Stephen went to stand closer to his father, who had the binoculars at that point, and they both watched in awe as the black cloud of boomerang-shaped birds gunned upwards, their screams reaching a crescendo, before fading, like the day.

'They probably arrived a couple of weeks ago,' Dad said.

'Arrived? Where from?'

'From Africa – they'll have flown over the Sahara Desert to get here, thousands and thousands of miles. They're migratory birds.'

'Migratory.' Stephen tried the word out for size. He'd heard it before but didn't know what it meant.

'Migratory birds,' said Tony, reading his mind, 'are birds that don't live in one place all year round. Once a year, either in spring or autumn, they travel thousands of miles, sometimes halfway across the world, to find the place with the best conditions to have their babies.'

'So, swifts come here in the spring, then?'

'That's right. The rest of the time, their home is probably somewhere like Africa. Then in May, when it's beginning to get too hot there and there isn't enough food, they fly all the way here to breed, then fly back home again afterwards.'

'When will they go back?'

'August, probably, even the end of July. Swifts have the shortest holidays in England of all the migratory birds, I think; they don't stay that long.'

'What, and then they fly all the way back to the Sahara?'

'*All* the way back to the Sahara,' confirmed Tony, passing the binoculars again, 'and further south than that.'

Stephen thought of the school summer holidays – still weeks away, but how quickly the end of them would come, by which point, these same swifts that he was looking at now, above the Essex marshes in England, would be back in Africa, making the same racket, but over the desert, dunes replacing bogs below them. It was epic. It blew his mind.

'How do they know when it's time to go back?' he said, watching as the swifts flew in manic circles above the creek.

'Oh, it's a complicated one, Steve,' said Tony. 'Basically, they come here to England to breed – with their true loves – because, you know, swifts mate for life. Each boy sticks with one girl and they have all their babies together.'

'Like you and Mum?' said Stephen and Tony gave a little laugh, amused. 'Yeah, like me and Mum. You could do worse than to take some life tips from swifts, I'm telling you.'

Stephen smiled, but it was delayed. He was too stunned to smile. He felt exhilarated, as if he'd just been told a huge secret.

'They build a nest when they get here,' continued Tony. 'Normally in the eaves of old houses or buildings – that's where swifts like to nest. Then, every May, when they come back to England, they go back to that same spot.'

'What, even if it's in a house just here, on Canvey Island?'

'That's right.'

They'd been so enthralled with the swifts that they hadn't noticed a woman with her dog appear. 'You seen the swifts?' she said. Her face seemed too young for her hair, which was completely white. 'Or should I say, heard them?'

They'd disappeared now, as quickly as they'd appeared, like a magic trick.

'They're nesting nearby,' said the lady, walking on after her dog, who was bounding along the banks of the creek. 'In the eaves of the old memorial hall. Go and have a look, before it gets dark – you might be able to see them.'

It was almost twilight as they walked back through the marshes, Tony keeping Stephen's pace, but only just, competing as they were against the light. There was still a final sliver of it, a band of orange on the horizon, like a bar of their electric fire back home – and a few swifts had gathered and were flying above them, as if they were coming with them, to guide them to their nest.

The memorial hall was a whitewashed building with a tall, pointed roof, like a church, about half a mile from the marsh, so it didn't take them long to get there. Now that Stephen had heard about the swifts, the prospect of seeing these miracle birds close up made the hairs on the back of his neck stand on end.

The whitewash of the hall's stonework glowed pearly in the twilight. His dad explained they never would be able to see *inside* a swift nest, because they were always hidden deep within walls and eaves of buildings, under loft floors, or in holes where the cement had come away. Not that Stephen minded. He could see where the entrance to the nest was because a flurry of birds – maybe five or six – were encircling it, flying in and out of the hole, making their screaming sound. Stephen liked the sound.

It was an excited squeal, not a frightened one, like you might make if you got some good news. It was a sound that Stephen – and Emily, to whom he would soon introduce the swifts – would come to associate with the arrival of summer.

His dad tapped the binoculars. 'See how that one nearest the entrance has got a feather in its beak?'

'Is that to make the nest warmer?'

'Yeah. And they'll have caught that feather in the air when they were flying. They do everything on the wing: they eat, catch stuff for their nests, even mate. They spend a couple of months breeding – like they're doing now – and the rest of the time, they never touch down.'

Stephen was looking through the binoculars, straight into, it felt like, one of the birds' large, pretty eyes. He could see its feathers close up – they were brown and velvety, not black as he'd expected. And he thought how amazing it must be to live practically your whole life in flight, but also how relieved you must be when you finally reached your nest and could rest. And just like that, he felt himself falling in love, completely bewitched by these beings whose existence he'd only just discovered.

Chapter Three

Emily

London, same day

The day began like any other. I was woken for starters from an anxiety dream, the only sort of dream I was having by that point, by the ping of my phone as a text came in. I sat up in bed and read it with one eye, the other not having quite woken up yet.

> Just thinking . . . a night in Bristol on the way down to Devon? Just the two of us? My treat. Xx

I suddenly remembered how, on the night Dan and Vanessa had come over, we'd all drunkenly agreed to go on holiday to Devon together. I held the phone in my hand, wondering how to respond, when it rang. It was James, of course, but it was also 7.37 a.m. I had to get in the shower if I was going to make it to work on time. Thursdays were busy. A queue would already be forming outside the council offices, south London's homeless all praying for a miracle, that they'd somehow sprung straight to the top of the housing waiting list overnight. People needed me. I slid to answer anyway.

'Hi!' I tried to sound as upbeat as possible.

'Hi, gorge, just a quickie 'cause I'm nearly at the office, but what do you think?'

'Um . . .' I felt an unpleasant twinge of irritation that he was putting me on the spot when I'd just opened my eyes. 'About . . . ?'

'About Bristol.'

'Oh, right.' I rubbed at my forehead and pulled back the duvet.

'Oh God, did I just wake you up?'

'No, no . . .' I lied.

'I did, I'm sorry. Go back to sleep immediately.'

I put him on speakerphone whilst I got up. 'No, honestly, it's fine.'

'I just think we should book somewhere if we're going to do it, because it's Easter and you know what it's like.'

'Sure,' I said, opening my wardrobe and pulling out a semblance of an outfit, tossing garments onto my bed.

'I've not got much on today so could book it in my lunch hour.'

There was a moment's silence whilst I pulled my night-shirt off over my head. 'Em, you there?'

'Yeah, I'm right here. I just need to get ready but I'm listening.'

'So, shall I book somewhere?'

'Sure, yeah. Look, I really have to go and have a shower now. I'll see you tonight.' James didn't officially live with me but basically did. It had happened almost without me noticing. He'd simply spent more nights at mine and fewer at his, not that I minded or blamed him. I'd seen stationary cupboards with more soul than his flat. 'I'll cook something nice, yeah?' I hung up, feeling instantly guilty, a feeling I was all too familiar with.

I stood under the shower, letting the glorious warm water pummel my head. My flat is lovely, don't get me wrong. Split-level, it's on the ground floor of a small, fifties block on a leafy avenue in a desirable postcode. I get to share this avenue with mostly cavernous Victorian terraces; front doors painted that sea colour (I believe it is Farrow and Ball 'French grey') that I've come to realise is code for 'middle-class tasteful'. Doing the job I do, I am more grateful than most to come back to my flat every night, but it needed a lot of work when I bought it, three years ago, and even then, I'd basically lived for several years on crisps to afford it. So many things in it have been pulled from a skip or a charity shop and lovingly 'upcycled' with paint and sandpaper in the garden I share with Seth, my neighbour who lives in the other ground-floor flat with his mum, Joan, who has dementia. I didn't scrimp on the shower, though: the head is the size of a dinner plate; the tiles alone cost – well, I try not to think about that. The whole thing worked out to more than my monthly mortgage, that's all I know. But that time in the morning before the madness begins, it earns every penny. It is my time to think and daydream, rather than careen through life, bouncing off the surface like a toboggan racer, which is how I tend to feel the rest of the time.

I decided to skip the armpit-shaving part of the proceedings and was getting out of the shower when Stephen arrived in my head, as he always did at some point before I left for work. Mostly, these thoughts came laced with anxiety: where was he today? How was he? What was he doing right now? Occasionally I'd just be treated to a memory – a lovely one. Today, it was waking up at some ungodly hour in the bedroom we shared when we were little, to find my brother wearing pyjamas and binoculars (which was basically how he slept), yanking the bedroom curtains open, the marshes there waiting for us, my duvet bright with the Essex dawn. 'Milly, get your lazy bum out of bed. Come on, we're going on an adventure. I've already seen a marsh harrier – we're missing the best part of the day!'

Oh God, but I miss you.

I got dressed and hastily liquidised the survivors in my fridge: an orange, some tomatoes and a floret or two of raw broccoli, resulting in something that looked like a GCSE geography soil sample. I downed it, holding my nose, with half an ear on the radio, where there was a programme about loneliness. Then I made myself a cup of tea, teabag still in, and drank it as I always did with the kitchen door open, looking onto my part of the garden and, in particular, the bird feeder I'd installed when I moved in, so excited to have some garden at last, and where, right now, a single blue tit pecked intently at the seeds inside. 'Do you have anything to tell me today, Mr Blue Tit? A sign, a message?' I liked to talk aloud to the birds sometimes. Seth had caught me once or twice and sweetly turned a blind eye.

The garden was finally coming alive after what felt like a never-ending winter: cheery daffodils and deep Malbec-coloured tulips, sheathed in rain this morning. The rain – it was bloody endless. I wouldn't have been surprised to see Noah's Ark sail into view.

When I first moved to London, seven years ago at the age of twenty-four, I lived in a shared flat in a tower block in Battersea Park, sleeping on a futon that used to tremble with the constant overground trains hurtling towards Victoria. Before I moved here – my own place! – I fondly imagined I'd finally feel grown-up and sorted, and glide around, probably in a waffle dressing gown, drinking green tea, luxuriating in my own space. The serenity! Yet, even though I do own a waffle dressing gown and have been known to drink green tea, how I imagined I'd feel then is not how I actually feel now. I can't really describe how I feel, except maybe scattered, restless. I have all my things around me, things I've chosen with love, and yet, it doesn't feel like I live here. Sometimes, when I open the front door, I feel like a visitor.

I made it onto the bus to work, the rain sloshing about the windscreen, the wipers set on manic, drenching any poor soul who might have been standing too close to the kerb. Mum called just as I was approaching my stop – meaning I sailed right past it. She wanted to download that morning's activity, the sum of which was that Deborah the nurse had been in. Mum cares for my stepfather, who is paralysed from the chest down and has lost the power of speech. It's a gruelling and thankless task. Deborah had told her about the aromatherapy she could have down the Mayfield Carers' Centre to help her sleep. I told her she should go for it.

All this meant I got into the office fifteen minutes late, by which point the queue was stretching right back to the entrance, scores of desperate people hoping this would be the day we'd be able to perform an act similar to the feeding of the five thousand: making a pitiful number of houses go around the millions who need one.

I went straight to the office kitchen, which acts as a cloakroom/staffroom, where Justine was standing at the kettle, waiting for it to boil. I love many things about Justine, who is my team leader (so technically my boss even though she's also my best friend), but her ability to make the perfect cup of tea – teabag left in, stewed so it's strong – is high on that list.

'Juss,' I began, taking off my dripping mac. 'I'm so sorry I'm so late. My mum called just as I was coming up to my stop – you know how she forgets I have a job? Well, anyway, it meant I missed it so I've basically legged it all the way from Blackfriars Bridge.'

Justine was holding out the mug of tea and I took it, gratefully. 'Look, when you practically live here, you do not have to apologise for being fifteen minutes late,' she said, taking a rather inelegant slurp from her own mug. 'And anyway, I'm not interested in your crap excuses. It's not even 10 a.m. and I've already deloused a five-year-old and talked my husband out of buying a caravan on eBay from someone who lives in Hull.'

I laughed, whilst experiencing a mild pang of envy at the busy, buzzy morning in a family home she'd had.

'Seriously, talk about working for the homeless – anyone would think you didn't have a home to go to yourself. In fact, do me a favour,' she said, holding the door open for me. 'Go home on time tonight, will you? You're starting to make us all feel guilty.'

I sat down, tucking my chair underneath the desk at the exact moment a voice came over the tannoy – 'Wendy Shaw to interview room twelve, please' – and something inside me withered. When I began this job nearly seven years ago, I was all guns blazing – Christ, I was so wide-eyed and idealistic back then, and, if not confident I could change the world, then hell-bent on giving it my best shot. Now, with the housing crisis in full swing, I obviously realise it's not my fault that there are 1.15 million people on the waiting list, but when you spend more of your day saying no than yes, when you realise this is a service where *not* helping people is generally seen as doing a good job, when you have to explain the housing crisis to people who already feel like life couldn't get any worse, it's hard to feel you're doing any good. In fact, you start to question how good you really are.

I got Wendy's details up on screen then watched as she stood up from her chair and made her way over, wearing a trademark pink baseball cap and heartbreakingly optimistic smile. She pulled the sleeves of her hoodie over her hands and sat down, resting her elbows on the glass panel of the kiosk that separates 'them' and 'us'. These days, I was feeling increasingly that I provided nothing but a gatekeeping service, as if this were Passport Control at an airport that I stood behind, rationing who got a roof over their head and who didn't, who boarded the plane to a life, and who stayed stuck on the ground. Because, really, life begins with a roof over your head, doesn't it? Without that, nothing can take off.

'Hi, Wendy,' I smiled, trying to sound friendly without being too cheerful. It's important not to give people false hope. 'How can I—?'

'Did you read my doctor's note?' she cut in, breathlessly, peering over the glass panel at my desk, as if I might have been hiding it. 'The note I brought in yesterday – have you read it yet?'

'Yes, I did . . .' I hesitated, hand hovering over the mouse, trying to bide my time before I had to turn Wendy back out onto the streets, as I'd done every single day for the last six months. 'And again, we had to make a judgement based on the information we had and I'm afraid—'

Wendy's face began to crumple. 'Don't tell me no. Don't tell me no again.'

'We've been through this, haven't we?' I said, gently, dying inside. 'I'm sorry but we do not have a duty to house you unless you fall into one of the priority categories, which, as I've explained, are being responsible for children, being pregnant, or having a severe mental or physical disability or illness, which . . . I'm so sorry, but this letter does not say you have.'

'But I have got a severe illness. I can't walk for starters.'

'I know,' I said. 'You're in an awful situation.'

I was aware of a voice over the tannoy again, the next person being called to interview room thirteen next door, where my colleague, Benjamin, did the same job as me, but I didn't catch the name.

'It's not just that you don't meet the criteria.' Criteria made me so cross. Sorry, love, but if you don't tick the box, you have to continue sleeping in one. 'There's also the fact of your eviction for rent arrears.'

I bit my lip as I glanced over her records on my screen for the umpteenth time. 'Which, as I've explained, unfortunately puts you in the intentionally homeless category.' Of all the tellings-off I have to deliver to grown adults in this job, the 'you've made yourself intentionally homeless' one is the absolute pits; I mean, you only have to look at the people who come in here to see that nothing about their situation is intentional.

Wendy gave a shuddery sigh. 'That wasn't my fault. You know that. I missed one meeting – one meeting with my key worker. My mum had a doctor's appointment that day, I had to go with her, but my money was stopped without warning. I had no money to pay my rent.'

I sighed, hating this. 'Wendy, I know it must feel harsh.' That was the understatement of the century. 'But this is unfortunately the system.'

'I just want my own front door.'

'I know, I know you do.'

'I just want my own set of keys. Is this too much to ask for a forty-three-year-old woman with serious health problems?'

I offered a small smile. 'I'm sorry, but right now it seems to be.' If this job had taught me anything, it's how many people's lives are, basically, impossible.

Wendy began to cry. I leant forward, so she could hear me behind the glass. 'You know if it were up to me, I would give everyone a house. I would give you a flat in a heartbeat. But I don't have that power and, most importantly, there are nowhere near enough properties for those in what is deemed as priority need, let alone those who aren't. The fact is, they're just not building enough houses. There aren't the houses . . .'

And it was then, as I was uttering those words, that I became aware of the voice. Not that I experienced it as a voice at first, as much as something visceral, a physical jolt of recognition. Wendy was saying something, but I couldn't focus on what, because I was drawn in by that voice next door. It was raised, but the tone wasn't aggressive, so much as exasperated, fuelled by injustice – and, just hearing it, a scene opened up like a flower in my mind: me, ten perhaps, so Stephen would have been fourteen or fifteen, and I'm standing barefoot in a summery dress in the spacious lounge of my mother and stepfather's house (our parents had separated by then). It's sunny, light showing up the dust motes hovering above the swirl-patterned carpet, and I am holding a box in my hands. It's a shoebox from a pair of shoes our stepfather bought me the day before, on one of the rather confusing, impromptu shopping trips he would sometimes take me on, where he'd spoil me rotten for no discernible reason. Inside the box is a tiny, injured bird, which I'm showing to Mum, who I imagine will surely share my deep concern. But instead it's just making her mad and fretful, as she so often was by that stage of my childhood. And now she's yelping, throwing her hands up, which knocks the box out of my arms so that the bird falls onto the carpet in front of everyone.

Our stepfather is bellowing at Stephen, not me, even though I was the one carrying the box, the one who dropped the bird – which struck me as unfair even then – and Stephen is shouting back, protesting that he just wanted to save the bird. And that voice, that young, male voice, was the same as the one that was coming from interview room thirteen at that moment, and it was saying: 'But you don't understand, you don't understand . . .' It had the same sense of powerlessness and despair. I couldn't hear every word but it was talking about being 'stuck on twenty-one points' (the points we award people to establish their level of housing need). 'How am I meant to get beyond twenty-one points?' he added, loudly. 'I'd have a better chance if I got on the booze or the drugs . . . I mean, what's the point? What the fuck is the point?'

Benjamin, the housing officer in room thirteen, was saying something in response to the voice, but I couldn't hear properly for the roar of blood in my ears, the kicking in of my nervous system; my mouth was suddenly stripped of moisture, every hair on my arms stood on end and my skin felt like it was contracting – a strange, out of body sensation – as if I was literally about to shed a skin.

Stephen.

Wendy was asking me something, and I was doing my best to focus, but the voice next door was dragging me under, like a rip-tide. 'Look, I know you're trying to help,' it was saying, 'but with the best will in the world, those places are full of addicts and lost causes. People pushing booze and drugs. I don't want to sound ungrateful, but I don't need that, mate, I really don't.'

'Stephen,' I said again, only realising I had said it aloud this time when Wendy said, 'What? Who's Stephen when he's at home?'

I stood up but my legs were jelly. I was struggling to make my lungs expand.

'You all right?' she said. I wanted to move but I couldn't. It was like one of those awful dreams where your brain is awake, but your body is paralysed.

'I'm fine.' My hands had begun to shake as I was gathering up some papers. 'But, look, Wendy, I'm sorry to do this to you, but can you excuse me? I've just got to check on someone . . . I'll give you a call later, okay?'

Before she could answer, I was already out of the door, about to barge straight into room thirteen, only to see the flaps of Benjamin's cord jacket disappearing at the other end of the corridor, the meeting obviously finished.

I ran down the stairs at the back of the interview rooms, the heels of my boots clacking on the blue-speckled concrete, hands squeaking on the handrail, bursting out on the ground floor, near reception. Stephen was nowhere to be seen but Benjamin, who had presumably used the lift, was on his way through the main doors.

'Benjamin!'

He turned around.

'Where are you going?'

'On a home visit. Why? Is that allowed?' Benjamin was a man of relentless, low-level sarcasm, but he had a heart the size of London, so was forgiven.

'Where is he? That man you were just interviewing?'

'Man?' he said, as if he'd instantly forgotten.

'That man you were with just now – the one who was getting upset, who was going on about being stuck on twenty-one points.' I was looking around me, in case he was still here. 'Where is he?'

Benjamin regarded me as if I was mad. 'I guess he's gone.'

My heart sank. 'What did he look like?'

Benjamin puffed his cheeks out. 'Well, like lots of them, to be honest – in need of a good night's sleep. Tall, er . . . he had a rucksack with him, I think. I tell you what, though, I did notice something odd about him.'

'Yeah?'

'He had a pair of binoculars around his neck, which

I thought was a bit . . .' My hand went to the top of my head. '. . . unusual.'

I froze in the archway of the council offices entrance hall, through which countless people had trodden over the years I'd worked here, me praying that one day Stephen would be among them.

'Actually, I've just remembered his name,' said Benjamin. 'It was Nelson, actually, Stephen Nelson.'

My face must have said it all.

'Wait,' he said with a small laugh. 'You're not related, are you?'

And in that moment, it felt like everything: our past, Canvey Island, the marshes themselves, came racing towards me like the clouds in the vast canopy of sky above them, stopping dead right in front of my feet.

'Related?' I managed eventually. I was laughing, with joy, shock, nerves, but mostly joy. 'He's my brother.'

Chapter Four

Stephen

London, same day

Despair, they said, was the one unforgiveable sin: to just give up on everything, resign oneself to eternal damnation. It was not something Stephen indulged himself in. Not even something he felt, actually, despite everything. Did he feel pissed off? Definitely. Frustrated? Regularly, especially when people chucked a Big Mac at his feet then walked off, as if he was a begging dog and should be grateful for every titbit flung his way, never considering he'd have the audacity to be vegetarian (he was) in his situation. Being homeless was a constant roller-coaster of emotion, you couldn't deny that. But no, he didn't do despair.

Until now, as he walked from the council offices in the drizzle. At least, he was pretty certain that despair was the right term for this gaping chasm of hopelessness in his chest. He stopped in a shop doorway to roll a cigarette, thinking about the way the housing officer – Benjamin, that was the name on his badge – had shrugged and said, 'All you can do is put your name down and wait like everyone else, I'm afraid,' in his shirt so cheap, you could see his chest hair through it. *I'm wearing a nicer shirt than that and I'm homeless, mate*, Stephen had wanted to say. But Benjamin was just doing his job, was just another faceless cog in the huge wheel that was steaming right over him. Not that he was the only one – he had comrades in these trenches, and that would have been a great comfort had he not had to give them up too.

He thought of the boys now, Lee, Scotty and Jimmy, down under the subway; they'd be well out of it by now, several cans down, wrapped in sweet oblivion. Stephen was one of the lucky ones, a rarity; he'd seen, both in prison and on the streets, what addiction did to people's lives, and had clung to the precipice himself. And although he still went on the odd bender, he'd largely nipped it in the bud. This had come at a cost – namely, leaving behind his friends and moving from the spot he'd shared with them in the Waterloo subway to the residential area of Camberwell to start life afresh. The move, however, had been emotionally difficult, because drinkers they may have been, but just 'drinking buddies' they were not. They were *real* friends, people he would have laid down his life for, and walking away from them had felt like trading in community for sobriety. Right now, it seemed there was a very fine line between which of the two he needed most.

Stephen walked down to the river. Big skies, horizons, those were what he craved when he felt like this. That, or wilderness: a hidden, overgrown cemetery; a sunlit wood – somewhere to take him out of himself. He spotted a peregrine falcon just as he reached the South Bank, which cheered him up, but not as much as it normally would. Then he parked himself on a bench in front of the Royal Festival Hall and watched the boats glide past, the Thames grey and swollen after days and days of rain.

A heavy weariness descended after the adrenaline of the morning, and he thought about curling up on the bench, letting sleep take him, but resisted. He thought too about beer, gulping down a cold one in one go, then pushed that thought to the back of his mind like a sofa up against a door. He felt foolish, truth be told. What had he expected when he went to the council today? To walk away with keys to his own pad? He wasn't that naive. Just a little hope, maybe, a reward from the cosmos for cleaning up his act these past three months – for 'choosing life'.

No, despair, he told himself, resolvedly, *is the unforgiveable sin*.

The sun momentarily came out and, like a plant, Stephen unfurled, stretching his arms across the top of the bench, and his legs in front of him, crossing his ankles. He tipped his head back and closed his eyes, felt the glorious warmth on his eyelids. How in the world had he got here?

Actually, he could remember the first night he ever spent as an official homeless person, as if it was yesterday. 30 August 2007: sleeping rough on a park bench in the grounds of the Imperial War Museum. He was almost four years out of prison (where he'd spent four years) and that afternoon, he'd come back to the hostel he'd been living at spectacularly hammered – a crime, unfortunately, with a punishment of immediate eviction. So, Stephen had stood outside on that late summer's eve, knowing that for the first time in his life, he had literally nowhere to go: no flat, no hostel, no friend's couch, no squat he could pretend was a 'lifestyle choice'. Judgement skewed, he'd considered calling Grandma and Grandad Paradiso – ever his supporters – to see if they could help. It was either a very good or a very bad thing – depending how you looked at it – that he decided against this, since unbeknownst to him, Grandad had died three days previously from a stroke; Grandma was to follow three weeks later, dead from a broken heart, no doubt. Stephen missed everything, including the funerals, of course. Still, he'd spared his grandma the upset of him being off his nut the last time she spoke to him and that was a blessing, he supposed.

It was a warm, sultry evening, and so the first couple of hours walking the streets was fine, liberating even. Just him and the city in some romantic embrace. But then he sobered up, the sun went down and with it the temperature: a warning of the long, cold nights soon to come. People went home, drew the curtains, closed their front doors, and Stephen realised he needed somewhere to bed down for the night. And so he'd chosen a park bench in the grounds of the Imperial War Museum. It had made sense to him somehow – like nature: the reassuring comfort of his own insignificance; the feeling there were far greater powers at work than his own internal battles. In that grand, pillared museum, which stood as if on watch over him, were stories of men and women, legions of them before him, who'd faced the horrors of war. Surely he could survive a night on a park bench?

And now here he was, a decade later, another day, another bench . . .

A wind picked up, blowing drizzle in his face, whisking the Thames into small white-caps. Stephen rolled a cigarette, and for some mad, fleeting second thought about calling his dad, and asking to come home. Then he remembered that 'home' for Dad was no longer his little house in Eden Court; it was a house Stephen had never been to that his dad shared with Sandra – a woman Stephen had never met. Also, he remembered what his dad had said the last time he'd seen him, thirteen years ago now, in 2005 – 'You're on your own now, sunshine, I can't help you' – and thought better of it. Still, he couldn't help his mind drifting to all the wonderful times he'd spent out on Canvey Marshes with Tony – just the two of them and the birds. Stephen still dreamt of those days sometimes, and for a few moments after he woke, that feeling of being close to his father, and safe, would linger and it was exquisite. Then in an instant it would evaporate, his present reality would reinstate itself, and it would take him all day to get over the loss.

The rain and the wind were not letting up, and Stephen was suddenly murderously ravenous. He dug in his pocket. He had £2.04 left from the money he'd earnt from his bird drawings that week: just enough. So, he walked away from the river into the labyrinth of Southwark streets to a corner shop he knew, passing a development site on the way: 'A hot location for an exciting new luxury lifestyle' it said on a sign plastered across the entrance, which made him laugh sardonically to himself. He bought his Pot Noodle and walked, then, taking the back streets to the hospital. He left his rucksack in his secret hiding place behind the industrial bins as he always did, and then the key was to walk through those revolving doors with confidence. Over the months he'd been doing this, he'd studied the security guards' comings and goings. He knew when one started a shift and the other clocked off and worked around it. He'd studied too how the doctors and nurses carried themselves, so that he could emulate them and not draw attention. He'd noticed how they walked, head up, eyes straight ahead – the walk of someone with purpose.

Trying desperately to mirror this, Stephen made his way to the downstairs staff cafeteria, which he was pleased to see was busy enough that he would blend in and where, crucially, there was a boiling water tap that all staff in the hospital could use to make tea, coffee or cup-a-soups. He filled up his Pot Noodle, regretting getting the Bombay Bad Boy flavour – possibly the most attention-seeking of all Pot Noodles – and praying nobody would rumble him.

Stirring the pot, he then found a seat on the farthest table in the farthest corner of the room and tried to fold himself into the wall, making himself disappear. Bending over the pot, he inhaled his food, sauce splashing onto his chin. When he was finished, he leant back and belched, unthinking, but loudly enough for a nurse sitting opposite him on a table two rows back to look up from her newspaper. She looked up at him over her glasses and he raised a hand, murmuring 'sorry' and offering a sheepish smile, praying he wouldn't be rumbled by a burp, for Christ's sake, that she wasn't about to turf him out into the wet and cold, because he didn't know if he could take any more. His prayers answered, she just gave a small smile of amusement and went back to her paper and Stephen watched her then, wondering what her home was like, this woman, in her mid-forties, he guessed. He imagined the warm light of the hall, maybe a radio on low somewhere. She'd have a partner, definitely, kids, likely teenagers, lounging around the television. He often did this – tried to imagine people's homes and lives and families, almost as if by doing so, he could teleport himself there, just to sample some simple comforts for a while: water from the tap; food in the fridge; a boiling kettle; clean sheets; a long, hot bath behind a locked door.

A home with a mother who wanted him there, who had not disowned him.

Food digesting, a wave of exhaustion washed over him and he leant his forehead on the window to be met, almost directly opposite, with the yolk-orange beak of a male blackbird that had just landed on the bough of a tree. He pulled back instinctively and watched as the blackbird opened its beak and sang, as if to him. Blackbirds often sang after rain, they said, and of all birdsong, the blackbird's was one of the most beautiful. Stephen couldn't listen to it now, though, for thinking of that July evening – his mother's thirtieth birthday party, years ago now – when a blackbird had sung too, and how, in a way, that had signified the beginning of the unravelling of his life. He'd read later that if you were to put a blackbird's feathers under someone's pillow, that someone would tell you their innermost secrets. He thought of that now and wondered if it were true.

God, he was tired. He closed his eyes, and quite without noticing it was happening, drifted off. Then, something pulling at his coat sleeve, a memory? A dream? A policeman tugging at his arm?

'Wakey, wakey, please, sir.' Stephen opened his eyes to find a security guard in a high-vis jacket yanking roughly on his coat sleeve. 'You need to leave immediately, otherwise I'll have to call the police.' Stephen sat up and, realising he'd drooled a little, wiped his mouth with the back of his hand. 'Quickly now, we don't want to make a scene in front of all these people.' Stephen tried to stand, but the fatigue was so heavy and his sleep had been so deep that he couldn't keep his eyes open.

'Come on, sir. Let's speed things up a touch, shall we? These nice people don't want you ruining their lunch.'

That woke him.

'Hey, I'm not drunk,' he said, wishing suddenly, so badly, that he was.

'Yeah, all right, mate, whatever you say.'

'I'm not,' Stephen protested. 'I'm just shattered.'

'Well, you're on something, you're all on something,' said the security guard, taking Stephen's arm as he walked, unsteady with exhaustion, towards the door.

'Look, I don't have anywhere to live, that's all,' he shouted as another security guard arrived to frogmarch him out, holding his arm so tight it hurt. 'That doesn't make me a drunk, all right? Or a drug addict, or a thief or a paedophile. It just makes me homeless.'

He could feel the injustice burn his insides, as well as the burn of people's eyes on him, but he was past caring.

'Off you go,' said the security guard, as soon as the automatic doors opened. Outside, the air smelt metallic: more rain was on its way. And in that second, he felt it: total despair. He'd committed the unforgiveable sin – and was about to commit another.

'Mother Duck'

June 1991

The car was warm as a bath with the sun, and the backs of Emily's knees were sticky against the cream leather. Next to her, Stephen, his hair gelled smartly to the side and dressed in a blue-checked shirt, read a sign through his binoculars. 'Welcome to Tow-cester,' he said, making 'tow' rhyme with cow, as they rolled into town.

In the front, Mummy and Daddy laughed.

'You pronounce it Toaster,' said Tony, who was suited and booted, at the walnut wheel of his Rover, which, after the kids, was his pride and joy. 'Now, isn't that a funny name for a town?'

'Toaster?' Emily said, absent-mindedly. She was busy watching out of her open window, as a lady, wearing an apron, came out of her shop and lifted her face to the bright blue sky. 'Why is it called Toaster, Dad?'

'I dunno, I guess it just popped up,' he said, followed

by a wheezy laugh. Stevie did a happy groan, and Alicia slapped her husband's leg.

'She's four, you daft sod! She won't get that.'

Not that Emily was paying attention. There was far too much to look at. Like the strings of multicoloured flags, hanging like sweetie-necklaces against the cloudless sky. People scuttling in and out of shops as if they all knew each other. And flowers. Lots of pretty flowers, hanging outside shops in baskets and on windowsills.

She caught her daddy's eye in the rear-view mirror. He winked and she gave him what she knew was a cute smile back.

'One thing I do know, kids, is that Towcester is a Roman town,' Tony carried on, 'and Watling Street, that we're driving along right now, was built by Roman soldiers – how about that? If you stay on it—'

Stephen, familiar with his father's fascination for all things Roman as well as bird-related, finished his sentence for him. 'It'd go all the way to Italy.'

'Exactly, Steve.'

'Oh, Tony . . .' Alicia flipped her vanity mirror down, and Emily watched in the gap between the car door and the front seat, as her mother stretched her lips taut and reapplied frosted-pink lipstick for the hundredth time since they set off. 'Stop it with the Rome drone, they'll be asleep before we get there.'

Not me, thought Emily, as she lifted her chin towards

the warm summer's breeze. It made her eyelids flutter; sunshine-bubbles played across them. She loved how the breeze blew her hair about as it did on the marshes back home, but also how the air smelt different here, of baking cakes and flowers and hot roads and happiness.

They were going to a wedding! Mummy and Daddy's friends Mitch and Tina's wedding.

'What happens at a wedding?' Emily had asked the night before, when Mummy had finished reading her a bedtime story.

'Well, it's just an excuse for a party, really. There's a lady and a man and the lady will be in a big white dress,' Mummy had said as she'd tucked her in. After she'd kissed Emily goodnight, she'd folded her arms and added with a strange smile, 'even if white's not her colour.'

They'd had to set off early. So early that the sun was only just getting up, and Stephen had said she could bring her Care Bears duvet. Now the day was hot; she and Stephen had long since taken their shoes and socks off, and the Care Bears duvet had been relegated to the floor. After forever on the big and boring road, they'd finally arrived in the town where the wedding was to be held and it felt to Emily as if everyone there knew.

Mummy and Daddy sang along to the radio.

'*I got my mind SET. ON. YOU.*'

'Mummy?' Emily said twice and, second time, her mother turned the music down.

'Yes, sweetheart?'

'Where will the party be?'

'Hmm?'

'The wedding party?'

Alicia had finally finished applying lipstick now, and was powdering her nose, twisting her shiny pink mouth from side to side.

'Will it be in the white dress lady's house, like I had my birthday party in my house?'

'No, you silly sausage. I hope not anyway. That would be very common . . .'

'What about in McDonald's, like Hannah's party was, then?'

Everyone laughed at that so she did too.

'Milly, it's a wedding,' said Stephen, amused and charmed as he so often was by her. He took her clammy little hand and spoke nose-touchingly close to her, so he could be sure she'd understood. 'It'll be in a church, okay? The man and lady will talk about loving each other, when you'll have to be really quiet . . .'

'Oh, she doesn't, not really,' sniffed Mum, looking out of the window.

'And then there'll be the party, when . . .' – Emily could feel the car slowing down – 'we'll have party food and probably a disco.' Now it was going so slow it was almost at a standstill. Emily and Stephen sat up like meerkats. Daddy turned the radio off. Everybody stopped talking.

The Toaster, it felt to Emily, was holding its breath, waiting for something. Was it the lady in the big, white dress?

Then Mummy squealed and clapped her hands together. 'Oh, my days, Tony, look!' And she stuck her head out of the window, one hand on her blonde hair, blow-dried at the crack of dawn before they set off. 'There's a mother duck with her babies trying to cross the road! Tone, stop!' She slapped the steering wheel, gold bangles jangling. 'That's why this man in front has stopped.'

Stephen launched forward between the two front seats. 'I want to see!'

'Yes, Daddy, please!' Emily pleaded from the back seat. 'I wanna see too!'

'Hang on!' said Tony, exasperated but laughing at the farcical situation. 'Like true Englishmen, we're all stopping for the ducks, don't worry.'

Stephen reached back and unclipped his sister's seat belt. Emily jumped on his back, like a baby koala bear. She was not missing this: a fat and quacking Jemima Puddle Duck was weeble-wobbling off the high street curb, her fluffy babies following her, like an upturned basket of eggs. It was a scene so entrancing as to, literally, stop traffic, because when Emily turned around, there was a tailback stretching right back and around the corner of the road that led into town.

'Oh, I can't bear it. I'm getting out,' said Alicia then, and everyone watched as she tottered, on her new, maroon patent sandals and a skirt so figure-hugging she could only waddle herself, towards the fluffy, quacking procession, all the time expressing little whoops of delight and waving her hands about.

Tony shook his head and tutted affectionately at his wife, then got out himself.

'Milly, come on.' Then Stephen crawled, Milly on his back, out of his father's side of the car declaring in full, rescue mission mode, 'There's a drain they could slip down. They could all die if we don't all help!'

In truth, it *was* probably a whole town effort to get Jemima and her ducklings across that road safely. Shopkeepers and cafe owners came out onto the pavement to watch and support. A burly truck driver played goalie, standing in front of the drain in the road, stretching his beefy, tattooed arms out and scuttling from side to side, trying to keep the ducks from falling down the gaps in the drain cover. All the while, Stephen and Emily sat on their haunches so as to be at the ducks' level and ushered them from the hazardous drop. 'Come on, you can do it,' they encouraged. 'We're not going to let you get hurt.'

And for the ten or so minutes it took to complete Operation Ducks Crossing, the whole of Towcester held its breath; you could have heard the town hall clock tick. And when the fluffy procession was safely on the other side, the onlookers erupted in spontaneous applause. To a four-year-old Emily, it felt like applause for the ducks, yes, but mainly for all of them: her and Stephen, Mummy and Daddy.

At the wedding reception – in a nice hotel, it turned out – she was on a high. As they queued for the buffet, she and Stephen spoke of nothing else. On 'Daffodils' table adults and kids whom Emily and Stephen had never met sat enraptured by their feathery tale and, as word spread to the wedding party, they were hailed as heroes of the day.

After they'd had their celebration tea, the dance floor swirled with discs of multicoloured lights and Emily sat sugar-doped and mesmerised as the lady in the big white dress, and the man in the soldier outfit, danced like Cinderella and her prince. At the disco afterwards, everyone said she'd had 'a second wind' as she and Stevie boogied as if this was the last night of summer, or even the year, Stephen swinging her around to the 'Time Warp', both of them kicking their legs to 'New York, New York'.

'She can't half move,' guests cooed, and Emily revelled in the attention. 'She'll sleep well tonight!' They must have known a thing or two these grown-ups, for although she fought it as long as she could, as soon as they reached the motorway – empty that time of night – Emily fell asleep in the dark, quiet of the back of the Rover, her face still flushed from dancing. Just before she dropped off, her sweaty head lolling against Stephen's shoulder who was also asleep, she had a thought: *That was the best day of my life.*

Chapter Five

Emily

After Benjamin had confirmed it was Stephen, I dashed outside to look for him. I ran up and down in the rain shouting his name. I probably looked quite mad, but I didn't care. No matter how much I tried to magic him into existence, though, he wasn't there. I'd come so close only for him to disappear again. The cruelty of it felt mind-boggling. I was aware of the city alive and pulsing around me, but I felt separate to it, as if I was in a glass box unable to reach outside to this huge gaping mouth that had surely swallowed my brother, gobbled him whole, not leaving a trace.

Devastated and reeling, I eventually had to go back inside to work. I was desperate to grill Benjamin about his interview with Stephen, but he didn't come back from his home visit, and it was probably for the best. By some miracle, I got through the afternoon, but my concentration was shot to pieces. I was in fight-or-flight mode, flinching at every tall, slim, youngish man who walked by; a birder on high alert, waiting for that sighting, yearning for it.

On autopilot, I got on a bus. The rain spattered relentlessly at the window as if the universe was trying to tell me something, to punish me for something, and the journey took an eternity, the bus stop-starting, wheezing its way deeper south, through the grey veil of drizzle in rush hour; all these thousands of people heading home. I imagined them opening the door to warm, dry hallways; to children, flatmates and partners. It would be dark in less than two hours and Stephen was out there, alone and homeless, in this city that felt vast as an ocean.

The bus stopped at Elephant and Castle and half of the passengers got off. I felt more space around me but inside, the tightness in my chest intensified. Should I get off too? Start looking for him? In fact, why was I just sitting there? I told myself I needed a plan, a strategy, that it was a stupid idea to just launch into the middle of London, trying to find one human among millions. Underneath, though, I knew what was really going on: the worry of what I'd say if and when I found him. The worry of whether or not he'd even want to be found.

We trundled, agonisingly, along the Walworth Road.

Stephen's voice slid into my head again, along with the injured bird from all those years ago. It was a willow warbler; Stephen and I had found it slumped at the bottom of the patio doors. I remember being horrified and asking if it was dead, and the way Stephen had lowered himself onto his knees, slid his hand, ever so gently, beneath its body, and told me to place my hand on its breast. 'It's alive!' he'd said. 'Feel its little heart. It's just stunned. It needs a bit of time to recover, but then it will be right as rain.'

That night, my stepfather had been the one to come and say goodnight, because Mum had taken herself to bed in one of her low moods; she was having a lot by that point, which I hated because I always felt it was something I'd done. As he switched off the light, he'd told me the warbler had not made it. And that, my first experience of death, had devastated me, and, even though it probably devastated Stevie equally, he'd been the one to comfort me. He always put me first. But who put him first? Who comforted him?

I lay my forehead against the cool glass of the bus window. *I have to find you. I have to make everything all right.*

You'd think my long-lost brother walking into my office on a random Thursday morning would be the shock of my life. Of course, it *was* shocking. Not to mention catastrophically disappointing when he then disappeared again. Yet, when I heard that voice, I also had the feeling of a master plan having come together, as if the last ten years of my life had all been leading to this point. You see, I've known Stephen was homeless for years. I've known from talking to Dad – the only person in our family he's kept in touch with. It was a major factor in me deciding on a career as a housing officer in the first place and I've fantasised about this day since I started, an idealistic twenty-something, convinced I could change the world and that miracles could, and did, happen. Why couldn't one of those involve my brother walking through those doors?

Over the years, I've never stopped looking for Stephen: I've searched records, called hostels and night shelters regularly, but he could have been anywhere. Maybe even abroad. There have been periods when I've feared him dead. (The insights my job has given me have not always been welcome.) Then there's been the relief every few months when he's finally called Dad, swiftly followed by the disappointment that he didn't want to be found, wouldn't even tell Dad where he was.

Now, though, he'd come to my council offices, so he was not only alive but *near*, and wanted to be housed. He wanted to get his life back on track. If he wasn't ready to be found *now*, then when?

James phoned just as I was walking up the path to my block. 'Hey, just checking in . . .'

'Oh, hi.' I felt generally unhinged from the day's events, not to mention a ripple of irritation at what I saw as his intrusion. For all James knew, I was still at work, busy with clients, and yet he was still 'just checking in'. *Don't be a cow*, I told myself. *It's sweet he's phoned.*

'How's your day been?'

'Um, fine, good.' I was rummaging in my huge, bottomless bag for my house keys, wondering why I never learnt to put them in the front pocket. 'Actually, I got off work early. I've just got home.'

'Ah, that's a shame.' He sounded disappointed. It made me feel pressured. 'I could have met you in town if I'd known.'

I kicked the post off the doormat as I walked in. 'Sorry,' I said, to a silent, empty flat.

'Not to worry, I'll jump on a bus and come over now. Maybe we can go for a drink? Thursday being the new Friday night and all that.'

What day it was, the approaching weekend, it all felt so meaningless; everything apart from finding my brother felt meaningless.

'Um, I can't really . . .' I said lamely.

I was standing, junk mail around my feet, hand clasped to my forehead.

'Oh.' His disappointment was palpable. 'Okay.'

I felt even worse. 'Look,' I said. 'Something big happened today.'

'Oh?'

'My brother . . . You know, Stephen, who I told you about?' I'd told him the bare minimum which is that I had a brother, who was probably homeless, and who I'd not seen for a long time and missed, desperately. 'Well, he walked into the council offices earlier looking for a flat.'

There was a long silence. It was several beats longer than it should have been before James said, 'Wow. *Wow.* Oh my God, Ems, well then, we definitely need a drink to celebrate—'

'But then he walked out again before I could talk to him and now I don't know where he is,' I cut in, my voice beginning to wobble.

'Well, we can talk about it,' said James, an air of desperation in his voice that was making me feel panicky. 'I'll help you decide what to do.'

I couldn't think of something I wanted to do less right now, which was a bad sign and I knew it.

'Look, James, don't take this the wrong way but I just want to chill, on my own. Is that . . . is that okay?'

Another pause, where he was obviously waiting for me to change my mind. 'Sure,' he said, unconvincingly. 'Of course, I totally understand. I've got some work I need to do anyway.'

'Oh, well then, great.' I said it rather too quickly. 'I will call you, though, okay?'

'Yeah, no rush. As long as you're all right.'

I paused. 'I will be,' I said. Who I was hoping to convince of that fact, I did not know.

It was after 6 p.m. and dark by the time I shut the front door behind me. The flat felt emptier than usual; I felt not just a visitor in my own home, but a stranger. Perhaps for comfort then, to feel closer to my brother, I went straight upstairs and took it out of my bedside drawer: *The Garden Birds Guidebook* he'd given me all those years ago, and, inside it, on the page with the wren on and the whitethroat, the folded piece of A4 on which Stephen had written our Top Five list.

1. Spot TWO rare birds in twenty-four hours
2. Go on a night birding woodland walk
3. See an owl in flight
4. See a seabird colony
5. Watch the swifts' migration from the Spurn Peninsula

Chapter Six

I read our Top Five list aloud, as if to communicate with him, wishing he might answer back with some clue as to where he was. Then I got changed out of my work clothes. I was starving but couldn't face cooking, so I stood in the light of the fridge and had a dinner of anchovies and gherkins straight from the jar, and several slices of ham. These fridge dinners were becoming more and more the norm of late. Basically, when James wasn't there, this was how I ate.

A tall, dark shadow flashed across the kitchen window and I jumped half out of my skin, only to see it was Seth. He waved, laughing at me clutching my chest. I shook my head at him, chidingly, then shut the fridge door and beckoned him in.

'God Almighty,' I said, opening the back door that led into the garden. 'I thought you were Freddy Krueger.'

'A flattering doppelganger!' he said, then, 'I'm sorry.' By the look on his face, I must have looked pretty spooked; I certainly felt it. Now he was standing in my kitchen, though, dripping wet and with his cagoule hood pulled tight around his face, he looked about as sinister as a garden gnome.

'What were you doing in this weather?'

'Putting the tarpaulin over the tomato plants.'

'I see,' I said, feeling ridiculous. 'Not about to break into your neighbour's house, then?'

'Not so much.'

We were laughing. I offered him a cup of tea. He accepted, although he couldn't stay – he never can, because his mum can't be left on her own for long.

'How is she?' I said when we were sitting on the sofa.

'She's okay. Poured a bag of flour over herself, though, yesterday, when we were doing some baking.'

'Oh Seth.'

'She claimed it was snow, she was having a jolly good time too, until I tried to get her in the shower and then, well, let's just say she was none too happy about it.'

I gave a small smile. 'Must be so hard.' Seth used to be high up as a designer in a creative agency, but gave it all up to look after his mum. Can't really go anywhere, do much; he's tied to her. It can't be easy. He never complains.

'Ah, she's all right, you know? She's happy enough in herself.'

I'd been talking about *him* – how hard it must be for *him*.

'She keeps me busy and on my toes. Anyway, what's your day been like? Before I nearly gave you a heart attack.'

'Well, actually, you're not the first person to do that today,' I said, and to my embarrassment and surprise, I found my eyes filling with tears.

The smile dropped from Seth's face. 'Oh God, you really are spooked, aren't you? What happened?'

'Well, you know my brother . . . ?' And I told him the story of hearing the voice next door.

'How do you know it was definitely him?' said Seth, when I'd finished. Seth knew about Stephen – this troubled wild child who I missed and adored. He didn't know I'd been searching for him, though. Hardly anyone knew. Not even Justine. 'Did you just remember his voice after all these years?'

'I must have. It did something to me. It was visceral, do you know what I mean? What really clinched it, though, was when I spoke to my colleague Benjamin, who was the one to actually see him, he told me he was wearing binoculars around his neck.'

Seth looked blank for a moment.

'He's a birdwatcher,' I said. 'Loves them, he's obsessed with them.'

A flash of understanding crossed Seth's face. 'The bird table.'

'Yeah.' I smiled.

I'd felt compelled to get one when I finally got a garden.

When I talk to the birds, I feel closer to Stephen, as if I'm somehow talking to him. Seth often puts food out for them too if he's doing some gardening.

'So, what you going to do now?' he said.

'Try and find him, I guess.'

'Will you take him in?' Seth seemed to want to help, rather than pressure me, so I didn't mind the questions.

'I don't know. I'd like to think I would, but then . . .' I realised who I was talking to, what *his* situation was. 'I know I am imagining how it will be, this big reunion, me "rescuing" him, but the reality is . . . I see how hard it is for you with your mum.'

He thought about this for a second, then shrugged. 'The way I see it, she looked after me for all those years I needed it, so now it's my turn to look after her. It's as simple as that.'

I went to bed around 10 p.m., lay on my back staring into the dark, knowing sleep was hours away yet. I could hear the rain slapping the window and thought of the marshes on Canvey Island. In particular, I remembered how I loved being out on them with Stephen when we were kids and watching a storm roll in. I used to love the way the sky would go battleship grey but the grass would become a vivid green against it. Then the rain would come, approaching in towering, diagonal sheets. It was best enjoyed under canvas then. There was nothing I liked better than camping out when it was raining, listening to it drumming against the tent while we were cosy inside.

How did the rain sound to Stephen tonight? Comforting, because he was in a warm bed like me? Unlikely. Did he even have a tent or shelter of any kind?

After fifteen minutes, I got up and went downstairs, opening the kitchen door to the garden. I watched the rain bouncing wildly off the decking. Then I took off my shoes and stepped out, barefoot, eyes closed, for as long as I could – half a minute of eternity – before I was freezing and, funnily enough, wet through.

Swearing, I ran inside, closed the door and stood there dripping. My little act of martyrdom, self-flagellation, or whatever it was, had achieved nothing but a puddle on the kitchen floor. I finally went upstairs again, took off my damp pyjamas and stood at the threshold of my room in a towel, drying off. I couldn't get what Seth had said about his mum out of my head. She had looked after him when he needed it and now it was his turn to look after her. Simple as that.

It *was* as simple as that, wasn't it? Of course I was going to invite my brother to live with me when I found him. And I was not going to give up until I had.

It was 10.38 p.m. Normally I wouldn't dream of contacting anyone, let alone a work colleague, at this time of night, but Benjamin had alluded in the past to strange nocturnal habits. I got the feeling he was lonely and figured he may even appreciate a text at this time. It seemed I was right, too, since he replied in seconds, instructing me to call him. I got dressed and went out front to make the call. Maybe I wanted to feel closer to Stevie somehow.

'Hi.' My voice sounded extra loud in the silent street. 'Thanks for talking to me so late; it's kind of important so I really appreciate it.' I hesitated. 'It's about my brother,' I said, eventually. 'Stephen Nelson – you saw him today? I was just wondering if he said anything about any services he might be using, you know, hostels he might be staying at, soup kitchens he might be going to, or just where he might be hanging out?'

'Okaay,' said Benjamin, thoughtfully but also obviously taken aback by the urgency in my voice.

'I really want to find him if possible, you see,' I said, feeling faintly ridiculous, as if this was a scene in a soap opera. 'I *need* to find him. I'm really worried about him, especially out in this weather.'

'Sure,' said Benjamin. 'Of course, of course you are. But, uh no, not really, he didn't mention anything. Actually, he gave me a bit of a mouthful when I tried to suggest a couple of hostels – about how hostels were full of addicts and that it was a flat he needed. If only it were that easy, hey?'

'I know,' I said. 'So, he didn't mention any specific area he was hanging out in?'

'I don't think so, no. I don't think . . . Oh, hang on . . .' Benjamin, I was fast realising, had a maddening habit of omitting crucial information until the very last second. 'Camberwell. He did mention Camberwell area actually, which is why I suggested a hostel there.'

'Camberwell? But that's ten minutes from me,' I said, looking to my right then my left, as if he might be walking down my street right now.

'Thames Reach on Camberwell New Road might be worth a visit. They do a soup kitchen, I think, in St Giles' church, which also has some crash pad facilities.'

My heart thumped with excitement. 'Thank you,' I said. 'You're a total star.' I went back inside to get a coat, then got in the car; the London night suddenly felt like a wide, black sea that I was wading into, full of promise and peril.

I drove out of my street, past the wisteria-strewn bay windows. I drove down Denmark Hill and into Camberwell where, only five minutes and a postcode away, the world changes: late-night grocery stores selling plantains replace delis that sell manchego and olives for a fiver a tub; launderettes and mobile phone repair shops replace organic cotton babywear boutiques. I parked the car near Camberwell Green end, briefly regretting my decision to turn down James's offer to come over tonight, to be with me now.

I walked along Camberwell New Road, squinting

through the rain to read the numbers, looking behind and around me, hyper-vigilant. This part of London is not really somewhere you want to be as a lone female at night. Eventually I found 464, a door between a solicitor's and a mobile phone shop. There was a panel beside the door that read 'Thames Homeless Reach Night Shelter', but it was graffitied over and anyway, the door itself was half boarded up, the only sign of human life an empty can of lager on the doorstep.

'You won't find anything there, love.' I started, then looked around to see where the voice was coming from to find a man sitting outside the Tesco Metro, three doors down. He was skinny, the jeans he was wearing voluminous on him. His face was ravaged and dirty and there were two well-worn plastic bags by his feet. 'They're all closed now,' he added. 'Austerity, innit?'

'Tell me about it.'

He took a little packet out of his pocket and began rolling a cigarette.

'How are you?' I asked.

'Good,' he said, visibly shivering.

'You don't look so good. Here.' I rooted in the pocket of my toasty parka with its fleecy hood, and dropped a couple of quid in the pot next to him. I've never been sure where I stand on giving homeless people money.

'Bless you, darlin'.'

'McDonald's will still be open on Peckham Road; go

and get yourself a cup of tea,' I said and he looked at me as if I was mad. 'So, was this the only night shelter?' I asked, nodding towards the boarded-up door. 'Are there no others that you use? Other hostels nearby or soup kitchens?'

'There are a few, but they're no good for me,' he said, scattering tobacco into his cigarette paper. 'I've had places in loads of them, but always got chucked out because of the drink.' At this point I noticed the top of a bottle peering out above one of the plastic bags. 'You're better off on the streets if you ask me,' he said, licking his Rizla and sticking it down. 'I'm too long in the tooth and too far gone these days.'

'Well, it's hard, isn't it?' I said, scrabbling for something useful to say. 'A vicious cycle. Life is hard, and so we drink, then life gets harder.' *Shut up*, I thought to myself. *What the hell do you know?*

He looked up at me. 'Oh, don't feel sorry for me, I'm a big boy, I'm forty-two.'

I tried not to look shocked – he looked at least sixty.

'I've got a family who loves me – my mum made me this hat for Christmas,' he said, proudly indicating the yellow bobble hat he was wearing. 'But she can't help me while I'm not ready to help myself.'

Stephen was ready, I thought. He was ready, at least there was that. He was sober, I'd heard him say as much.

'I've buried more friends from alcohol than I have from

drugs, but you live by the gun, you die by the gun.' As if demonstrating his point, he took the bottle out of the plastic bag, unscrewed the cap and took a long slug.

'What's your name?'

'Damian.' He swallowed, wincing, holding his hand out.

'Pleased to meet you, Damian,' I said, shaking it. 'I'm Emily. Actually, I'm wondering if you might be able to help me. I'm looking for my brother. He's homeless and I'm told he hangs out in Camberwell – you might know him? Stephen Nelson? Not the most memorable name.'

Damian frowned, then shook his head.

'He's thirty-five,' I persisted. 'Tall, dark hair, although it's maybe a bit grey by now. You might have seen him with a pair of binoculars around his neck,' I added, at which point a light flickered in Damian's eyes and, for a fleeting second, I saw the person he maybe once was.

'Birdman?' he said. 'I know Birdman! We call him that 'cause he loves the birds – he draws them, don't he?'

'Does he?' I beamed, delighted. An image flashed up in my head of us sitting in the hide on the marshes and, across Stephen's lap, a sketchbook, open. He did love drawing birds. I felt closer to him knowing he still did.

'Listen,' I said, having got his attention now, 'I'm desperate to find him. It's a long story, but I can help him, I need to help him. Do you know where he might be?'

Damian's face clouded over then. I waited while he

took a few drags of his cigarette. 'Look, there's a few regular places I know. If you swear you won't tell him I sent you, then I'll tell you where I think he might be.'

I pressed my hands together. 'I swear.'

I drove badly, anxiously, perching forward in my seat. *You know the subway in Waterloo? The one with all the tunnels, the cinema in the centre?* My stomach flipped when he'd said that, because I knew only too well the state of the homeless guys who hung out there; I'd even looked in that subway in the past for my brother, only to hear from Dad he was in a completely different part of London, or – more often than not – that he wouldn't say where he was at all.

I turned on the radio to distract myself. The Hollies' 'He Ain't Heavy, He's My Brother' was playing. I had a dark laugh at that and switched it off. Turning right into the Old Kent Road, I thought how desolate and unforgiving this part of the city looked at night: the roads so quiet, decades of pollution making buildings look as if they'd been dredged up from the seabed; bargain furniture shops, pound shops, shuttered shops and pubs. Still the bargain basement on London's property Monopoly board.

I parked behind the London Eye and walked to the subway, feeling a whole new frisson of intimidation. Condensation ran down the white-painted brick walls of the tunnels, which, together with the harsh strip lighting, gave the impression of walking through the corridors of a mental hospital. I could hear voices – men's voices. They were shouting, aggressively; a row was underway. I stopped for a moment, the madness of the situation suddenly hitting me. What was I doing? Wandering the underbelly of London on my own after midnight. But I was on a mission now, a mission to find my brother. The argument seemed to die down, the voices sounded nearer and I thought I must be getting closer to the group – my brother hopefully among them – and I felt a flash of exhilaration at the prospect that I was seconds away from him. I imagined how I might hug him, tell him I loved him, that his nightmare was over and that I was taking him home in a warm car, to a warm bed and warm food; the sheer relief he'd feel, his face like the guys at the Glasgow soup kitchen where I used to volunteer when I was a student, when I opened the door in the morning to them. We would talk about this moment in years and Christmases to come, which we'd spend together, with his wife and children possibly, a roof over his head, life back on track.

When I found the source of the voices, however, Stephen wasn't among them. 'Cheer up, love, might never happen,' said one, followed by a ripple of laughter from the rest. I walked on, my pulse throbbing, hope and dread jostling as I turned each corner. The voices I'd passed were growing fainter – just ghostly echoes – but now there were more, different voices, and one in particular that stuck out, agitated, shouting in what sounded like panic. I turned the next bend and stopped dead in my tracks; I felt something like an electric shock shooting along my neck and shoulders then travelling down the backs of my arms. There was a huddle of men sitting on the floor, and one who was standing up, but with his head and arms hanging forward, like a rag doll. He was swaying, as if he was drunk, but he didn't look drunk; he looked terrifyingly deranged. He kept lifting his foot, attempting to take one step forward, then stepping back again – repeating this action over and over, as if he'd been lobotomised, or he was a zombie.

'Look at him,' the one voice shouted again. His speech was slurred, clearly very drunk himself. 'He needs an ambulance. Someone call an ambulance, for Chrissake.' But the men just carried on with whatever they were doing, drinking, smoking, staring blankly into space, as if this was a perfectly standard way for someone to behave. I was so shocked by the nonchalance that I failed to realise that the guy who'd pleaded for an ambulance to be called was my brother.

When I did realise, my heart, my breath – everything stopped.

He was sitting on layers of cardboard, his rucksack, which he was leaning on, against the condensation-covered wall. He was wearing no coat, even though it was freezing, just a dirty, pale-grey jumper, torn at the hem. The collar of a red gingham shirt underneath. There they were – the binoculars around his neck. He had his head on his knees now, a burning cigarette in one hand, empty cans by his side.

I was standing ten or so metres from the group but the smell was undeniable: urine, cigarette smoke and cheap booze. I made myself step forward.

'Stephen?' I said and my voice sounded weirdly high and echoey in the tunnel.

No response.

'Stevie?' I said again, a little louder, when he didn't answer, and I stepped closer, but not too close. I was petrified, I realised, of my own brother. Of what he might have become, of what life might have done to him, of how – it dawned on me horribly – he might feel to see me after all these years. My heart was beating so fast that I couldn't get a full lungful of air, and my toes flexed inside my trainers, preparing to run. Nobody need know I'd even come; I could just forget all about it.

Then Stephen looked up at me with bloodshot, unfocused eyes.

'It's me,' I said. I wanted to reach out but did not dare. 'It's Milly – your sister.'

He squinted at me and tried to take a drag of his cigarette, but he couldn't coordinate his movements and kept brushing the cigarette against his cheek instead. If there was pain, he didn't seem to feel it. He eventually managed to get it to his mouth and took several, slow drags, eyes narrowed at me, cheeks sucked in, gaunt and pale as wax. The zombie man was still hanging there, arms outstretched, failing to take a step, the others either ignoring him, or too wasted to remember he was there. Stephen exhaled, resting the back of his head on the wall.

'It's your sister,' I said again and Stephen's lips curled. His eyes swam but he was looking straight at me. He exhaled a plume of smoke, slowly.

'I haven't got a sister,' he said, finally.

'Barnacle Geese'

October 1991

Emily was standing on 'her' stool – painted by Grandad Paradiso to look like a toadstool – so she could reach the stove; Grandma Paradiso's hands hovered around her hips, in case of any wobbling. 'That's it,' she said, as Emily held the spoon over the pan and watched, her mouth watering, as the syrup poured from it like liquid gold. 'One more spoonful of that, and then we're stirring.' Adding the golden syrup was Emily's favourite bit about making toffee apples; she liked to make a show of holding the spoon high, so as to get the thinnest, longest drop; then wiggle it, so that when the viscous amber hit the hot pan, it made sizzling patterns, like writing in the air with a sparkler. On the kitchen worktop, the apples – picked that morning by Emily and Stephen from the tree in the mini orchard at El Paradiso – lay on parchment, rosy in the late afternoon light, waiting to be toffee-dunked.

Outside, beyond the wooden veranda, at the fringes of the olive-green marshes that stretched towards the sea, Emily could see flames the same colour as the syrup racing upwards into the misty blue sky, where a faint moon was already out, like a worn patch on faded denim. Stephen and Grandad had spent all afternoon building their bonfire while she'd been cooking with Grandma. She watched her big brother now, gathering armfuls of dead leaves and then – with a little run-up – throwing them onto it, Grandad Paradiso next to him, supervising. The earth-scented smoke drifted in through the window and mixed with the burnt sugar smell of the toffee, which was bubbling ferociously now, like a magic potion.

'Grandma, can we do the water trick to check it's done?' said Emily, excitedly, and Grandma leant forward, Emily catching the familiar and lovely scent of the talc she used, and surveyed the contents of the saucepan.

'Yes, in a minute.' She held one finger up. 'But it's not quite there yet. Keep stirring.' She went to the sink to fill up a bowl with cold water, ready for the trick, whereby you dropped hot toffee into it, and, if it set hard immediately, it was ready.

Emily thought it was the tap making the honking noise at first. This house made all sorts of noises, because it was made from all sorts of things: clapboard and chicken wire; corrugated iron, slate tiles and old rubber tubing. When it happened repeatedly, however, getting louder, as if it was getting nearer, coming for her even through the window, she ducked, instinctively, her hands gripping her blonde pigtails, only to see Stephen running towards the house in his wellies, a plume of bonfire smoke behind him, and she gasped, thinking he might be hurt, until she saw that although his mouth was open, it was a smiling mouth, his eyes wide, his arms flapping at his sides. 'Milly, quick!' he called, and now she could hear what he was shouting, and a smile spread across her mouth too. 'Come outside! You have to come outside.' And he burst through the back door, straight into the kitchen. 'Quick, Milly – now. You have to see this!'

'But she's got her toffee apples to finish . . .' Grandma trailed off, befuddled by the sudden whirlwind of urgency that often accompanied her grandson, especially if there were birds involved.

Emily was already getting down from the stool, padding across the lino after her brother in her red-stockinged feet.

'She's got no shoes on.'

'I'll carry her!'

'Your mum and dad will be back any minute.'

Stephen was already out the door.

Emily followed him until the edge of the wooden decking, which was damp with sea mist, where he crouched down: Emily's cue to put her hands on his shoulders, so he could wrap his arms around the back of her knees and hoist her up in a piggy back. He strode then off the raised veranda, up the short garden path and through the gate, rusty from decades of briny air. 'Look,' he said, pointing to the sky. She was already looking, because how could she not? An air show, with flickering dark shapes making giant arrows in the smoky blue sky.

'Aeroplanes!'

'No,' laughed Stephen. 'They're geese!'

'Pardon?' She couldn't hear him over the racket, which was tuneless, yet joyful, like the tooting of toy trumpets, coupled with what it sounds like to camp in a gale, canvas buffeted by the wind.

'Geese!'

'Yeah, oh wow, there are thousands of them!'

Emily put her hands over her ears like a pilot donning protective head gear, as she watched the honking and yipping Vs gun over her head.

'It's called a skein,' said Stephen.

'What is?'

'The shape, the V formations they're flying in. Do you know why they fly in that arrow shape?'

Emily shook her head and Stephen must have felt it because he said, 'To help each other. It's teamwork. See how each goose flies a bit above the one in front? It's so it can pull it along, at the same time as protect it from the wind; it helps them all save energy. They take turns being right at the front too, and just go to the back and give another goose a turn when they get tired.'

'Like when we take turns being in front on the scooter?'

Stephen hoisted her up a bit. 'No, that's just 'cause you demand to have a go in the front,' he laughed. 'You can't even move, I'm so heavy!'

Emily had nothing to say about that.

'If one goose gets injured, a couple of geese from its flock will stay on the ground with it until it's okay again and then they'll find a new flock,' added Stephen. 'They always stick together.'

Emily tipped her head back. It made her tummy flip like it did when she went high on the swing. The sky was blue and looked never-ending. It seemed as if the geese arrows were going over her head, behind her, and all the way under her, in a full circle, and she was suspended in a ball of sky. With the funny tummy feeling, she felt she might fall, but that would be okay, because Stephen was holding her. He would always hold on to her. If she fell, he would catch her.

Chapter Seven

Stephen

London, Friday morning

Hoping to God nobody could see him, Stephen was rifling in the big commercial bin when something flashed in his peripheral vision. He turned his head quickly to see a fox, trotting brazenly across the yard behind the mini supermarket in the bright morning. The sudden movement made his head thump harder. He couldn't work out if he was nauseous or ravenous; he just knew he had to get something inside him quick, if things weren't going to take a drastic turn for the worse. He was in luck: the bin was full of perfectly good products all with yesterday's sell-by date and he pulled out an Innocent berry smoothie, falafel bites with a sweet chilli dip, a Finest roast beef and horseradish sandwich on malted brown bread and a Devonshire cream lemon curd yoghurt.

Discarding the sandwich – obviously no good for a veggie – Stephen opened the smoothie as he walked, downing it in three quick gulps, shoving the empty plastic bottle in his pocket; he'd keep that and fill it with tap water later. He tore open the falafel and rammed them into his mouth so quickly that he had to take a half-eaten one out again, as there wasn't room to chew them all. He turned left at Southwark Street, where several blank-faced people emerged from the tube station, noses glued to their phones. It was just coming up for 11 a.m. the day after Stephen's first bender – his first taste of alcohol come to that – in many months and, at the vanishing point of Southwark Street, the sun was high, bleaching the post-storm London sky a creamy lemon colour.

After two weeks, the rain had stopped, lending an extra stillness to the morning, an extra calmness. But Stephen, in his delicate state, was feeling horribly overwhelmed; car horns startled him, the glare coming from glass office blocks blinded him. It was a brand-new day, but also another day to get through, and Stephen wasn't sure at this point how he was going to do it.

Pausing to adjust the rubbing straps on his rucksack, he turned off the main road and into a shady churchyard, where he found a patch under some bushes to sit down and eat his yoghurt. The earth was still wet after the rain, but it was gorgeously cool and refreshing against his toxic skin, and anyway, his jeans were already filthy again after twenty-four hours on the street, and now he had no clean spares. He leant back, using his rucksack as a beanbag – albeit one about as comfy as a bag of stickle bricks – and peeled the lid off his yoghurt, then dug inside the pocket at the front of his rucksack where he kept plastic cutlery for such occasions. Among the spoons, Rizla papers and fag butts, his fingers touched a small, folded piece of paper. He took it out and unfolded it. It was a receipt for food from Marks & Spencer: boeuf bourguignon, potatoes dauphinoise, a bottle of Chianti for £16. This confused him, since he'd never bought anything from Marks & Spencer's in his thirty-five years on this planet; he'd not even got to the dizzy heights of rummaging in their bins. But then he turned it over, and written on the back in blue biro was the following:

Nutbrook Avenue, SE22 1BD / 07775601743
Please call or come any time. Milly xxx

The words 'please' and 'any' were underlined twice, although something greasy, presumably in his rucksack pocket, had blotted the paper and the house number was no longer legible.

Stephen stared at the message, yoghurt forgotten. There was a falling sensation in his stomach, a sudden vertigo. Fragments came to him, blurred and disjointed: a tunnel; echoing voices, laughing and talking; someone asking if he was all right; a hand on his shoulder. And then, out of this scene, like a dream, a woman with blonde hair and a full mouth, a heart-shaped face.

A face he'd once known so well. A face he'd never imagined he would see again.

Stephen felt sick. He leant over to the side, rucksack still attached, like a diver rolling overboard, and spewed barely digested falafel and smoothie onto the grass. He retched and retched until, finally, nothing more came out. He spat, wiped his mouth.

Jesus, he needed water. He needed water badly. He thought about getting up and going to find some, but he felt horrendous: bilious still, his head so scrambled he could weep. He turned on his side and lay there, very still, hardly daring to breathe in case another wave of nausea hit him.

He awoke to a jabbing in his side. 'Birdman,' someone said, then Stephen heard gentle laughter and couldn't work out if it was real or a dream.

'Nah, it's all right, he's warm, he's alive.'

Was that the same voice or a different one? Stephen opened his eyes.

'Just checking you weren't dead, buddy,' another voice added, and Stephen sat up, feeling so woeful, he almost wished he was. He looked around him. The sun was in his eyes and he couldn't have told you the day, time, season, not least because Lee, Jimmy and Scotty were sitting next to him and they were from another time, another life. The idea he might be back there filled Stephen with horror.

Please let me be dreaming, he thought, sitting with his

knees drawn up, head in his hands. There was the hiss of a can being opened, then the smell of hops.

'What time is it?' said Stephen.

'One o'clock,' said Lee.

He'd been asleep for two hours and if anything felt worse.

Scotty had a four-pack and a clanking bag full of God knows what else. Stephen felt temptation rising, but knew that that would be the worst idea in the world.

'Where've you been?' Scotty said. 'You disappeared for months.'

'He went and found some real friends, didn't he?' Lee said, lighting a cigarette, giving a phlegmy laugh. He unscrewed the cap of his vodka bottle, took a swig and held it out to Stephen.

Stephen eyed it. He ground his back teeth. A few swigs of that, get a bit drunk today, just today, and it would make his hangover go away; his shame at having got in such a state last night too.

'Come on then, my arm's falling off,' said Lee.

Thank God he came to his senses.

'No thanks, mate,' said Stephen. Then he hauled himself to his feet. 'I'm off, lads.'

'Aye, course y'are,' laughed Lee, bitterly. 'Course y'are, laddy – where? Where the fuck are yer going?'

'Somewhere else,' said Stephen, mostly to himself, putting on his rucksack. 'Just somewhere other than here.'

Chapter Eight
Emily

We are human beings. You cannot expect human beings to live like this.

My last client – Mr Adebayo – had been tough. Standing in the corridor after the interview, getting some air, I couldn't get his voice out of my head.

Not to mention that of my brother's.

Mr Adebayo and his family had been living in a B&B since being evicted a year ago, through no fault of their own, which was all too often the way. There were four of them in one room. His daughter had to do her homework in the bathroom they shared with two other families because it was the only place she would not be disturbed. His wife suffered from heart problems because of the stress.

'Are you going to tell me you can't do anything?' he'd said, at one point. 'Because that is all that we hear.'

And I'd thought, *Mr Adebayo, that's exactly what I'm going to tell you.*

I leant my head on the cool of the windowpane, looking

onto the street. I hadn't slept and was so tired, I felt I could fall asleep right there.

'Emily?'

I looked up, relieved to see Justine walking down the corridor with her school ma'am-ish stride, even though she's not remotely a school ma'am-ish person, clutching files to her chest, blowing her Titian fringe out of her eyes. She stopped when she saw me and put her hand on my shoulder. 'Emily, my love, you all right?' And then, of course, as is the law when you're not, and someone asks you if you are, or God forbid is nice to you, I burst into tears.

'Okay,' said Justine. 'Let's get some lunch.'

'So, he just looked at me and said, "I don't have a sister."' We were in Pret A Manger at lunch rush hour. All the seats were taken, so we were sitting on stools by the window, having to lean in so that we could hear each other.

Justine shook her head slowly, small, wise eyes narrowed in concern. 'But you say he was really drunk?' she said, and I nodded.

'Like, totally out of it,' I explained. 'Paralytic and filthy. Juss . . .' I felt terrible for what I was about to say, but I had to tell someone. 'And this must never, ever be repeated. God strike me down and all that. But the smell down there in the tunnel . . .'

'Oh God.'

'It was like nothing else, and he's my own brother, you know? My big, hero brother who I grew up with, who I worshipped. I mean, Jesus, to see him in that state . . .'

Tears again. It was true I was in shock. It had been far worse than I'd imagined, although I don't actually know *what* I'd imagined.

Justine was rubbing my arm. It felt good to tell her this stuff. 'There was this one poor guy,' I continued. 'He was standing up but hanging forwards like a zombie, picking his foot up then putting it down, unable to take a step, like a ketamine-fuelled show pony or something. Honestly, I thought I'd seen it all. I thought I was pretty un-shockable, but oh my God . . . And the worst thing was, nobody was taking much notice of him, like this was normal, like they saw it every day.'

Justine bit into her hot chicken and mozzarella wrap. I'd been too busy talking to even touch my crayfish salad.

'Spice,' she said, catching a bit of melted cheese that had escaped with a cupped hand and guiding it back.

'Spice?'

'This hideous drug they're all taking. It's becoming rife, especially among the homeless. It's been nicknamed the "zombie drug" because it makes them look like that – like zombies. I think it's some kind of synthetic cannabis thing but it's so bad, so dangerous.'

I stared at her, horrified. Spice. *Of course. Of course that's what it was.* 'Oh God, what if Stephen starts on that too?' I said. 'What if he's already on it?'

'Oh, he won't be.' Having seen my horror, Justine was clearly backtracking. 'He would have been on it at the time if he was hooked. They do it all the time, once they are. Em, honestly, he was probably so drunk, he didn't know what he was saying.'

I looked out of the window. 'Oh no. He knew all right.' At that point a blackbird landed on the window ledge and I became aware I was looking at him, rather than at Justine, whose stare I could feel on me. 'He knew what he was saying and he knew who I was.' The blackbird met my eye with its glossy, black, gold-rimmed one, hopped twice along the sill then flew off.

'I suppose I just wasn't expecting it to go how it went . . .' I added, after a while. 'That's what hurt. I don't know what I expected, some sort of bloody fairy-tale reunion probably.' What *had* I expected? I hadn't thought it through at all. 'I feel like such an idiot. Anyway . . .' I'd said too much, opened the gates to a conversation I didn't want to go any further with – one that would inevitably lead to places I didn't want to go. I loved Justine, she was loyal and fun, but we only met two years ago, making her a relatively new friend in my book, and I told nobody more than this about my brother: he was homeless, I missed him and would never stop looking for him. Even if I feared that he no longer wanted to be found. A fear that seemed to have just been realised.

Justine sighed in a way that said, *what are we going to do with you?* Outside, the sun was burning through cloud, but the pavements were still dark and shiny.

'Look, Em,' she said, suddenly. 'I'm not going to ask you to go into the whole shebang and I don't want to pry. I'm only interested in you not looking so bloody miserable, because honestly, I can't bear it. But how were things when you last saw your brother? I mean, does Stephen have a reason for claiming to not know who you are?'

And there it was. I didn't blame Justine for probing but it made my scalp prickle. 'I was really young,' I began, fiddling with the scrunched-up napkin in my hands. 'I was only twelve when he went to prison. I missed him so much – I've never forgotten that aching feeling of longing for someone, you know? It was like he'd died. But to be honest, it was also scary having a brother in prison. Even embarrassing at times. Kids at school said nasty things, people on Canvey talked . . .'

'Did you visit him?'

'Only once. I found it too hard. He'd caused our parents so much trouble, so much grief. Mum didn't talk about him – his name was taboo. Dad tried, but Stephen and he were really close and I think he had a lot of sadness about how he'd ended up, guilt probably too, and I was just too young to know how to deal with it. Then, I was at Glasgow uni, so not exactly close . . .'

I was aware I was rambling, not answering Justine's question about what happened when I'd last seen my brother, but if she'd noticed, she didn't say anything. 'I didn't think when we met that we'd put everything behind us and it would all be hunky-dory or anything, I just wanted the opportunity to help him. I've been desperate to find him for years – it's basically why I went into housing in the first place.'

'I know,' said Justine. 'And yet, what were the chances of him actually walking into your office? It's meant to be. You're meant to have him back.'

'God, I hope so. Thank you – thank you for saying that.'

'Benjamin's gagging to know the backstory,' she added, stirring sugar into her coffee. 'Not that he's letting on. He's always bloody there when I turn around, though, going, "Oh, hullo there, Justine. Heard from Emily at all? I do hope she's okay about . . . you know, her private matter."' I laughed at Justine's impression of mole-eyed, geeky Benjamin – God bless him. It was a relief to lighten things.

'Listen,' I said. I felt the need to confess. 'Before I left Stephen, I gave him a piece of paper with my address and phone number on. It said to get in touch any time, that's all.'

I was pushing some crayfish around but I could feel Justine looking at me. 'And how do you think you'd feel if he did turn up at your house?' she said, after a pause.

'Well, thrilled,' I said. 'I mean, obviously.' Talking about it had ignited a new and glorious hope, a determination not to give up. And yet jostling alongside it was the downward drag of anxiety, a feeling I could not shake that my brother showing up had set in motion something huge – something that once started, would quickly become unstoppable, like taking the handbrake off an empty car, and watching it roll downhill.

'Cuckoo'

July 1992

Stephen handed Emily the buttered baguette, in a bowl so big her arms barely reached around the sides.

'Right, so I'm going to take some more drinks out, and you're going to go around everyone with the bread, okay, Mills?'

She nodded, one hand creeping over the side and into the bowl.

'And no eating it!'

'I'm not!'

'Not even a nibble. If Mum catches you, she'll go mad.'

Emily stomped outside with the bowl and into the garden. Alicia's birthday barbecue had fallen on a scorcher of a July weekend. Emily had spent most of it in the paddling pool, and was still in her swimsuit, damp curls peeping out from beneath her red baseball cap. From the kitchen door, Stephen watched his sister's progress; he could hear the guests cooing over her cuteness, bursts of laughter that seemed muffled by the sunshine.

At the bottom of the long lawn, under the weeping willow, his father was behind the barbecue. Tony had brought all the meat from his shop that morning, and was completely in his element. Best of all, though, Stephen could see Mum laughing, glass in hand, looking resplendent in her new blue dress. Relief washed over him at her obvious contentment.

She'd not been herself recently – Dad could do nothing right. Last week, Stephen had been woken by her hoovering while crying at 5 a.m. But today was her birthday, the sun was shining, she was happy and that's all Stephen needed to make him happy too.

He picked up the tray from the side, already loaded with his next round of drinks, and carried it outside. He was taking his role as wine waiter very seriously. Tony had shown him how to pour 'the shampoo', as he'd called the champagne, and how to tilt the glass so that the bubbles didn't fizz over the rim, and Stephen felt grown-up as he made his way through the party.

'Excuse me, would you like some champagne?'

'Ooo, champagne,' said a lady with jet-black hair piled up on her head. 'Now that's what I call a proper knees-up.'

'Actually, it's better than champagne,' he said proudly, as she took a glass. 'It's Asti Spumanti – the best money can buy.'

She snorted with laughter – 'Aw, isn't he adorable?' – and to Stephen's bafflement so did all her friends. He smiled politely and moved on, doing a quick check for his sister's whereabouts, to find she was doing handstands against the garage in front of an audience of enraptured toddlers sitting cross-legged on the driveway.

His mother called to him then: 'Stephen, we're dying of thirst over here, bring us some bubbles, darlin'.' And he looked over to see she was standing with several people, including – his heart sank – Mitch Reynolds and his wife, Tina, the ones whose wedding he'd been to on The Day of the Ducklings (which is how it had gone down in Nelson family legend). Dutifully, Stephen walked over.

'Here he is,' said Alicia, sweeping his fringe out of his eyes. Stephen felt his face grow pink. 'The little sommelier. You're doing a brilliant job.' She put her empty glass down and took two of the three full ones left on the tray, sipping from one and giving the other to Mitch, who put his empty on the tray without so much as a glance at the person holding it.

'Say hello,' his mother said. 'You know Mitch and Tina . . .'

'Hello,' said Stephen.

'This is my boy, Stephen,' she said to the rest of the group; Stephen counted six people who were standing in a semicircle, with him – he now felt keenly – right in the middle of it. 'My little nature lover.'

Mitch and Tina and his parents had met at the Canvey Island Social Club and been friends for pretty much as long as he could remember, sometimes coming over on a Saturday night. Tina was nice, friendly even, but Mitch? Stephen wasn't a fan. His parents were always going on about how he'd fought in the Falklands War and was a war hero who'd got medals for his bravery. All Stephen knew was that the man had never paid any attention to him – except once.

His mum had invited some friends over for a fondue evening. 'How old are you now?' he'd asked Stephen, in front of everyone.

'Eight, nearly nine.'

'Really?' he'd said. 'I'd have said seven at the most.'

Stephen had felt the need to go to the privacy of his bedroom and do several karate chops, imagining Mitch as his opponent, in his wardrobe mirror. He didn't care how many bravery medals he had, he'd never forgiven him.

Tina suddenly clapped her hands. 'Oooh!' she said to the rest of the group. 'This young man's not just a nature lover but a nature saviour.'

Stephen beamed.

'He and his sister . . . Don't you remember, Mitchell? At the wedding reception? They stole the show telling us about how they got that duck and her ducklings across the road; caused a traffic jam on Towcester high street! They were heroes.'

Mitch frowned and pursed his lips, looking skywards, as if thinking about this. 'Yeah, course I remember,' he said, running a finger along the black stubble of his jawline. 'I'm sure I do.'

'Gosh, and isn't he the spit of Tony?' Tina carried on. Stephen was beginning to feel very self-conscious with all these adults studying him. 'Doesn't he look like his dad?'

'Don't say that to the poor lad, scar him for life,' said Mitch, which everyone seemed to find very amusing. 'I'm only pulling yer leg, son.' He patted Stephen's shoulder with a large, tanned, ring-adorned hand. 'I'm just messin' with yer.'

Stephen looked to his mother with appealing eyes but she just giggled into her glass. She was definitely tipsy now.

'Take no notice of him,' said Tina. 'Mitchell, please will you go to the car to get my cigs? And the Ambre Solaire, I'm still burning to a crisp here.'

Mitch jangled the car keys in his pocket. 'In the glove box?'

Tina nodded.

'And I better go in and wash some salad,' added his mother, when Mitch had walked in the direction of the front of the house. 'The meat's nearly ready. Stephen, go and give your dad that last drink, will you?'

'Hello, Steve,' Tony said cheerfully, when Stephen had

sidled over to the barbecue, grateful his mum had given him a get-out clause from having to stay and talk to grown-ups he hardly knew. 'You earning yer keep? Good lad.' Stephen felt a sudden wave of gratitude for his father's very existence. 'And you've brought your old man a glass of shampoo, I see? Fantastic,' and he reached over and took the last glass on Stephen's tray. Stephen stood next to his father and watched his father flipping burgers like a pro. 'I'm putting you on some corn on the cob, don't worry,' said Tony, reading Stephen's thoughts. 'You and Milly can have a whole baguette of garlic bread to yourself, eh? How about that?' he said, giving him a fatherly nudge with his elbow.

'Can we?!' said Stephen, straightening up excitedly.

'Yeah,' said Tony. 'Just don't tell your mother.'

The evening was at its peak now and a blackbird was singing its smooth, summer's song: those three or four fluting notes, topped off with a flourish. Low sun flooded the garden as Stephen went to the kitchen to get more champagne. As he walked through the open back door, he stopped, his heart banging against his chest at what he saw: his mother at the sink, her back to him; Mitch standing so close their bodies were touching, his hand on her bottom.

He must have made a sound because his mother yelped, softly, like a puppy, and the two adults sprang apart.

Alicia turned around. 'God, don't creep up on people like that, Stephen, it's not nice. What are you wanting anyway?' She had her hand to her throat, which Stephen noticed was blotchy. Mitch was looking out of the window.

'More drinks.'

'Right, well, get on with it then,' she said, snappily but not unkindly. 'I've got to take this salad out.' And she tipped the salad from the colander that was in the sink into a bowl she had ready on the side, and walked out.

After a few seconds, during which Stephen stood frozen to the spot, holding his breath, Mitch said, 'Right, well, you'd better get a burger down you if you're going to grow into a big, strong lad, hadn't you?'

'I'm a vegetarian,' Stephen said, as Mitch brushed past him, on his way back out to the garden, leaving a waft of cigars and aftershave behind him.

A month later – a Sunday in early August, a week before his tenth birthday and days after he'd said goodbye to his swifts, his first experience of love, if loving meant pain when the object of your love disappeared – Alicia announced she was leaving his father to be with Mr Reynolds, and Stephen knew his world had ended.

Chapter Nine

Like most people, I suppose, I don't have many memories before the age of five. There are vague recollections of Mum and Dad still living together in Merlin Drive and of us being a regular family of four, and those memories are generally lovely: visits to Grandma and Grandad Paradiso; snuggling on the sofa on a Saturday night, hoping not to get sent to bed too early; summer days – too many to count – spent simply roaming the marsh with Stephen, often only coming in when it was teatime. I think I remember feeling sad when Mum and Dad split, but I was only five and a half so can't be sure.

Apart from those few, hazy memories, I only really remember life being Stevie and me at Dad's during the week, and at Mum and Mitch's most weekends, where there were largely two states of play: being in the house where things were fraught – particularly between Stephen and Mitch; or me and my brother being happy as Larry playing and exploring outside. Just the two of us and acres and acres of space. Sometimes we'd go to visit our grandparents at El Paradiso. Mostly, the adults, though, were out of commission. In fact, when I think back to that part of my childhood before Stephen went to prison, it's as if those figures, our parents, are shadows in the background, or else players in their own plays, plays that didn't have much to do with ours. Mine and Stephen's.

I got off the bus just by Lordship Lane and walked the five minutes home, fighting the feeling – even though I've been here for two years – that 'here' still doesn't feel like home. I could hear the phone ringing as I was rooting (as ever!) in my bag for my front door keys. It would be Mum, I knew it. She's the only person who calls me on the land-line, as if driving home the point that she can't get hold of me, because I'm 'never in' whereas she doesn't need a mobile phone, because she's 'never out': she can't leave my stepfather, Mitch, who needs round-the-clock care. She uses that phrase a lot – 'round-the-clock care' – as if she doesn't want anyone to forget it, not that I ever could.

Usually, I'm running around the flat like an idiot, looking for the damned phone, but it was in its cradle for once, on the hall wall. 'Hi, Mum,' I said, as breezily as I could muster, shrugging off my coat, but guilt was already sloshing around my insides like too much wine. I pictured myself in the tunnel last night, looking into Stephen's bloodshot eyes, tucking that piece of paper with my contact details into his rucksack pocket. God, if she knew. And yet, I wished she did, and that I could tell her; tell her how her son needed her, needed both of us. That she had to forgive him.

'Hello, love,' said Mum. 'You're in, finally, then?'

'Mum, you're actually lucky to catch me at this time; normally I stay at work later.'

'Oh? Oh, I am lucky then – and how is work?' She rarely enquired about my life, so I was suspicious.

'Oh, fine, good. Well, you know, hard,' I said, caught off guard. I walked through to the lounge area and sat down in an armchair. I pictured the scene at her end: the front room of their bungalow in Bridlington, the curtains closed, the world shut out; Mitch sitting mannequin-like, strapped into position; the hoist equipment dangling from the ceiling; his oxygen tank.

Without warning a flashback arrived. The beating heat of that June day. The sky almost navy blue, and Mitch, lying on the patio, eyes a fixed stare, blood pooling from his head. Paramedics clustering around him, calling out urgent instructions. Mum approaching the house now, in the copper Peugeot. Her getting out, glamorous in Capri pants and heels, and her face falling, then turning to panic as she sees the police car, Stephen's face in the back of it, the waiting ambulance, then me, standing sobbing on the garden path, a policewoman with her arm around me. 'What's happened?' says my mother, fingertips to her lips. 'God help me, what's happened?'

How I longed to tell her about Stephen.

I hauled myself back to now. 'Anyway, how are you, Mum? Deborah been today?' Deborah comes twice a day so that Mum can have a lie-down, do some housework or even go out, a rare occurrence but something that was beginning to happen more often at that time, which I was thrilled about.

'Yes, she's been, she was great, I just didn't have her here long enough, as ever.' She paused, just to let that sink in. Not that she needed to drum up sympathy from me: I felt it, her pain, her bitterness, all the time. I pictured her wiping Mitch's dribble and felt wretched for her. 'He's not doing well,' she added. 'He's had another chest infection, a raging temperature.' I felt tightness in my chest too. Sometimes it physically hurt when she told me this stuff; as if I had to feel some pain to cope with not being able to do anything practical to ease *her* pain.

'He nearly had to go into hospital but the doctor came over and managed to stabilise him – unfortunately.' She paused. That word hung in the air. 'I only mean because I would have got some respite.'

'I know, Mum. It's all right, I know.'

'Anyway . . .' I could hear her fiddling with her St Christopher pendant. 'I've been talking to Sheena.'

'Sheena?'

'My friend from B.R.A.S,' she said, quickly, bashfully, 'my friend' not being a phrase that often left my mother's mouth these days. When I was young, she seemed to have countless 'friends' who all abandoned her after Mitch became a tetraplegic, crippled wheelchair users not really fitting their idea of aspirational living or what a Falklands hero should look like, I expect.

'Oh, Sheena!' I couldn't hide my delight that Sheena was still on the scene, not to mention the fact that Mum was still going to B.R.A.S, a local meet-up of women who'd had mastectomies due to breast cancer, and who got together for coffee, cake and support every other week. My mother is not a 'joiner', especially when it comes to groups of women, of which she is very suspicious, so I'd been thrilled when she said she'd started going, if only for the fact she was getting out of the house and having a break from Mitch for a while.

'And? What did Sheena say?'

Mum paused. 'She says I should think about finding a residential home, that I've done my bit, that I need to hand over the burden and have a bit of a life for myself, you know, before it's too late.' There was a pause. 'So . . . I've decided I'm going to,' she said, and it was as if I felt something lift, options open, hope.

'Do you think that makes me a terrible person?'

I couldn't formulate a response; I was still trying to take this mind-blowing news in.

'Emily? Say something.' She sounded tearful.

'No,' I said, 'I don't think it makes you a terrible person, Mum, I think it's wonderful.'

I put the phone down and burst into happy tears.

'Turkey'

Christmas 1992

'Well,' said Alicia. 'Happy Christmas, everyone. Cheers!' and she raised her glass of wine and Emily lifted her beaker of lemonade with the glittery curly-wurly straw she'd got in her stocking and clinked it against her mother's. 'Cheers, Mummy!'

'Yes, a very merry Christmas to you all,' said Mitch, raising his glass too, and he clinked with Emily's and then held it out to Stephen, who sat with his arms by his side.

Emily leant in towards her brother. 'Deeby, you've got to do the cheers,' she whispered over the Christmas songs that were playing on low. She was wearing the party hat from her cracker, which was far too big and had slipped over one eye. 'That's what you have to do at Christmas. You just have to do it.'

'That's right, darling,' said Mummy. 'Good girl. Stephen?' Emily watched Stephen slowly lift his cup and clink it with Mitch's, then as Mitch did the same with

Mummy, after which he stood up, leant across the table and kissed her on the lips. It lasted a really long time.

'Now, who wants what?' he said, rubbing his hands together. 'Bearing in mind all the pigs in blankets are mine.' Emily felt her heart nose-dive and looked to her mum who was laughing, pouring more wine. 'He's only joking, sweetie. You can have as many as you like,' she said and she served up the mini sausages to everyone except Stephen, who didn't eat dead animals, then she served the vegetables and potatoes. All the while, Mitch was carving the turkey up at the table with a giant knife and fork. 'Santa Claus is Coming to Town' was playing, one of Tony's favourites, and Emily had a sudden pining for her daddy, for him to be the one standing at the table, cutting the turkey, not her stepdad, but she'd seen Daddy that morning for presents, so it was okay.

'Who's for leg and who's for breast?' said Mitch. 'Because I'm a breast man, that's for sure . . .'

Alicia snorted. 'Oh Mitchell, behave.'

'Twenty-eight English pounds' worth of gold standard turkey here. You won't find better than this.'

'Gosh, well, just the lean breast for me, Mitch,' said Alicia, taking another sip of her wine.

'Leg, please,' said Emily, bouncing lightly on her chair. 'And all the crispy skin!'

'All right, all right. It's the grown-ups first and certain greedy piglets last.'

Mitch served Alicia, then himself, followed by Emily. Then he put a couple of slices of breast meat between the giant knife and fork and leant across the table to put them onto Stephen's plate. Stephen moved it. Mitch rolled his eyes. 'It's Christmas Day, Stephen,' he said. 'And as I said before, on Christmas Day in my house, when I have paid for the best turkey money can buy, I don't think it's too much to ask . . .'

Stevie said he didn't like it and that Mitch couldn't make him eat it.

'Come on.' He held the meat out again. 'You'll never grow big and strong like me if you just eat rabbit food.'

'He doesn't eat dead animals,' said Emily, matter-of-factly and, she thought, helpfully.

'Don't you want muscles?' Mitch said, ignoring both of them. 'Or do you want to stay weedy? Because it's survival of the fittest out there, Stephen, I can tell you that.' And he put the meat on Stephen's plate.

'But I don't eat meat,' said Stephen, simply.

Mitch blew his cheeks out and glared at Stephen. 'Christ, I need more wine and a cigar for this kind of nonsense,' he said, as he left the table and strode into the kitchen, muttering. 'Don't wait for me, it'll only get cold!'

From where she was sitting, through the glass partition separating the dining room and the kitchen, Emily watched as her stepfather (he and Mum weren't married yet, but they would be and she'd been told to call him her stepfather) opened the back door and stood on the patio, smoking his cigar; she could smell it too, wafting in. Stevie smiled at Mummy, who smiled back, but it was a naughty kind of smile. Then, quick as lightning, Stephen opened the serviette up on the table, stabbed the turkey on his plate with a fork, picked it up (leaving a slice – because he wasn't stupid) and transferred it to the serviette, wrapping it up. Emily looked over at her mother who smiled again, conspiratorially, then back at her brother who put a finger to his lips. Emily giggled, feeling excited to be part of a secret. A game between her and Stevie and Mummy, the very best kind.

Mitch strode back in, chest puffed, holding a new bottle of red wine and a bottle opener. He made a show of popping the cork and pouring the wine. Emily hummed along to the music.

'What you have to learn, Stephen,' he began, 'is a little respect for your elders.'

'Leave him be, Mitch, will you?' said Alicia, gently. 'You can see he's done well. Look, he's nearly finished that meat.' Emily caught her mother's eye and bit her lip.

Mitch looked over at Stephen's plate and held both palms up. 'Well, there you go,' he said, sitting down and laying his serviette on his lap. 'That wasn't that bad, was it? What was all that fuss about?'

Stephen shrugged. 'I've no idea,' he said, cutting into

a potato. Emily had to think of something sad so that she didn't laugh.

At the beginning of the May following that first Christmas since her parents' split – which had turned out to be a good Christmas, actually – Emily sat in the front seat of her dad's blue Astra as they pulled into the drive of his new house on Eden Court. She'd been to a friend's house for the afternoon, and Dad had just picked her up. It was a sunny, warm evening and the front lawn was a riot of buttercups and daisies. As the car slowed, Stephen shot out of the front door. He'd been playing footie in the back garden with his friend Moose and was wearing a white vest and blue, silky football shorts; stick-thin legs poking out the bottom and his binoculars, as always, hanging around his neck. They banged against the car as he stuck his head through Emily's side, unable to wait till Dad had even come to a stop. 'Oi, do you mind?' said Dad, still trying to manoeuvre the Astra over the gravel. 'You're scratching my bloody car.'

'They're back!' said Stephen, so overcome with excitement that he was panting like a puppy. 'They're back, I just saw them. Can I take Milly to see them, Dad? Now? Please?'

Next thing, she and Stevie were free-wheeling down country lanes, him giving her a croggy on the BMX, the thick, grass verges curving ahead of them in a spearmint-coloured explosion of cow parsley. At Canvey Memorial

Hall, which Emily only knew as 'the white church', they stopped and got off. He lifted her onto his shoulders in one, pro, big-brother move.

'Okay?'

'Yeah.' She felt perfectly safe.

'Now, just look up.'

That's when she saw them for the first time. There must have been about eight of them, black against the sky, making a squealing sound, as if they were excited; as if something was about to happen.

She gasped, because it felt as though the occasion called for it, but she didn't really know what she was dealing with. 'What are they?'

'They're swifts,' said Stephen. 'They've flown all the way from Africa for the summer to have their chicks on Canvey Island. That's their nest inside that hole.'

Emily was mesmerised by the concept of birds home-making like humans. It made her think of the Beatrix Potter books Grandma Paradiso read to her; of Mrs Tiggywinkle and Jenny Wren and creatures that lived inside tree trunks and did ironing wearing cloth caps. She badly wanted to know what it looked like inside the hole too. Were there different rooms like in her Fisher Price toy treehouse? Did it open up into a cave of tunnels?

She told Stevie she loved the swifts.

'Aren't they cool?' he said. 'But we've got to make the most of them, Mills, do you know why?'

That's when Stephen told her how they were only here for a short while; that come August they'd fly back to their other home in Africa.

'And then we never see them again?' she asked, watching them. It wasn't dark yet, but the moon was already out, but faint, just an impression like a potato print. Stephen said they came back every May no matter what to have their babies.

'I love them so much,' Emily announced again, and Stephen laughed and said he was glad and he loved them too.

'We can totally count on them, you know, to come back,' he said. 'They'll never let us down, not like people can. They're our swifts, Milly, mine and yours.'

'Mine and yours, Deeby,' she parroted. And then she scrunched up her fists by her mouth and gave a little squeal of excitement. It sounded just like the swifts.

Every year after that one – 1993 – they welcomed the swifts back to Canvey. Stephen was able to predict their homecoming, almost to the day – the end of April, the first week in May – which always amazed Emily, as if he had a special 'in' with Mother Nature. All she knew was that along with the sudden warming of the earth, the unfurling of Dad's chrysanthemums in his tiny back garden, she and Stephen would look up, one still evening, and there, high in the sky, would be a couple of dark, arrow-shaped dots, cruising silently. They were back!

The one-hundred-day holiday romance would begin again, then, and they'd stand barefoot and pyjama-clad on the dewy lawn at dawn with the binoculars, attend their evening rooftop screaming parties at dusk, watch as they flew in and out of their nest in that secret crevice of the memorial hall, bringing twigs and gossamer, making their summer home.

Chapter Ten

Stephen

'Can I help you?'

Stephen, who was on his knees, rucksack still on, peering through the glass of the block's entrance, was aware of the woman's voice behind him, but chose to ignore it the first time.

'Hello?' she called again, but he still didn't move; he merely watched the woman's reflection in the glass of the door. 'Excuse me. Can I ask what you're doing?'

Stephen stood up then and turned around, hitching his trousers up, to see that the voice belonged to a woman standing across the road. She had dark reddish hair, sunglasses on her head, and a little girl of about seven, he guessed, by the hand.

'Er, oh, hi.' Stephen wiped his nose on the back of his hand and pulled down his shirt. 'I'm looking for Emily.' He'd walked the four miles from Southwark to East Dulwich and his voice was hoarse with exhaustion, his mouth sticky. Even he knew he was dangerously dehydrated. 'This is the address I've got for her.'

The woman carried on looking at him from under one hand, which was shielding her eyes from the sun. The other was now around the girl's shoulders, pulling her in closer. The little girl was watching Stephen with the same, hard frown as her mother.

'Do you know Emily?'

Stephen hesitated, shifting from one foot to the other. 'Yeah, yeah, I know Emily.' He was beginning to find the woman disconcerting, very unhelpful. 'Do you?'

'Yes, I know Emily.'

'And she lives here, does she?' added Stephen, conscious to keep his tone friendly. 'I'm just trying to work out which number flat.'

The woman carried on looking at him. The little girl, who was in her school uniform, looked up at her mother, as if she too was confused by this weird exchange.

'It's one of the bottom ones, but don't ask me which one,' said the woman, eventually, stony-faced.

'Great, cheers,' croaked Stephen, and he lifted an arm to give a friendly wave, but before he had a chance, the woman had turned her back and was unlocking the door to her own house, a beautiful double-fronted Victorian number, wisteria across the front – the sort of house Stephen had only ever seen on films. He watched her go inside with her daughter, turning around to glance at him as she closed her yellow front door behind her. Only when he was sure she was inside did he turn and ring number two's buzzer. It seemed as good a bet as any.

He stood and waited. Inside his trainers, one of which was more an open-toe sandal now due to the gaping great hole in the front, the soles of his feet burnt, his blisters throbbed. It felt like someone was trying to prise his hips apart, they were so sore from walking and from sleeping on concrete. He buzzed again, leaning his forehead on the glass panel and closing his eyes. Then, footsteps. He opened his eyes and pressed the palms of his hands and nose to the glass to see tight-clad legs walking down the hallway, sunlight glinting off them, a black skirt, a light-coloured top, blonde, wavy hair to her chin. The door opened. It was all he could do not to fall inside, cartoon comedy style.

Emily gasped, slapping both hands to her mouth. 'Oh my God.' The colour literally drained from her face, even though Stephen had always thought it was only a figure of speech. 'Oh my God, you came.'

Stephen leant on the door frame with one hand. 'Hello, Emily,' he said.

There was a moment, from the look on her face – exactly the same face as he remembered, same deep-set blue eyes, bee-stung lips, just more defined, as if childhood had been chiselled away – where Stephen thought that maybe she'd changed her mind, that him coming was all a horrible mistake. But then she said, 'Come in,' and she opened the door as wide as it would go. 'Please, seriously, just get inside.'

In the sunny, parquet-floored hallway, Emily tucked her hair behind her ears and took a step back, looking him up and down as you might survey the wreckage of your home after a flood. 'My God, Stephen,' she said, hand over her mouth. It was a shocked whisper. 'Jesus Christ.' Then, putting her hand lightly on his back to steer him and indicating her front door at the end of the entrance hall, she said, 'I'm down here.' He went with her in silence.

Once inside, he watched her watching him as he took off his rucksack.

'Hello,' she said, shyly, once he was standing there, free of it. She was hugging herself, rubbing the tops of her arms, tearful. 'So, what do you need? I mean, what can I get you first?'

'Water, please,' he said. He couldn't think about anything else. He felt he could drink a lagoon of it and it still wouldn't be enough.

She quickly brought him a pint of water, which he downed, practically in one go, before holding out the glass, which she refilled again and he drank again, while she waited, handing it back to her.

'Ready for a cup of tea now?' she said, smiling, even though she was crying.

'Just about, I think.'

'And, like, toast, soup? What . . . ?'

'Honestly, just a cup of tea would be incredible.'

Emily instructed him to sit down, which he did, on a huge sofa that was beautifully soft and stylish like everything in the open-plan room – and so comfortable, he feared falling asleep, instantly. He watched her at the shiny kitchen area, filling the kettle, mainly to stop his eyes closing, because they were so heavy and the room was so quiet and warm, just a radio burbling on somewhere. Everything felt woozy. He was in that sickly waiting room between intoxication and sobriety. He wanted to sober up. He wanted to sober up and feel normal more than anything else in the world.

He scratched his filthy head and watched her get two mugs from a cupboard above her head, put two teabags in them with shaking hands, then pour water in, all wordlessly, except asking him if he took milk or sugar and him saying black and two, please. 'Still got my dirty sugar habit, I'm afraid.' Nineteen years, more or less, and now he was here, and she was here, his baby sister, the light of his life growing up; he'd have died a hundred times over for her, and yet, right now, she felt like a stranger.

She handed him the mug of tea and sat down next to him, wiping tears away with her cardigan sleeve. Stephen was too wrecked to access those same emotions. He was in survival mode. He suspected he stank to high heaven, though, and some part of him did care what Emily thought, but he was too exhausted to do anything about it apart from shuffle up a little.

She curled one leg up on the sofa and alternated between blowing on her tea and sniffing, loudly. She was smiling too – really smiling. She looked so pleased to see him. 'I don't know where to start,' she said and he gave a small smile.

'Me neither.'

'I didn't think you'd come. Well, I didn't think you'd even find my note . . .'

'I was confused by the Marks & Spencer receipt at first, I must admit,' he said, and she laughed through her tears. 'I thought, when did I buy a bottle of Chianti and dauphinoise potatoes?' And she gave a little shake of her head that told him she was more than a little bit embarrassed at having given him *that* receipt, her luxury lifestyle exposed.

'How have you been?' she said, and he was about to answer with 'great' or something utterly ridiculous but she immediately said, 'Sorry, stupid bloody question.'

So he said, 'Living my best life, as it happens,' as a joke, an ice-breaker or a dig, he didn't know which. He just knew he felt a sense of shame so big at being in the state he was in that he could barely look at her. But she didn't laugh, she just looked solemnly down at her cup of tea.

'Anyway, what about you? How have you been? Good? By the looks of things,' he said, glancing sideways at her, not able to look at her square on. 'Who is this grown woman in front of me?'

There was a pause, then she blurted, 'Jesus Christ, I was so worried about you last night.'

'Yeah, I'm sorry if I scared you,' said Stephen, not that he could remember anything, which was only adding to his anxiety. 'That hasn't happened for a long time, by the way.'

Emily just nodded.

He looked down at his right hand, fingers splayed, mottled with bad circulation. 'So, how did you find me? I mean, how did you know where to come or where I was? Why *did* you come?'

And Emily reached out to put her tea down on the coffee table, then put her hand on top of his. It was warm from the tea. 'Shall we leave that till you're feeling better?' she said, her eyes swimming with tears, and he nodded. He was in no state for big discussions right now.

'I'm really glad you came, though,' she said, and he could tell she meant it. 'I'm so glad you came.'

'Me too.'

She insisted on making him toast. Afterwards, when she was at the sink washing up, he lit a cigarette and at the sound of the lighter sparking, he watched her flinch and turn around.

'Sorry. It is okay, isn't it . . . ? You don't mind?'

'Um, sure.' She wiped her hands on a tea towel. 'Here, but let me give you this.' She brought him something to use as an ashtray before opening two of the room's large windows.

'Thanks,' said Stephen, who would later look back to this moment and wonder how he'd ever thought it was okay to just spark up like that. 'Never needed this more, I'm afraid. Sorry, do you?' He indicated the tobacco tin.

'Ah, no. No, thanks.'

So many things he did not know, whereas he used to know every single thing about her.

The cigarette was the nail in the coffin, however, because after that, he felt so wasted that he lost the power of speech. Emily said she'd show him where the bathroom was so he could have a bath or shower before getting some sleep, and asked him if he had any spare clothes, to which he replied he didn't. 'My boyfriend James leaves stuff here all the time,' she said, calling from a room off the kitchen where she'd wandered off to. 'So I'm sure I can find you something.' Stephen clocked the existence of a boyfriend but was too tired to enquire any further.

'Thanks,' he said, simply. 'That would be great.'

Emily came back with two towels, and some items of clothing on top – jeans, a T-shirt and a jumper (ironed).

'I hope they're okay, they're all I can find,' she said, handing them to him. Then she asked him to follow her up a short flight of slatted stairs, and around the corner. 'Here we go,' she said, holding the door to a bedroom open. 'Just, you know, make yourself at home. You can have a lovely hot shower or bath – the bathroom is this one.' She indicated the room opposite. 'And my room is next to it, just along the hallway.' Take as long as you like, use whatever lotions and potions you like; it's like Boots in there.'

It was a small but spotless room. Stephen walked inside and stood at the foot of the bed.

'Well, just shout if you need anything,' said Emily. 'Well, maybe not actually shout. I'm just downstairs after all.' She stepped forward and touched the side of his face, then, before she left, and he flinched, not with displeasure or discomfort but because it was the first time he had been touched with tenderness in as long as he could remember.

Stephen put the towels and clothes on the floor, sat down very slowly on the edge of the bed, just the tips of his fingers pressed down at either side of him, as if unsure the bed was actually safe. It was a small room, but one that with his artist's eye he could tell had been put together with care and thought – even if it felt like some other universe to him, a totally foreign land, the only window to the world he knew a small one, with a neutral-coloured blind, above the double bed.

He ran his hand over the bed then lifted it off as if

the surface were hot. The bed was made with a pristine, Christ, what looked like an ironed white duvet cover, like a hotel, the kind of hotel he'd never been in, that's for sure, but how he imagined classy London hotels to be. There was a chest of drawers at the foot of the bed in front of him, on which there was a glass bottle with sticks coming out of it, which Stephen worked out was giving off the floral scent in the room – overpowering to his nostrils – a small, white alarm clock and a dressing-table style mirror through which Stephen saw first his own reflection – an ill-looking, unshaven, filthy fucking disaster – and behind which he saw various cushions arranged at the top of the bed in velvet and fur and jewel shades that matched the headboard which was also velvet and purple. Behind that, the wall was papered in a jade and silvery migraine-inducing floral pattern that reminded him of the wallpaper in Mum and Dad's house hallway, circa 1990. But hey, what did he know about home decoration? He caught his reflection in the mirror again, which was terrifying in itself since he was as pale and waxy as an embalmed corpse, had eye-bags like dead mice and a bloodied scratch on his cheekbone that he couldn't remember getting. Then he looked behind him, first right, then left as if the cushions or the flowers on the wallpaper might spring alive and attack him, like he didn't trust them or, more to the point, he didn't trust himself with them, with a room like this.

As he turned his head back, something on top of the chest of drawers glinted, catching the last remnants of his consciousness, which was dwindling by the second. It was a small, silver photo frame in the shape of a heart. Stephen leant forward and picked it up to find it opened in two. On one side was a photo of Emily, arms around a couple of other girls when she was at university – he could tell because he recognised the building behind them which was blond sandstone and unmistakably Glaswegian. On the other side was – Stephen's heart jolted – a picture of Emily with Dad. They were standing on the snow-covered marshes, the sea a glacier-blue line behind them, wrapped up as if on a walk. It must have been taken in the last few years because Emily looked the same as she did now – a woman, not a girl, face slimmed out, cheekbones in all their glory, and Dad looked like his own father, like Grandad Nelson; the same as Stephen remembered him, just with greyer hair, the jowls looser.

The two of them didn't look entirely comfortable together, it was true, but they were standing side by side, Emily's head tilted towards Dad, smiling in the winter sun, and Stephen's stomach twisted with a sad envy. He shifted forwards on the bed and looked again.

The last time he'd seen his father was in 2005; he was twenty-three. He'd been out of prison for two years by that stage, and was struggling. He pictured the pair of them sitting opposite one another at the table in the dining room of Eden Court, eating – he can't remember what, he just remembers the food not going down, the pain he'd felt in his throat, trying to get his words out. It had been winter then too, and he and Dad had been spotting birds on the marshes, which he'd enjoyed, but it had been nothing like it was as a child when they'd gone out together to the edgelands, a joy, actually, and always a respite from his worries.

Stephen remembers the gas fire being on full, the room sweltering. 'I need some help, Dad,' he'd finally said. What it had taken to utter those words. His dad had looked up from his plate and across at him, as if Stephen had just asked him to help bury the body of a man he'd killed earlier.

'Help?' Tony had said, mouth open in confusion or disgust, or both – Stephen couldn't quite tell. 'What sort of help?'

All the help! Stephen had longed to cry. *Just help me, for God's sake! Help me to find a way out of this chaotic nightmare I'm living. Help get me a roof over my head so I'm not sleeping in my car – the car I can't afford to run – every night. Help to get rid of the demons from the past, the voices that sit on my shoulder and whisper in my ear like a fucking demented parrot, especially in the small hours of the morning when I'm so scared and so cold, I rattle like a windowpane in the wind. Help me to stay alive, basically.* But he hadn't said any of that; of course he hadn't. Instead, he'd said, 'Just a bit of money for a deposit so I can get a flat.'

'I thought you had a flat,' his dad said then, sounding alarmed.

'I have.' Stephen had lied through his teeth. He'd not had his own four walls for over a year. 'But the landlord's selling it. I can pay you back,' he'd added, when his father didn't say anything, already wondering how the fuck he planned to perform that magic trick. Then he'd seen the look of exasperation on his dad's face. 'Or maybe I could just come back and live here for a bit? Just to sort myself out.' The look had worsened.

Tony had put his elbows on the table, clasped his hands beneath his chin. After what felt like forever, he'd said, 'I love you, Stephen. You're my son. But you're twenty-three. A grown man. Do you know what I was doing at your age?'

Stephen had shaken his head, feeling like he might die, right there, from shame. 'I had a baby, a wife, my own business. Every Saturday, I used to get up at 4 a.m., drive to Smithfields in London to pick up stock, and be back to open up shop by 8 a.m., then work a full day. That was on top of my normal working week. Being a butcher isn't easy, you know, it's not working in a lovely shiny office. It's early starts and long hours on your feet. But I did it, because I had responsibilities. I had a family that needed providing for and I would not have had it any other way, even if your mother would have.' A rare dig because he was dignified, Stephen's father; he might have lost his wife to another man, but he hadn't let it destroy him, he'd got back on his feet. 'I would not have dreamt in a million years of asking my parents for help. Not in a month of Sundays. What have you achieved, eh? Absolutely sweet F.A., if you don't mind me saying, except stress and trouble. And you know what else?' Tony had pointed a finger at his son and Stephen winced. 'It's not the going to prison I am talking about here, or even the reason you went – in fact, I wish you'd pushed that ladder a bit harder. It's the fact you came out of prison and I offered you a chance at a good steady job here, a life on Canvey. But you got into drugs and drink, you pissed it all up the wall. So, no, I can't help you. It's time to stand on your own two feet, to be a man.'

Later, when Stephen was leaving to catch his train, his dad had shoved several rolled-up ten-pound notes in his hand. 'That's just so you don't bloody starve to death. But don't you dare ask for any more, because I don't have it.' And this, Stephen remembers this: his dad had not been able to meet his eyes, such was his disappointment. He'd walked back into the house. 'You're on your own now, sunshine,' he'd said, lifting an arm in the air, 'and don't spend it on booze.'

He had.

*

Stephen sat there on the end of the bed, the rose glow of a sunset filling the room along with the memory of his father's fathomless disappointment. But there was also a glimmer of hope, a tiny one. Like a searchlight on the far-away ocean. Had something changed? Was that why Emily had come looking for him at this point in time? He put the picture frame down and, intending just to rest for a little while before having a shower, sank back onto the crisp, white duvet. *Take your dirty clothes off at least, you moron,* was his last thought. And then, blackness.

Chapter Eleven

Emily

I crept down the stairs and stood at the bottom, my hand over my mouth. I'd hoped and fantasised about this happening for my whole adult life, and now I'd got it, and my brother was here, in my house, and, yes, I felt elated – I felt like opening the front door and screaming it to the whole street – but I also realised I had concentrated so much on finding him that I hadn't thought ahead as to what might happen afterwards, and I felt terror at the life-changing, overwhelming responsibility of it all; of the potential now, with the arrival of Stephen, for the past to come bubbling up like molten lava.

I wandered in a daze into the middle of the lounge. The last of the day's sun formed an oblong on the dining table, and through the far window of this downstairs space, I could see the blossom on the cherry tree bobbing in the breeze like balls of antique-cream lace. I was aware of wanting to hold this moment in my hand and savour it, to be fully present in it, whilst being simultaneously aware that I was unable to do so, because it did not feel real to me, and how this was one of the ironies of life: you wished and wished for something amazing to happen then when it did, it was so amazing, it blew your mind like a fuse, so you couldn't process it.

It was half past six on a Friday evening. Normally at this time I'd still be at work. On that rare day I was home at a normal time, I'd be cooking dinner, probably with James if he didn't have a council meeting. Afterwards, we'd sink into my huge sofa to watch trashy TV, me marvelling at just how relaxed James could become so quickly, switching from work to home mode in as much time as it took him to take off his tie and change into trackie bottoms, beer in one hand, the other around my shoulder. Meanwhile, I'd be sipping my beer, hoping it would take away the voices and faces of the day, so that I didn't have to think about the single mum who would be back with her baby now in her bug-infested flat, or Mr Adebayo's daughter doing her homework on the bathroom floor – or my mum spoon-feeding my paralysed stepfather, or my brother on the streets. My brother, who was now safe, upstairs in my house.

So why did I have the nagging feeling that the real worrying began now?

I needed to do something useful, something to calm me down. I went back into the lounge. Despite having the windows open, it still smelt of cigarettes, and Stephen's filthy rucksack was propped up against my wall

– repainted only a month ago – which, I was dismayed to find, provoked a flicker of annoyance in me. Eyeing it for a moment first, I seized the rucksack, as you might seize a muddy dog by its collar, and dragged it over to the washing machine, where I began to empty it, holding each item between thumb and forefinger (and, crucially, away from my nose), shoving everything into the washing machine before I could even decipher what was what: trousers, pants, everything seemed to have turned the same shade of mushroom, and it all smelt awful. I told myself to get a grip. It was not me who'd had to live like this for God knows how long. This rucksack was the sum of Stephen's possessions, of how it had ended up for my brother. This was the same kid who had run with me over our edgelands and leapt over creeks. The same adolescent who had stood in wonder with me at so many dawns and dusks, roared around Canvey with me on his BMX, who had taught me everything I knew about nature and many more things besides. He had protected me, sacrificed so much for me and this is how the world had repaid him?

Angels really did end up in hell far too often.

After dealing with the main compartment, I then went through all the pockets, quickly, not wanting to pry, just to empty everything out so I could then wash the bag too. The contents mostly consisted of smoking paraphernalia and half-used packets of wipes. I tipped up the rucksack, just to be sure I had everything, and a notebook – black leather, a single elastic band around it – fell out. I half opened it – as I said, rifling through Stephen's belongings seemed wrong – and out slipped one of those plastic wallets, and inside it, a piece of A4 paper, which had obviously been torn in two at some point because it was sellotaped together down the middle. The hairs on my arms stood on end when I realised what this piece of paper was, when I read my brother's childlike bubble writing.

Our Top Five by Emily and Stephen Nelson
(aged eight and a half and thirteen)

1. Spot TWO rare birds in twenty-four hours
2. Go on a night birding woodland walk
3. See an owl in flight
4. See a seabird colony
5. Watch the swifts' migration from the Spurn Peninsula

My mind flashed back to when we made the list, by torchlight, in our little tent on one of the many mini camping adventures Stevie used to take me on. I had the exact same list, in the exact same handwriting. Stephen had made me a copy and I had kept it, all these years, tucked inside the book about garden birds that he had also given me.

His list felt like the matching piece to mine, the other shoe, and an idea formed in my head: we'd made a pact, actually, our 'passport to freedom'; we had something that bound us. Something that transcended the nightmarish events that unfolded that day, in the June of 1999. The day that tore us apart.

Did he feel the same? Was this why he'd kept it all this time? Did he look at it and think only of how we were then?

Was it a sign he forgave me?

I put the notebook with the list tucked back inside in the kitchen drawer to keep it safe, then the contents of the rucksack on a hot wash, the swishing and whirring of the washing machine bringing a soothing, welcome return to normality. I sat and watched it, trying to process the events of the evening, then I turned to the rucksack itself, lay it on the draining board and began scrubbing at the straps, pushing down the rising pressure in my chest, this potent mix of joy and anxiety.

The phone rang on the side – 'James Carter – Palmer' flashing up, which is how I'd saved James's number when I'd met him that first night at the Palmer estate residents' meeting.

I left it for several rings, staring at it, before eventually picking up. 'Hello, James Carter Palmer.'

He laughed then tutted. 'Have you not changed that to something less formal yet?'

'No, but I will, I promise.'

'Anyway, guess where I am.'

'I dunno, at a council meeting?'

'Nope, much more exciting.'

'Oooh, let's see, a hot yoga class?'

He laughed. 'Um, no, I'd rather stick needles in my eyes.'

'A casting for the new Bond film.'

'Ah! So, you do find me attractive?'

'Yes, obviously!' (That has never been the issue.)

'Well, good, anyway, because I'm walking down your street.'

I stopped, cloth in hand. 'What – down my street?' I parroted idiotically.

'Yes, down your very street. I know we hadn't arranged to see one another tonight, but, well, you already spurned me last night and I want to hear all about your brother.'

'Oh,' was all I could manage before undertaking a farcical last-ditch attempt to erase any sign of my brother – not because I was ashamed; I just wasn't prepared. At all. For any of it. I removed the damp rucksack from the draining board and shoved it in the linen cupboard, sprayed a room scent everywhere, and tried to look normal, no doubt failing miserably.

The intercom went. I looked skywards. Then buzzed to open the main entrance, before opening my front door to see James walking down the hallway, holding a huge bunch of yellow roses.

He stood on the mat outside my flat, looking handsome in his new Italian wool suit and holding out the flowers.

'Wow, are these for me?'

'For you . . .' he smiled, a little sheepishly. 'I feel like I didn't make a big enough deal of your brother showing up, then disappearing, come to that. That was huge. I should have called you back last night to talk about it more. I should have insisted. I want to help you, I really do.' He paused, tipped his head to one side, attempting to look past me. 'You going to let me in then?'

'Oh, yes, yes,' I said, and I opened the door properly and he stepped into the hallway, stooped to kiss me (I've always been a sucker for a tall man), then carried on inside, telling me he'd brought dinner and wine . . . I squeezed my eyes shut, then the door.

'I hope M&S ready meals will do. I got these fancy chicken-in-creamy-sauce things,' he said, getting the goods out of the plastic bags and putting them on the kitchen island while I stood biting my thumbnail behind him. 'Yeah, they look grand,' I said, weakly, remembering that Stephen was a vegetarian when we were kids, and probably still was.

'Oh, and also . . .' He gave a comical, flirty flicker of his eyebrows and brought me towards him. 'I booked the Bristol hotel.'

'Oh, brilliant.' My heart was thudding so strongly, I felt sure he'd be able to feel it against his chest.

'Yeah, it's got a beautiful roll-top bath.'

I thought of Stephen upstairs. I'd not heard my bath or shower running yet; maybe he was asleep.

'I'll just do the flowers,' I said, releasing myself from the embrace and going over to the sink. I filled up a tall, blue vase with water and began trying to arrange the flowers which were beautiful, although in truth, I've never liked roses. As well as the strange, grand gesture shopping trips my stepfather would spring on me, he'd also make grand romantic gestures where Mum was concerned. His favourite of these was to fill their bedroom with dozens of red roses, which Mum never seemed pleased about – perhaps because, I later worked out, these gestures often followed a row, either between Mitch and Mum, or Mitch and Stephen. Often, all three of them.

Still, I brought the vase of flowers over to put on the coffee table, praying the scent might disguise any residual odours of my homeless brother. 'Bristol is such a cool city,' James carried on, behind me. 'Actually, have you ever been to Bristol?'

'James, I've got something—'

'It's got fantastic shops – and I'm all for clothes shopping, you know. I love a supermarket sweep of Reiss like the next woman.'

'James, can I just—'

He paused, he sniffed. 'What's that smell?' he said and my stomach lurched.

'What, the roses?'

'No, fags,' he said, alarmed. 'I can smell cigarettes. Emily Nelson, have you been smoking?'

'No,' I said, as if I was fifteen and it was my dad who was asking. I watched as James's eyes fixed on the coffee table, where the two empty mugs that Stephen and I had drunk our tea from stood side by side. He blinked at me and gave a short, incredulous laugh. 'Oh my God, have you got a man here?'

'Yes,' I said, flattered, I must admit, by the crestfallen look on his face. 'James I've been trying to tell you, to get a word in—'

'A man?' he said. Poor James – his face was a picture. Then we heard shuffling about, the creak of floorboards, a lock slide, bath taps go on. James laughed mirthlessly, eyes wide in total disbelief. 'Jesus, Em—'

'It's not a man,' I cut in, quickly, covering my eyes. 'Well, it is.' I placed my hands together, my fingertips touching my lips, as if in prayer. 'So,' I said. 'My brother's here.'

James's mouth hung open and I could not help but notice that if his face had fallen at the thought I had a man here, there had been a facial landslide to learn that that man was, in fact, my homeless brother. He closed his mouth again. 'Oh,' he said, blinking. 'Oh, wow. When? When did he arrive?'

'About two hours ago. Isn't it amazing?'

'Yes. Yes! Em, that's so amazing.'

'But, oh God, he was in such a state, James. He's a wreck, it's heartbreaking.'

'Shit, poor guy, I mean, wow.' James was clearly lost for words.

'I know, I know. Look, let's just have some wine,' I said, going to the kitchen, not sure what else to do. 'And put the food on. You can meet him when he comes down. I can't wait for you to meet him. The thing is, I think he's veggie . . .' I said, picking up the ready meals and studying the instructions on the side, not a word of information going in. James appeared to be frozen at the kitchen island. 'I could put some pasta on for Stevie,' I added, mainly to myself.

'Um, yeah,' he said. 'Whatever you think.'

I poured us both a glass of wine and handed James his, then stopped. 'Oh actually, probably not a good idea, thinking about it. Stephen obviously had or still has a drink problem, might have a drink problem, I mean, and I don't – you know . . .' – I lowered my voice – 'want to make him feel uncomfortable.'

James's eyebrows went up but he said, 'Sure, sure,' and handed me his glass of wine and I poured both back into the bottle.

'So, what I don't get is how he got here,' James said, keeping his voice down at least, as I set the table. 'And how he knew where you lived.'

I laid down the fork I was holding. 'Because I gave him my address,' I said, aware there was irritation in my voice. What did it matter how he got here? The fact was, he was. 'Look, last night, I went out looking for him. Benjamin from work gave me some information about where he might be and I just had to go there, I couldn't sleep, I couldn't just do nothing. And I found my brother. Aren't you pleased for me?'

'Course I am.' I wasn't sure how I wanted my new boyfriend to be taking this, I just had a feeling it wasn't like this. 'I'm just shocked, that's all. I mean, Jesus, what are the chances of that? What are the actual chances? So, what happened then? How come he didn't come back with you last night?'

'Well, he was very drunk and he didn't recognise me, which, you know, he'd be forgiven for, considering it's been so long.' I didn't believe this for a second but it was what I was telling myself.

'So what did he say? What does one say to their sister who's just turned up out of the blue after, what, going on twenty years?'

'Since I saw him properly, yes. Since we last lived together as brother and sister. Well, actually . . .' I suddenly felt tears threaten, all the shock and stress of the last few hours catching up with me. 'He said, "I haven't got a sister."' And I shrugged as if to say, *what can you do?* when really, I'd been devastated by that. 'So,

I just wrote down my address and phone number and tucked it into the pocket of his rucksack, said he'd be welcome any time.'

James was holding my hands, nodding. 'Right,' he said. 'Right, I see.' He narrowed his eyes. 'But he was, like, off his head?'

'More or less. You know, you might need a drink if you had to sleep on the streets in the rain and the wind.'

'Oh, and likely more than that, I didn't mean . . . It's just . . .'

They say you see someone's true colours when disaster strikes or a big event happens. Now something had, I wasn't sure I liked the shade. I didn't know this man very well. I'd only known him five months after all, and there was something about that rabbit-in-the-headlights look about him that made me recoil, as if this had upset his smooth and lovely middle-class life. As if this was an inconvenience.

'What is it?' I said. 'You seem . . . I dunno. Aren't you happy for me?'

'Yes,' he said, emphatically. 'Absolutely I am.'

'You will be nice to him, won't you?'

'No, I'll be an absolute bastard,' he said, which did amuse me. I rolled my eyes. Then I stopped, because as if on cue, the floorboards creaked and we both looked up to see Stephen walking down the stairs, hair still wet and shaggy from the bath. When he saw there were two of us, he stopped.

'Hello,' I said. 'Feeling better?' He still looked a wreck – just cleaner.

'Much better. Thanks. The bath was an absolute dream.'

'This is Stephen,' I said to James. 'Stephen, this is James.'

James walked over and, taking Stephen's hand with both of his, shook it firmly. 'Hi, Stephen, it's great to meet you,' he said, smiling warmly. But then I watched as James looked my brother up and down, and, realising he was wearing his clothes, went a deathly shade of pale.

Later that evening, after Stephen had gone to bed, we were watching TV when James turned to me: 'So you know that jumper you lent him?' he said, with a grimace. 'I honestly wouldn't mind but the thing is, it is Burberry, and also' – this was the clincher – 'it's kind of handwash only.'

I should be grateful really, because I'd suspected this relationship was not going to last the long haul, that something about James – us – wasn't right. Now Stephen had turned up, I was acutely aware that there was only room in my life for one of these men, and James had made my decision easy.

The next morning I uttered those words I'd become accustomed to over the years: 'It's not you, it's me.'

If I didn't know how bitingly true those words were in my case, then my brother was about to show me.

Chapter Twelve

Stephen

Stephen had arrived on the Friday evening. After emerging briefly, chucking some pasta down his neck and meeting Emily's boyfriend, whose name immediately evaded him, he'd crashed. For that first weekend, he'd slept like the dead, waking intermittently to find Emily sitting on the side of his bed with a cup of tea or a bowl of soup, feeling simultaneously overwhelmed with gratitude and desperate for her to leave, so that he didn't have to go through the humiliation of her seeing him in this state.

And then, on the third day, or it might have been the fourth, he opened his eyes to a clear blue sky, birdsong, and some bloke – who was not the boyfriend – standing over him. 'Morning,' said the man, who was smiling and had a head of mousy brown curls, which only contributed to his general air of affability – not that Stephen would let any of that fool him. He sat up gingerly in his sleeping bag and scratched his head, which hurt for some reason. 'Don't worry,' he said. 'I'm moving on.'

The man's smile dropped from his face then. 'Oh no, you don't have to move,' he said, waving his hand in front of Stephen who was confused to see he was not in his sleeping bag on the street at all, and that this guy was probably not a policeman. (Policemen didn't usually wear gardening gloves, after all, or have a trowel in their hand.) Stephen appeared to be in someone's garden – a lovely garden, with a long lawn, trees in full blossom, borders of tulips and pansies. There was even a bird table in the corner. It occurred to him that maybe he'd died, and this was heaven.

'Sorry if I woke you up,' said the man, quite cheerfully. 'You looked very comfy there. It's just my mum's wandering about talking to the flowers.' He gave a waft of his hand that told Stephen there was an explanation to this story that he wasn't going to get into right now. 'And I didn't want you to wake up and freak out.' Stephen – utterly disoriented by this situation, unable to work out if this was real or one of those madly realistic dreams – looked across to see that yes, there was indeed an elderly woman in a purple nightie, bent over, chatting to the violas. Maybe he was on a mad trip. 'I'm Seth, by the way,' said the man, sticking his hand out, which Stephen shook, rather gormlessly, still half asleep and very confused.

'Hi, I'm Stephen.'

'I like your style, sleeping al fresco; lovely to be in the fresh air. I hear you're Emily's brother?'

'Er, yeah.'

'Me and my mum live in the other bottom flat so Emily and I share this garden.'

'Ah,' Stephen said, things making sense now. He could already feel the glorious calm of sobriety settling on him like a cool sheet. It was such a relief.

'Basically, my mum's not well,' said Seth, after a long pause. 'She's got dementia, so, she does sometimes go a bit free range, wanders about at funny hours.'

Stephen looked down at the duvet he now saw he was wrapped in, as well as the fact he was sitting slap bang in the middle of the lawn. 'Well, I think you can probably tell I'm no one to judge,' he said and Seth laughed.

'Yeah, I don't suppose. It's just a few people on this street and around here can be a bit . . . po-faced, that's all, a bit curtain-twitchy, you know. They get all antsy when anyone's doing anything out of the ordinary, like singing in public or wandering around.'

'She's got dementia, for Christ's sake,' blurted Stephen. 'It's not like she's doing it to annoy people and anyway, a bit of public singing is to be encouraged if you ask me.'

Seth gave a little laugh. He sounded relieved and this made Stephen feel good. 'Well exactly, but you know how it is, people can be . . .'

'Arses.'

'Precisely.'

To Stephen's surprise, Seth didn't seem to be in any rush to leave, to get away. He informed him it was Monday morning and that Emily had gone to work and then they chatted for a while about the garden that Seth mainly tended. Stephen wanted to know if they got many birds, and what kind, and Seth confessed to not knowing much about them but explained that Emily had instated the bird table when she moved in and that he liked feeding them and watching them and that he should probably pay more attention.

As Stephen began to point out a few birds, he realised he'd not done this very often in the last twenty years: have a 'normal' conversation with a 'normal' member of society – even less so about something he felt knowledgeable about.

After a while, Seth carried on with his weeding, chatting to his mum who seemed quite happy. Now that Stephen had woken up a bit everything about last night began slotting into place. He'd been unable to get to sleep in his bedroom. Those first forty-eight hours of being comatose were over, and the general post-bender restlessness had set in. But also, the bed had felt so high off the ground and the sheets like a many-tentacled sea creature that wanted to tangle him up until he panicked and couldn't get free. He'd gone to the toilet twice, banging his head on the door frame of the bedroom each time (that'd be why his head hurt), then tried sleeping on the floor, where he realised it wasn't the ground he craved so much as the wide, open sky. And so, in the dead of night, he'd taken his duvet to go and sleep in the garden.

Sleeping on the streets, no matter which position he got himself in, the concrete would jut, mercilessly, into his hipbones and every one of his vertebrae. Wrapped up in his duvet, on the grass, he'd felt like the Princess and the Pea in comparison. The navy-blue sky was plush, like velvet, and the stars so bright without the city smog and dense clusters of inner-city towers in the way. There was something else, too: he'd felt something foreign engulf him and it had taken him a while to recognise it was the quiet. Yes, this was still London, but not the London he knew. Not the unforgiving streets. Here, in his sister's garden, in leafy zone two, the sirens were faint and few and far between. There were no drunk passers-by kicking him; no traffic – or not at the level he was used to anyway – or echoing voices or squealing alley cats. Just the sounds of a normal, residential garden in the 'burbs as far as he could tell. A low breeze, the distant rustling of the odd creature and this had soothed him, like a lullaby, into the most satisfying sleep.

He had no idea what time it was now, or what day for that matter, but from the sun's position, he guessed about 10 a.m. He thought he'd better venture inside, a concept so foreign to him he put it off for a good twenty minutes, smoking two more cigarettes back-to-back. He felt cheeky doing so in this beautiful garden, but if Seth even noticed, he didn't let on. Seth's mum eventually adjourned her conference with the violas and Seth said he'd better take her inside.

'What are your plans today?' he said to Stephen. 'Are you going anywhere or just staying in?'

'That would be a first,' Stephen grinned. His mate Scotty's face flashed up. Him and Scotty had a mordant in-joke where one would say, 'What you doing tonight, mate?' and the other would say, 'Oh, staying in again, I think,' and they'd crack up because if you didn't, you really would crack up, and not in a laughing way.

'Course,' said Seth, with a little chuckle. It could have been the light, but Stephen was sure he was blushing.

'Anyway, I've just got to take my ma in, but I'll come back and give you some local info, where the shops are and so on, if you like?'

Stephen said that would be great and watched Seth go, thinking what a nice bloke, there must be a catch. Then he closed his eyes and tilted his face to the spring sunshine, feeling a strange and wonderful peace wash over him.

He must have half drifted off again, because he only came to when Seth brought him a man-sized mug of tea – he could have kissed him right there, he was so grateful.

Seth told him where the newsagent's was for tobacco and so on, and where the local boozer was. ('Don't think I'll be needing that, mate,' Stephen said. 'Much less trouble without it, I think.')

James came up in the conversation and Stephen noted Seth wince.

'I think James is no more,' he said.

'What?'

'Em told me yesterday when she told me the wonderful news about you arriving.'

'Shit, I hope it wasn't anything to do with me.'

'No, I think he might have been on his way out anyway.'

'Oh, that's good then,' said Stephen. 'I mean, not good-good but not . . .' Seth was pressing his lips together.

'Emily lent me some of his clothes,' said Stephen, darkly. 'These clothes I'm wearing, in fact.' He tugged at the hem of the jumper. 'It's fucking Burberry.' Both men snorted with laughter.

'You should have seen his face,' said Stephen. 'When he saw me in it.'

Seth was chuckling. 'I met him once or twice, actually. Nice guy. Really nice guy, just kind of . . .' He paused.

'Corporate?'

'Yes!' Seth said. 'That's exactly it. And I wouldn't have put Emily down as corporate. She doesn't strike me as that kind of girl, but maybe I'm wrong. She has had quite a lot of boyfriends come and go . . .' He realised how that sounded and stopped himself. 'Does she go for the corporate type usually?' he added, as if he'd been weighing up whether to ask or not, and decided to go for it.

'I don't really know,' said Stephen, getting out his cigarette papers. 'I've not seen her for years, have I? But let's just say, Seth, I'd be bloody disappointed if she did.'

Seth smiled.

'Yeah, me too,' he said.

Stephen ventured inside, through the back door to the kitchen that Emily had left open. It felt odd being here on his own without her, a bit as if he was trespassing – he'd certainly broken into enough empty buildings in his time. Something on the fridge caught his attention. A sheet of light blue paper. On closer inspection, it was a note that Emily had left with things like how to put the heating on, where the spare key was and the nearest park (*Dulwich – some good birds there!* she'd written, which made him smile.) There were basic instructions as to how the coffee machine and the shower worked, and the fact she'd left lunch in the breadbin. Stephen went straight to it to check, as if he didn't quite believe it, but there it was, wrapped carefully in foil. Quiche, he discovered, on further inspection, and what looked like hummus and salad sandwiches. At the end she'd included the numbers of her dentist and doctor just in case he had 'the time or inclination to call them' to make an appointment to register. (Unlikely. He'd not been to a doctor or dentist in twenty years.) *That cough needs attention*, she'd added, sweetly he thought. Then: *Really looking forward to seeing you later. Emily x*

She'd typed the list out on the computer and printed it out and Stephen was touched by this effort as well as the thoughtfulness of the list itself. The 'looking forward to seeing you' bit made him smile from ear to ear.

After almost three days out cold with exhaustion, it was like seeing the flat for the first time, and there was no denying it was pretty special. In fact, he tried to remember ever being in a home so beautiful and drew a blank. The homes Stephen had lived in or frequented in London were of the squats and shady drug dealers' hovels variety; a room in a house in the arse end of Tottenham that he'd been evicted from when they realised he was signing on.

He'd once, for several months, about a year after getting out of prison, in one of his fleeting 'getting his life together' interludes, got himself not only a girlfriend – fallen head over heels in fact; that fire burnt out hard and fast – but a flat on the twentieth floor of a 1960s high rise in Vauxhall, which had huge windows from which he could watch the birds and was his paradise, until the private developers moved in. But this . . . this was the sort of stylish home he'd only gazed through the windows of, imagining the lives of the people inside. This was a world in which he'd never had a day pass, never mind belonged: the world of huge sofas and giant televisions in cupboards; of shiny coffee machines and Persian rugs; of kitchen islands and art on the walls. And yet here he was, in one of those homes, his sister's no less as an invited guest, and he felt a sudden wave of gratitude and optimism so big as to move him to tears. It felt to Stephen like waking up on the deck of a boat having survived a great storm, to see a sunlit beach coming into view.

Gleefully, he made himself a cup of tea (a kettle was a thrill enough; perhaps he could graduate to that exciting-looking coffee-making contraption later). Then he drank it, savouring every sip, allowing himself a snoop, just a little one, at the photos dotted around: there was Emily as someone's bridesmaid, then at her graduation, still with her puppy fat. There was one of Emily underwater, scuba diving, waving at the camera, and with a girl with red hair outside what appeared to be a London theatre, looking cute in a bobble hat, and more like the little sister he remembered than the grown woman he'd seen when she opened the door. There was, of course, a photo of Emily with their mum too, in a cafe or restaurant, and Stephen bristled at the evidence of life lived without him, of a relationship from which he had been cruelly excluded. After seeing the one with Dad he was prepared, and he allowed himself the indulgence of picking it up for a moment. He noted how time had not been kind to his mother. But then she'd been through a lot for her fifty-five years on this earth and he could see it in the lines around her eyes – the pained look in them. She'd only been twenty when she'd had him and for some reason, Stephen had not considered this until now, looking at the picture of the middle-aged woman in front of him. What had he been doing at twenty? Doing time in prison, that's what, developing a drug problem, with a criminal record for GBH. He was thirty-five now – fifteen years older than his mum was when she'd had him – and he still didn't have his shit together. Far from it.

He stared at the picture and felt sympathy, guilt and respect for his mum, all rolled into one. He thought back too to the meeting they'd had in the September of '92 – the first time he'd seen his mum since she left to be with Mitch – in a diner on Canvey promenade, of all places. She'd said it was 'nice to see him' – her son, who only three weeks earlier she'd tucked into bed and nagged to do his homework – and the sadness had been so big, it had felt more like panic.

Stephen remembers how he'd sat there, unable to swallow the ice cream he'd been eating for the lump in his throat, and asked her why she didn't love his dad anymore and, more to the point, why she did love Mitch Reynolds. She'd trotted out the stuff about him being a very respected man, a medal-winner, a war hero, and Stephen had wondered what the point of winning medals was if you were going to go around stealing people's wives, people's mums.

'I'm going to tell you something,' Alicia had said, 'that you're probably too young to understand now but maybe one day you will.' Then she'd told him how she'd been destined to go to London and be a model, how she'd met his dad instead and none of that had materialised; did she not deserve another chance at life? she'd asked. And he hadn't understood one bit, how Canvey Island was not her paradise as it was his. But now perhaps he did, and he experienced a choking feeling of empathy for her, an urge to reach inside that photograph and give her a hug.

Wasn't it funny how life turned out? A chain of events over which you had little or no control. No fairness to the hand you were dealt. The twists of irony. She'd not got to London – but he had. 'And I can tell you that the streets are not paved with gold, Mum,' he said out loud.

Stephen looked at all these photos, now he had thirty-five years of this strange life he'd lived under his belt, with sadness but also gladness, that at least one of them had had a good life, and that it was Emily.

Not likely to be ringing any doctor or dentist, Stephen decided to go out and explore his new territory, find a spot on the high street and get settled with his sketchpad. Maybe he'd make a bit of cash, and buy Milly some flowers. It was coming up to midday as he stepped out onto Emily's street, and the sun was warm for April, the trees that lined this avenue of smart Victorian terraces chandeliers of blossom. Stephen had had a long bath – he was making up for lost time. He'd also had a shave and was wearing his freshly laundered clothes. And he felt a thrill, that for the first time in his adult life he might, just, be able to pass as a normal person – even as one of the people who lived on this street. (If you didn't look down, that was, since the trainers with the humongous hole were unfortunately a dead giveaway.)

When he got to the main strip of Lordship Lane, however, his confidence waned. Lordship seemed a fitting name, since there were no bookies here, no dismal, half-empty grocery stores selling over-ripe tomatoes outside; no launderettes and pawnbrokers. Here, delis, vintage stores and 'wine and cheese merchants' jostled with upmarket bistros with pavement seating and cafes with blackboards advertising 'poached eggs on sourdough toast' for £7 (£7!). Stephen walked the entire length of it, stepping off the kerb and onto the road if need be, swerving – from habit more than anything else – out of the way of good-looking parents in sunglasses pushing buggies, and couples, walking arm in arm, looking at the pavement deep, it seemed, in conversation. All these highly functional people with functioning lives. What were they discussing? he wondered; what could be so important when merely surviving wasn't?

He stopped and peered in an estate agent's window to see that a flat like Emily's would cost in the region of £400,000 and actually laughed out loud. Then he walked on, averting his gaze from the wine merchant's window, feeling like a man on day one of the rest of his life. And yet along that length of road, he saw not one homeless person, not even one poor-looking person come to that, and by the time he reached the end, he realised he was not just a foreigner here, but a foreigner alone; an expat without an expat community. What was this place? This bubble his sister had chosen to live in?

At the end of the high street, he was relieved to find things got more real. There was a Co-Op with a newsagent's next to it, and so, feeling less conspicuous, he sat himself cross-legged down in front of it, his sketchbook on his knee. He may still have had great holes in his shoes and stuck out like a sore thumb but he hoped his holey trainers passed for boho artist rather than waif and stray piss artist. And anyway, he had sandwiches in his bag, his head straight and a place to go back to tonight where someone was looking forward to seeing him. So, for now, there was hope. There was so much hope.

*

Stephen made £6, which he used to buy a few essentials for the house – milk and teabags. Then he went to Dulwich Park, with a plan to pick some wildflowers for Emily but found only cow parsley. Around 6 p.m., just as the sun was dipping and the birds were beginning their evensong, he made his way 'home', enjoying this concept in his head as much as the journey itself.

As he approached Emily's house, something unusual caught his eye, up on the right side of one of the cherry trees. He stopped, bringing his binoculars to his eyes, and was delighted to find it was a long-tailed tit – rare in a London street. He'd just got in the zone, that wonderful trance-like state where he had no awareness of anything except the view through his lens, when he heard a child's voice calling, 'Hello.'

He looked up to see a little girl with long, brown hair, wearing what appeared to be a pink ballet costume, standing on the front garden wall of a house across the road. It was the same little girl, he realised, that he'd seen when he arrived: the daughter of the cold, unfriendly woman who'd eyed him as if he was a criminal. Come to think of it, the daughter had given him exactly the same look.

She didn't look cold now, though; she was smiling at him, arms outstretched, trying to keep her balance walking along the wall. Stephen winced. 'You be careful now, that wall is high,' he said.

'I'm good at balancing,' she said, pushing one side of her hair away from her eyes. 'It's because I do ballet, I've just been.'

'That's nice,' smiled Stephen.

'I'm grade three now.'

'Wow, you must be good.'

'Are you a tramp?' she said then, and Stephen laughed despite himself 'Um . . .'

''Cause my mum says you are.'

'Right.' Stephen stopped laughing. 'Did she now?'

'What are those flowers?'

He'd forgotten he was even holding any. 'Oh, it's only cow parsley. They're a pressie for my sister who's being kind at the moment, letting me stay.'

The little girl giggled and made a comical face, scrunching up her nose. 'They're not very nice.'

'Oh,' said Stephen, vaguely amused.

'I've got an idea, though, I can get you some better flowers. Wait there.' And she jumped down from her front garden wall onto the pavement side. 'You won't go, will you?'

'No,' said Stephen, curiously. 'No, I won't go.'

He watched her go inside her house then crossed the road, and rolled a cigarette whilst he waited. Two minutes later, she came skipping out holding something that Stephen realised were a pair of scissors, waving them in the air. 'What you got there?' he said, but before she answered, or he could protest, she began using them to cut at the roses in her front garden.

'Hey!' said Stephen, going around to her side of the wall. 'Hey, hang on, I'm not sure—'

'It's okay,' said the girl, with an expression that struck Stephen as far more grown-up than she looked. 'Mummy's got absolutely loads. She won't mind, honestly. And your sister deserves much nicer flowers than those . . .'

'Parrot'

September 1994

That Saturday evening, Emily was lying on her belly doing a colour-by-numbers of a parrot, when Stephen flung open the bedroom door, went straight to the built-in wardrobe and flung that open too – a very good sign.

She looked up from her parrot, felt tip between her teeth expectantly.

'Milly, get your things together, we're going camping.'

'Yesss!' She loved these nights – there'd not been one for a while – the ones where, out of nowhere, Stevie would announce they were going camping and they'd just GO – out on the marsh. It always felt like the best surprise, the most exciting adventure. It felt as if he'd just announced they were running away, which they kind of were, or going on holiday somewhere far away on an aeroplane *right now*, or disappearing through the wardrobe to Narnia, to a magical wonderland – which was how the marshes felt to Emily, so wild and empty and full of the potential to get lost, while at the same time feeling absolutely safe, because she'd be with Stephen, and so they'd never get lost.

After he'd taken her to meet their swifts last May, he'd told her how birds had a compass built into their brains, so they always knew their exact position in the world at any one time. They knew their north and south. They trusted the stars and the sun to guide them where they wanted to go. It was why they were able to find their way from Africa to the nest in the eaves of the memorial hall every year. Because their brain remembered the patterns and the way. And Stephen was like this, she thought, he was like a bird. Stephen could find his way home from anywhere.

There'd been perhaps four of these impromptu camping outings by that stage, in the two years of their new lives, spending every weekend at Mitch and Mum's, and Emily knew the drill now. Stephen would get out the Adventure Escape Kit, whilst she put her pyjamas on under her clothes; tonight, quite a lot of them, it being September and growing chillier, especially at night, and especially on the open shore where there was only the tent for cover.

The Adventure Escape Kit, as Stephen had called it (she'd loved that), was something they'd created after the first time they'd gone camping on a whim and ended up starving, freezing and not sleeping. Stephen said they were never to make that mistake again; they were to be prepared like proper adventurers next time. And it had been fun, thinking of all the things they needed in their kit, for their secret club. After some refining, it now comprised of a small tent, two mats, sleeping bags, two blankets (they'd learnt that lesson the hard way), a small camping stove, one pan, a tin opener, two Flora margarine tubs for eating out of, plus cutlery. There was also a hotchpotch of food they'd stored away: currently, tins of Spaghetti Hoops, Murray Mints, some pink wafers, several cartons of Um Bongo and a flask for water. There was also Stephen's Danger Mouse torch and a pair of scissors. Matches, of course, to light the stove and, if there was enough wood around, a campfire.

Stephen always wanted to leave quickly – that was the thrill of it – but tonight he was really in a rush. Emily felt as if they had a train to catch as he bustled her out of the door, one welly on, still pulling on the other.

She noticed he was wearing his tracksuit and his trainers were all muddy.

'Did you go running with Mitch?'

'Yeah.' Stephen was fixing her rucksack on her back. 'Why else do you think I'm red as a giant tomato?'

Emily looked back at him and grinned. It was true. He was red and puffy, especially his eyes.

'Was it fun?'

'Would have been better if you'd been there. Come on, let's go.'

'But we have to tell Mummy.'

'Don't worry, she knows,' said Stephen and he took her hand and they walked down the garden path, out the gate and along the lanes to the marshes, which were always waiting for them, like open arms. The silky evening air after the dusty radiator heat of the house felt like pure happiness, pure freedom, and Emily could see the blue line of the sea in the distance, the layer of fiery setting sun above it. Over their heads, the ocean of sky was streaked with pink clouds. They played a game of cloud-watching as they walked to find a camping spot. There was a giant mouse, a wispy shark and – 'A parrot!' Emily was the first to spot it. There it was, with its hooked beak and its giant wings stretching up and, behind it, the long, feathered tail.

They walked for maybe fifteen minutes along the edgelands, the September breeze carrying with it the occasional waft of the mudflats; of clams, mussels, snails and crabs. Mitch and Mum said it smelt like rotten eggs, but it was the best smell in the world to Emily. They eventually found a decent spot, a boulder providing a little shelter, and put up the tent. It was only as they were doing this that she noticed.

'Where are your binoculars?'

'They got broken. I dropped them by accident.'

She gasped. 'But Daddy got you those.'

'I know, I know, it's all right. I'm going to get them

mended,' he said, as he knocked in a tent peg with a stone. 'Or I'm going to get new ones anyway, don't you worry.'

'Daddy will be sad.'

'He won't because we're not going to tell him, okay? We're just going to sort it out – he'll never know.'

Emily felt relieved about that. They lit the stove and ate Spaghetti Hoops out of margarine tubs by torchlight.

'Milly?' said Stephen when they were cosy in their sleeping bags later. He looked directly at her and spoke intensely. 'You must never let anyone control you, okay? Never let anyone make you feel small.'

'But I am small,' she said and Stephen laughed.

'I don't mean it literally. I mean, like, you must never let anyone make you feel bad, like there's something wrong with you or you're not good enough.'

'I won't,' she said, with some confidence, propping herself up on her elbow. 'I am good anyway. I am a really good girl, Mummy says.'

Stephen smiled. 'Yes, you are and if anyone ever hurts you, or makes you feel bad, I'll kill them! Okay? I will literally kill them.'

Emily blinked, startled. 'Okay,' she said, not sure whether she liked him saying that or if it made her feel scared.

Then he rolled onto his back and, after a few moments, said, 'Where's the paper?' He sat up in the sleeping bag.

'The pad and paper? I want you to help me with something.'

Always one to want to help her big brother with any project big or small, Emily reached over to the Disney rucksack and brought out the pad and pens she always brought camping.

'You know the Top Five, Mills?' he said. 'Peter Trussell's Top Five birding experiences that's always in my *Young Ornithologist* magazine every month?'

Emily nodded eagerly. She knew the article all right; she ripped them out and kept them for him, put them in plastic sheets in a ring binder, personal organisation not really being Stevie's thing.

'We're going to make our own one,' he said. 'We're going to decide right now what our dream Top Five bird experiences are. And as soon as we're old enough – when nobody can tell us what to do' – he pulled off the pen lid, rolled up his jumper sleeves with purpose – 'we're going to do them, together. Travelling all over if we have to. Are you in?' He dipped his head so his kind, hazel eyes were level with hers.

'Definitely,' she said, with an emphatic nod.

They had fun making it. Gosh, did they have fun: brainstorming first, weighing up the options, eliminating, cutting, adding – even a little arguing. Finally, though, around midnight, they had their Top Five:

1. Spot TWO rare birds in twenty-four hours
2. Go on a night birding woodland walk
3. See an owl in flight
4. See a seabird colony
5. Watch the swifts' migration from the Spurn Peninsula

'This list,' said Stephen, ceremoniously, when they'd done, 'is our passport to freedom.'

Chapter Thirteen

Emily

'God, it's like a film,' Justine declared, as we walked to the bus stop together after work that first Monday after my brother arrived. The sun had that extra-bright glassiness that only happens in April, as if announcing its first proper outing in months. 'I mean, things like this just don't happen in real life.'

'You don't have to tell me,' I said. Justine had been on home visits all morning, so I'd only got the chance to tell her my news after lunch.

'It must be amazing to have your brother back after all this time.'

'Oh, it is.' Since he'd arrived, I'd also developed a twitch in my eyelid. 'I mean, it's a miracle really.' I could it feel now, as we crossed the road, going berserk. 'Although I've hardly seen him, to be honest, because he's mostly been asleep. He has so loved that comfy bed.' It had been so nice to provide him with that bed. A simple thing but a massive one, it turns out.

Justine was nodding eagerly, walking at her usual

breakneck speed. I was almost having to break into a jog to keep up.

'God, Juss, there is a bus every five minutes, you know . . .'

'Sorry, I can't help it. I'm so excited for you!' she said, squeezing my arm, and I smiled, leaning into her.

'So, what was it like when he actually turned up on your doorstep? Was it like Davina's *Long Lost Family*? God, I love that programme.'

'Really? I wouldn't have had you down as sentimental.'

'Are you kidding? I love a good blub at a family reunion. When Davina says, "Barry, we've found your mother, but she's in New Zealand and has only got two days to live," that's my favourite part. God, I'm a mess at that bit!'

I laughed. 'You surprise me.'

'So, did you cry your eyes out?'

'A bit.'

'I bet you just clung on to each other.'

Justine's family were very close, very touchy-feely. It was something I'd observed at her thirtieth birthday party, and it had stirred up those all too familiar feelings of envy I always had towards families that showed such easy warmth towards one another. Justine's family hugged when they passed in the hallway on the way to the toilet, for God's sake, never mind after not seeing one another for half their lives.

'Well, actually, we were quite shy with one another. You have to remember, I've not seen him for years.'

'Yeah, I s'pose so.' Justine sounded mildly disappointed. 'Must have been surreal.'

'Just a bit.'

It had taken me by surprise how much. It felt like a dream in many ways – in that way that dreams connect random elements and people and put them together. Here was my brother, but I didn't recognise him out of the context of my childhood.

'So, what did he say about claiming he didn't have a sister? Was it just that he didn't recognise you?'

'I don't know,' I said. 'Like I say, he's been asleep since he got here. He was on his knees with tiredness, so there's lots of ground not covered.' This was, of course, the understatement of the century. 'Also, he's got some idiosyncrasies I'll have to get used to.' We reached the bus stop, which was heaving, people spilling out over the curb. 'Like, this morning, for example. I got up to find he wasn't in his bed, but had taken his duvet to sleep on the lawn.'

'Oh dear,' said Justine, pulling a mock-horrified face. 'Well, that's going to wreak havoc with your fancy White Company bedlinen for a start!' I gave a little laugh, then sighed.

'I feel bad about James,' I admitted.

After I'd ended it on Saturday morning, when Stephen had rocked up just the night before, I'd called Justine and told her. 'It's one in, one out with you, isn't it?' she'd said.

'I think he really liked me.'

'They always do.'

'But it just wasn't right,' we said at the same time, which made us groan then laugh. Justine patted my hand. 'You just concentrate on Stephen,' she said. 'And everything will come right.'

How I hoped for that to be true.

I was looking in the direction of the bus, but I knew Justine had a big question brewing, I can always tell; there's this energy coming off her.

'So, Em?'

'Yeah?'

'When was the last time you actually saw your brother?' she said, and my stomach rolled. 'You said you were twelve or something?'

I swallowed. 'Well, that was when we were last living together – you know, with our parents.' I still had my head in the direction of the bus. 'Then he came to see me in Glasgow when I was a student, but it was complicated. He'd already gone off the rails by then.'

I could sense Justine nodding, out the corner of my eye. There was a long pause.

'Can I ask you another question?' she said then. I was beginning to wish she wouldn't. 'And you don't have to answer me. What was Stephen in prison for?' I did turn to face her then, but tried not to look too taken aback. 'I mean, was it, like, bad?' she said, and I nodded. 'What, like, the worst?' Her small, shrewd eyes were searching my face.

'No, not the worst,' I said, my stomach clenching. 'I mean, he'd still be in prison, wouldn't he, if it were the worst?'

'Yeah, yeah, of course. Obviously, yeah.'

'But it was serious, like, someone got hurt.'

Justine nodded again and bit her lip, obviously dying to ask more but not wanting to overstep the line.

'But I trust him,' I hastened to say, realising how faintly ridiculous that might sound given what must be going through Justine's mind right now. 'You'd like him.' Justine gave a small, understandably reticent smile. 'He isn't a violent person – at all. He's a really lovely, good person. Funny too – nobody could make me laugh like my brother when we were little. Life has failed him in so many ways. The system has failed him, you know?' I knew she did, doing the job we both did. 'And now it's up to me to help him. I really *need* to help him.'

I'd told Justine I'd last seen Stephen at uni in Glasgow, but that wasn't the whole story. I didn't tell her he'd hitch-hiked all the way from London to see me that freezing December night, or that I basically turned him away.

I was only three months into my new student life, after all, and my new identity, come to that, which was a carefully constructed hybrid of the real me, and some other girl called Emily Nelson, who did not have a paralysed, brain-injured stepfather, nor a brother who lived in this continent, let alone on the streets. No, my brother lived in

Kenya; he'd gone there to build a school, like the hero he was, which was why I didn't see him. It was a story I'd overheard in a cafe once and stolen for myself. I told it so many times those first three months that I believed it too. I'd only just begun to forge a new life for myself away from Canvey Island and my past, which seemed to lurk around every corner there, whispered on the tongue of every passer-by. A past that, through no fault of his own, starred my brother. This meant that when he showed up a wreck, about as unheroic as it is possible to look, that night, I was horrified – terrified my narrative was about to be blown like canvas from a tent frame in a storm, exposing the truth.

My student halls that first year in Glasgow were your standard 1970s-block-on-campus affair. We each had our own room – generously sized for halls, or so it seemed from talking to friends of mine at other universities. It was one bathroom between two, however, and when I say bathroom, I mean basically a wet room with a toilet in it, between the two rooms. Luckily, the girl I shared a bathroom with – a Cornish girl called Bex – had already gone home for Christmas that weekend, as had most of the other girls on my corridor, leaving just me and two others. 'The hardcore posse' we called ourselves, staying until the bitter end of term rather than running home to Mummy and Daddy as soon as we could. The sad reality, of course, was that we each only had a dysfunctional home to run back to – and I, for one, was not looking forward to another

Christmas on Canvey Island with just Dad, even less in Yorkshire with Mum and Mitch. I couldn't bear to see the bitter twist of her mouth as she fed and washed him, or the constriction I felt at not being able to mention my brother. I couldn't stand to see what my mother's life had become and hear, all the time, what it was supposed to have been. The shattered hopes and dreams.

'And to think I was once a beauty queen,' she'd say as she cut Mitch's fingernails, like she might, at any minute, just cut off his fingers. 'Miss Canvey Island.'

I couldn't take it anymore.

It was about half past seven and we were getting ready to go clubbing that night, a last hurrah before the holidays. It was around that time that my crush on Ollie Smith, a guy on my Psychology course, had reached a fever pitch. We'd had one snog during a tequila-themed freshers' night, and there was talk of him being at the club that night. This was back before every student had a mobile phone, when nights out held so much more anticipation. My plan was to seduce him – tonight was the night. So I was a couple of vodkas down and giddy by the time the intercom in the hallway went, telling us there was someone downstairs. 'Show Me Love' by Robin S was blasting from my room, which was awash with Clinique Happy as I answered it. I still can't listen to that song or smell that scent without my skin prickling with self-loathing.

The line crackled and then a voice said, 'Hello. Can I

speak to Emily Nelson, please?' and, of course, I knew. My heart rammed against my ribcage so hard I thought it might shoot right out. I remember running down the two or three flights of concrete stairs and pulling open the main, heavy-duty door of the building, the Arctic wind blasting in. There was no snow yet but it was imminent; everyone knew because of the damson-coloured sky that hung over Glasgow, heavy as an udder with it. I stood there in my silver-sequinned miniskirt and spaghetti-strap top, barely feeling the cold due to the shock of meeting my brother's eyes, which were red-rimmed and wet with tears, the wind, or both. I'd last seen him five years previously, in the visitors' hall of HM Prison Feltham, an experience I'd sobbed through, until my mother had taken me home. She never took me again. Mind you, she didn't go either.

'Stevie? Wow, what . . . ? Is that you? Oh my God.' The words toppled out of my mouth, breathily. I even managed a smile, although inside, I was dying. Faint. Dry-mouthed.

'Hello,' he said. He was clearly emotional with exhaustion, unshaven, and had aged about twenty years in four. To an eighteen-year-old me – a fairly immature one at that – he looked like any other druggie I'd seen on the streets of Glasgow, and I admit it, I was scared.

'Can I come in?' he said, and I'm ashamed to say my first thought was *No. Christ, no! Nobody can see you, nobody can know you're my brother, not the one building schools in Kenya*. But then, what kind of witch turns their own brother away? So, I let him in – of course I did – and I reached up and put my arms around him in the entrance hall and he clung on to me, but for me the embrace was awkward, resentful even. He smelt, he was a bag of bones and I was totally out of my depth, not to mention at the height of the selfishness of youth. Plus, there was Ollie Smith . . . He was my second thought. The shame about that still runs deep.

I was the one to pull away from the hug. Stephen was needy and vulnerable, which scared the hell out of me, because I'd never seen him like that. Even in prison, he'd been dignified. My big brother, my hero. 'What's going on?' I said. I knew he'd gone AWOL but he looked . . . there's no other way to put it, he looked like a tramp.

'I'm sorry, I'm so sorry . . .' He was crying and he kept apologising, over and over. 'I'm sorry to do this to you, but can I stay?' he said, desperately, and my heart lurched again. I was praying nobody would come down the stairs or through the front door. 'Just for a bit – I've got nowhere to go.'

'What, nowhere?' Trying to disguise my horror at the situation wasn't going well. 'The thing is, it's not allowed,' I said. 'If the warden found out, I'd be in a lot of trouble. I'd be fined. I'd probably get kicked out!' I was pulling out the big guns now.

In the end, I did smuggle him into my room because I didn't know what else to do. Luckily it was at the far end of the corridor – eleven rooms away from Joanna and Mel, the two other girls, so to this day, they don't know he even came. I still went clubbing that night, leaving my stowaway brother with strict instructions not to leave the room. And, after all that, Ollie Smith wasn't even there – which was probably for the best, since my plans to take him back were obviously well and truly scuppered now. But to this day, I cannot believe my behaviour that night. I can't believe my selfishness or how wrapped up in myself I was. How utterly immature.

The next morning, hungover and panicked, I found Stephen a room at a homeless hostel. It turned out I could be very mature, very resourceful, when necessary. I had a cursory cup of tea with him then left, telling him I'd be back the next day. I could not handle it. I could not handle the responsibility and shame every time I looked at him; I could not bear his suffering.

The next day I did go back to the hostel but he'd checked himself out that morning. I felt flooded with relief, then guilty at the relief. And that guilt has grown over the years, the surface of it calcifying to create a wall I never look behind because I know the guilt I'll see there runs deeper than I can cope with.

So, yes, that was the last time I saw him.

I saw the commotion as soon as I turned into my street that evening. Julia Turnbull was at the centre of it, naturally.

She was outside her house, still in the fancy yoga gear she seems to live in, despite being about as yogic as Basil Fawlty, addressing my brother – who was sitting on her wall – in a raised, angry voice. As I got closer, I saw that Stephen was holding a bunch of pink, blowsy roses in one hand, and in the other, a lit cigarette. *Wow*, I thought, half impressed, half dismayed. Judgy Jules, as Seth and I call her, would not be taking this well.

I walked closer.

'I have asked you several times,' Julia was saying, through gritted teeth, 'to please get off my wall.'

'And I have said,' said Stephen, calmly, 'I will, when I've finished my cigarette.'

'You've already stolen my flowers!'

'But I haven't,' he said simply.

'You've totally wrecked my beautiful rose bush.'

'I told you, I've not been near your bush,' said Stephen, which, deliberate or not, made me snigger, making Julia turn and see me, standing directly opposite her house on the other side of the street.

'But you're holding them, for Christ's sake,' she said, furious now, and making that even clearer, knowing she had an audience.

'What's going on?' I asked, the Boots bag containing the numerous bottles of vitamins and minerals that I'd bought to bolster Stephen swinging against my leg. I noticed that Eliza, Julia's seven-year-old daughter, was standing on the front step, the door open behind her as her mother made a scene on the pavement.

'What's going on?' said Julia Turnbull, who even when she's not pissed off (a rarity) has unfortunately got a face that looks like she is: sour mouth, cheeks devoid of any fat, which make her look older than she probably is. 'What's going on is that this man – your brother, I gather – has not only helped himself to several roses from my front garden, but is now refusing to move from my wall. Also, the smell of his disgusting cigarette smoke is drifting through my house.'

'Shut the door then,' mumbled Stephen, rolling his eyes – and something about the pure cheekiness of it made laughter bubble up. I swallowed it down fast. Stephen took another drag of his roll-up, raising his eyebrows at me. I raised mine back, the corners of my mouth beginning to curl up. I had to look at the floor. I was proud of him. Although if he had helped himself to roses out of Julia's garden, he hadn't done a very good job. The stems were all different lengths and they were toppling out of his hand.

'She's accusing me of something I didn't do,' he said, matter-of-factly. 'So, it's the principle. Anyway' – and he stubbed out his cigarette with his foot – 'you can have your flowers, don't worry.' He said it pleasantly enough, not sarcastically, as though trying to placate a toddler having a tantrum. And he hopped down off the wall before placing the roses on top of it.

'But Mummy!' Eliza rushed over then, looking distressed and tugging at Julia's floral Lycra leggings.

'Eliza, go inside, please. This is none of your business.'

I crossed the road then. 'Come on,' I said, putting my hand protectively on the small of Stephen's back, guiding him across to the other side. 'Let's just go and get a cup of tea.'

There was a second and then, the sound of little footsteps on the path.

'Hey, but don't you want them?' and Stephen turned around then to find Eliza standing on the pavement, as if calling to him from the shore as he drifted helplessly away. 'Don't you want the roses I gave you?' she said, close to tears, and Stephen looked at me, and I, confused, shrugged back. Then, after sauntering back across the road to Eliza, Julia looking on, open-mouthed, hands on hips, he bent down to her level.

'Your mummy doesn't want me to have them,' he said. 'So, I think it's best . . .'

'But I do,' pouted Eliza, who's the sweetest child – she must get if from her father. She went then to gather the flowers from on top of the wall and handed them to Stephen.

'Okay, well, thank you,' said Stephen and he winked at Eliza who beamed back. 'Milly loves them, don't you?'

'I do,' I frowned, even though, as I've said, me and roses aren't a good match, but I wasn't going to start getting into that now.

*

Back inside, Stephen told me the full story: how Eliza had taken pity on the cow parsley he'd got for me, and taken it upon herself to cut some of her mum's roses. He wasn't going to dob her in, though, that wasn't his style.

'I'm really sorry for causing trouble on my third day here,' he said.

'What? God, don't be ridiculous.' I was trying to arrange the flowers in a vase, easier said than done when most of the stems didn't reach the water. 'That woman is a witch. She's given Seth – the guy who lives in the flat next door – grief a few times about his mother. Like he can help it. Seth's mum's got dementia.'

'I know, I met them both today,' said Stephen, who was looking kind of awkward, standing in the middle of the lounge passing a hand repeatedly around the back of his hair, which, despite washing it, still had a strong scarecrow vibe. 'What a sweet lady and a lovely bloke.'

'What, Seth? Yeah, he really is.' Seth and I had become good friends since he'd moved in a year ago.

'He told me about James,' said Stephen. 'I'm sorry to hear that. I hope it wasn't anything to do with me.'

'Not at all,' I lied, with my back to him still. 'He just wasn't right.'

Behind me, I could feel Stephen nodding. 'Cool, I get it,' he said.

*

Stephen helped me prepare tea, me attempting to avert my eyes from his overgrown, filthy nails as he chopped onions and peppers, trying to remember at what temperature all germs were exterminated. Thank God James wasn't here – James, being the sort of person who pretended to be laid-back about these things, just as he tried to be laid-back about his Burberry jumper when it turned out he was the sort of person who wouldn't eat from bowls of crisps or nuts at a party. And wiped down salt and pepper shakers after homeless people used them: I'd caught him in the act, that first night Stephen arrived.

My brother had been here three nights and yet, I'd hardly had the chance to speak to him.

We sat down, stir-fry on our laps, half watching *Grand Designs* of all things, the sound of Stephen shovelling noodles in almost drowning out Kevin McCloud. Afterwards, Stephen went to smoke in the garden and I, wanting not to waste another second of being alone with him, asked if I could join him.

The sun had set, the garden was in silhouette. There was just a bank of clouds sitting, like the separated cream of the milk, above an apricot sky. The evening air smelt of spring: damp grass, new beginnings. We made small talk about how this was our favourite time of year: everything bursting into life, the promise of things to come, and it was just lovely, and I was simply trying to enjoy the moment. Then, out of the blue, he looked up and he said, 'The swifts will be here soon,' and my blood stopped dead, or so it felt.

'They will,' I said, as though that word, that concept, had no more meaning for me, were no more loaded, than if he'd said, 'Lovely drying weather we're having.' I felt sweat prickle my temples, although it was cool out here in the garden. The pause stretched far beyond what was comfortable.

'I meant what I said by the way,' Stephen said eventually.

'About what?'

'About the fact I don't want to cause any trouble. I'm so grateful to be here. Honestly, I feel like I've been in the lap of luxury these last few days, but I'll be on my way soon. I don't want to outstay my welcome.'

'But I don't want you to go,' I said, realising in that moment how much I meant it. I'd been all over the place for the last few days – lurching from elation one minute to overwhelmed the next. Irritated too, occasionally, when clearing away his little trail of Rizla papers and tobacco, found everywhere – and I mean everywhere, even on top of the toilet cistern. But I did not want him to go.

'Really?' he said. He looked genuinely surprised.

'Really,' I smiled.

'Okaaay,' he said simply, nodding slowly, but I couldn't *not* notice, as he turned his face, how the edges of his mouth had curled up.

'So, I want to help you get settled,' I said, encouraged

now, excited, as if the decision had been made: he was here long-term and I could help him; I could make things right. 'I want to help you find a job. I know someone who runs a cafe on Lordship Lane. I bet I know loads of people who need a handyman . . . Did you manage to call the doctor today? Or the dentist?'

Amusement flashed across Stephen's face.

'God, sorry,' I groaned, catching myself. 'I need to shut up, don't I? I need to calm the hell down, stop trying to run before we can walk.'

'No, it's nice you care,' said Stephen, but I suspected he was just being polite. That he'd rather not be harassed by his little sister of all people. 'I've not had that for a long time.'

I felt a pang, a shot of something like shame in my stomach.

We sat in comfortable silence for a while but I had a question I needed answering before I felt I could move on. I wanted confirmation and yet I didn't. 'Stevie?' I said, eventually, and it felt nice to use my childhood name for him for the first time since he'd arrived. 'There is one thing I wanted to ask.'

'Go ahead.'

'The thing you said in the tunnel.'

Stephen frowned as if to say, *I have no idea what you're talking about*. 'I was a mess,' he began, somewhat sheepishly. 'I was a complete—'

'You can say that again. But do you remember what you said to me?'

Stephen shook his head, once. 'I remember seeing you, though. I remembered as soon as I found your note in my rucksack.'

'Really?'

'Yeah. Because you haven't changed,' he smiled and, turning so that he wasn't looking directly at me, he passed his cigarette to his right hand and held out his left for me to hold. I took it, unable to stop myself from beaming. 'You're still my little Mills,' he said. 'Just a taller, older version, with a posh flat and ridiculously extravagant kitchen gadgets.' He grinned, sliding his eyes in my direction. 'And a corporate boyfriend.'

'Ex-boyfriend.'

'Anyway, unlike me who bears no resemblance to the person I once was—'

'Oh no, you do,' I was quick to cut in. 'You're still you. You still do exactly the same facial expressions like that silly, alarmed face that always made me giggle.' He did it and it did. 'You still can't be cool when you're excited about something.' Stephen smiled shyly at the ground.

'So, you did know then? That it was me, when you saw me in the tunnel?'

Stephen frowned. 'Of course.'

'Because you wouldn't acknowledge me at the time. You said, "I haven't got a sister."'

His mouth fell open. 'Did I?' He looked genuinely appalled. 'What a dick, what an attention-seeker,' he said, and I felt relief wash over me. So he didn't hate me! He didn't resent me.

He put his hand on my shoulder then; squeezed it, massaged it with his thumb, just as he used to when he wanted to reassure me in a public situation where he couldn't just give me one of his bear hugs. Then he shuffled up the decking – he seemed to hesitate momentarily – and reached out, put his arms around my neck, drew me close, and we did hug then, for a long time, in the garden that was now shrouded in darkness and yet alive with birdsong, and I had to stop myself from bursting into tears with the relief and the joy of it.

It felt like a watershed moment, as though there were things that could be discussed now. But not everything. I didn't know if we'd *ever* be able to discuss *everything*.

Stephen had my hand clasped in his and resting on his knee. 'Look,' he said, with a sigh. 'I want you to know that me saying that in the tunnel – "I haven't got a sister" – it was just a knee-jerk reaction. It was just what I was feeling at that exact time. A kid lashing out.'

'It doesn't matter,' I said.

'When you've spent as many years as I have surviving on your own, you get used to it. You put barriers around yourself to protect yourself.'

'I know,' I said, not knowing, not really. 'But you're not alone now. I'm here, I've always been here.' I knew this wasn't true, that I hadn't been – but Stephen thanked me anyway.

I made tea and Stephen made a roll-up. I only smoked these days when very drunk, but the occasion felt like it called for it so I asked him to make me one too. Then I brought cushions out and blankets from the sofa, and we sat on the decking and talked in a way only long-lost siblings with a problematic past can: like highly skilled pilots, circumnavigating tricky terrains and weather fronts, knowing where there might be turbulence and avoiding it, keeping things nice and smooth.

'So, what did you do after Glasgow?' asked Stephen and I told him about my wayward years, between twenty-one and twenty-four, before I realised I wanted to work in housing. About the rubbish boyfriends and terrible jobs; so many terrible jobs. So many terrible boyfriends, for that matter, all of them fizzling out.

'Potato grading was the worst, the absolute pits' – before deciding that no, it was actually working in a frozen pizza factory where, in my fleeting vegetarian years, I got moved to the pepperoni topping department, only after my colleague was signed off with frostbite.

'That's not true!'

'No word of a lie.'

He laughed properly then, starting me off, and we

giggled like we used to do all the time as kids, especially in the darkness of the bedroom we shared; playing silly games we made up, inventing characters to amuse but also, often, to distract us from the stuff going on somewhere else in the house, the shouting and arguing that was happening more and more frequently, and became worse as time went by.

This was my opening. 'Stevie, you know that night you came to see me in Glasgow?' I said. 'That last night we saw one another?'

'How could I forget?' he said. His expression was unreadable.

'I am so sorry.' I put my hand on his. 'The guilt about that has eaten away at me ever since. Palming you off like that – what was wrong with me? I came to the hostel, you know, like I said I would, the next day.'

'I'd checked out, though.'

'Yeah. Why?'

He sighed, heavily. 'I guess I realised I needed to stand on my own two feet. That it was unfair to rely on you, my little sister.'

'I should have invited you to live with me, though, or at least stay with me for a while.'

'Oh, look, you were eighteen. What else were you meant to do?'

'Where did you go?' I asked, not wanting to know the answer.

Stephen smiled, but it was a rueful smile. 'I was okay. It was a tough time, I won't lie, but I got by. I had my birds. They've saved me.'

Thank God, I thought. *Thank God for the birds.*

We smoked. Then he said, 'So . . . how's Dad?' completely without warning and if I was shocked, which I was, I tried not to show it.

'Oh, you know, same-same, just a bit grumpier.' Stephen gave a small laugh but it sounded nervous. 'You know he moved in with Sandra a few years ago?'

'Yeah, we do speak very occasionally. He seems happy enough.'

'She's nice, you know – when you get to know her. Homely. Good for him.'

'I'm pleased for him, you know, after everything.'

There was a pause. I knew what was coming next and was bracing myself.

'And Mum?' There it was. Stephen was studying his hands; I took a deep drag of my roll-up.

'Good,' I said. 'Well, not good but, you know, coping.'

'Do you see her a lot?'

I thought of the last time, back in February. We'd had vegetable pasties from the baker's for lunch and I'd begun to say how Stephen loved them when we were little, always chose them for his birthday tea, but she'd spoken over me, deliberately changing the subject.

'A few times a year,' I said vaguely. I went up to

Yorkshire every two months without fail, but it seemed unnecessary, rubbing salt in a wound, to tell him that. 'It's quite hard, you know. She's so . . .'

'Yeah.'

There was a very long pause. I was glad we'd got music on low on my phone, and that I'd asked for that cigarette, then Stephen said, 'So, does she – Mum – does she ever, like, mention me?' And he looked at me then with such hopefulness in his eyes that it killed me. And I crossed my fingers on the hand that wasn't holding the cigarette, because I was about to lie.

'Yeah,' I said. 'Of course, often.'

'Really?'

If the hopefulness killed me, then the happiness in his eyes now finished me off.

'Really,' I said.

He couldn't hide his smile. 'Will you tell her that I'm here, you know, when it's the right time?'

'Of course,' I said. 'Obviously I will.'

'Cool,' said Stephen, and he squeezed my hand. 'That's important to me.'

'Better go and get the blankets in,' said Stephen, at midnight. 'They'll get all dewy and wet if we leave them out there.' A memory then, immediate like a reflex: us, as kids, sitting outside our tent on one of our camping trips and Stephen, face illuminated by the campfire, saying the exact same thing: 'Bring the sleeping bags in, Mills, they'll get damp.'

Then there was, of course, that one specific camping trip.

'Oh, that reminds me,' I said, jumping up. 'Just a sec.' And I went back inside, opened the kitchen drawer and took out the notebook I'd found, the list inside. *Our* list.

I came back, plonked myself down on the cushions and handed it to him. 'I hope you don't mind, I found it in your rucksack pocket when I was taking everything out to clean it.'

Stephen unfolded it.

'I can't believe you've kept it all this time,' I said. 'So have I – I've still got that copy you made me too.'

He didn't look up.

'Seems like a lifetime ago, doesn't it?' he said and I noticed how he'd gone red in the face, and hoped I hadn't embarrassed him by drawing attention to the fact he'd kept a childhood list.

'And yet like last week. Did you rip it at some point?' I asked, indicating the sellotape down the centre.

'Dunno, must have done in a fit of frustration perhaps that I'd never get to do them all. Good old Peter Trussell, eh? He'd probably be about a hundred if he was still alive.'

'He was ninety-odd then, wasn't he?'

'We thought he looked it. He was probably about sixty. I lived for his columns.'

'I know you did. I used to cut them out for you and keep them in a folder, like your little secretary.'

'Did you?'

'Yes, I bloody well did! And set you quizzes about birds, and played "nature programmes" where I had to be the creature and you were David Attenborough doing the commentary. We'd play it for hours, don't you remember? Often when we went to Grandma and Grandad Paradiso's house.'

It seemed like light years ago now. Grandma and Grandad Paradiso had been dead eleven years. Stephen smiled as it came back to him. 'And here, in the bog-land of Canvey Marshes, you'll find the lesser-spotted Emily Nelson foraging for cartons of Um Bongo before her annual hibernation.'

'Excellent impression, although I'd argue I had the harder job, what with my acting repertoire having to span from wombat to ostrich. Do you remember I broke my wrist doing an excellent impression of an orangutan for the purposes of your David Attenborough show?'

Stephen chuckled properly then. 'Oh God, yes, I felt guilty about that for years – haven't got over it, in fact.'

'I remember making that list,' I said after a pause.

Stephen smiled but didn't look up.

'I remember everything about that camping trip. I loved those trips – you always made them so exciting.

Do you remember the Adventure Escape Kit that we kept in the wardrobe at Mitch and Mum's?'

'God, yeah, that was years ago.'

'I remember you marching into our bedroom that evening that we ended up making our Top Five, flinging open the wardrobe and pulling out the kit. It was all so sudden and totally thrilling. And on this particular trip, you got quite serious, I'll always remember it. You started saying how I must never let anyone control me or make me do anything I didn't want to do and then you looked at me, so seriously and you said if they did hurt me or do anything, then you'd kill them!'

'Christ,' said Stephen, looking down at his hands. 'Intense.'

'Then you asked me to help you make this list. You said we'd do it when we were older, when nobody would be able to tell us what to do . . . "Milly," you said.' I made wise, intense eyes. '"This is our passport to freedom!"'

Stephen smirked. 'Wow, I was quite the philosopher.' He pulled a funny face at me. 'Like, proper deep.' I was laughing.

'Have you ever done any of them?' I asked and Stephen shook his head.

'I haven't, no. Maybe that's why I carry it with me all the time, just in case one day I get round to it.'

'Yeah,' I said. 'Maybe that's why I've kept mine too.'

Chapter Fourteen

Stephen

When Stephen was in prison he would dream, almost weekly, about the time when they had been a normal family; a time when they would eat together, a six-year-old Stephen sitting on a cushion at the dining table so that he could reach, the TV burbling in the background, a little Milly in her high chair. A time when his dad would kiss his mum when he came in from work, and she would kiss him back; when Stephen might catch his parents laughing at something while they were driving somewhere, and he'd watch the cats' eyes on the road until his eyes were heavy, and then he'd fall asleep in the dark quiet of the back of the car, his mind blissfully blank.

As is the case with most dreams, it would be the feeling, the emotions of that dream, rather than the events themselves, that would linger long after Stephen was woken by the turning of the key in his cell lock at 7.30 a.m.: happiness, yes, but mainly safety, belonging.

Towards the end of his four-year sentence and for a short time after release, Stephen became preoccupied with getting that feeling back. To be part of a family again – *his* family. Not only did he want it, but he believed he could have it. His mother had only come to see him once in prison, but she'd written every week without fail. The letters contained little of substance: she'd tell him how the damn squirrels had been digging up the lawn again, or how the washing machine was on the blink. She never asked Stephen how he was; she never asked him anything, but she'd taken the time to write regularly, and Stephen hung on to that fact. He apportioned hope to it – too much hope, as it turned out.

The depth to which he'd missed his mother over those four years inside had come as a shock. It had been primal, the longing arriving with no warning, like a wave, knocking him for six. He'd be sitting eating his breakfast, or lying awake at night, listening to Hobbs, his cellmate, snoring as if he'd never put a foot wrong in his life, and find suddenly he yearned for her smell, her touch. He yearned for her as an infant might yearn for their mother – which was, he worked out in the many hours at his disposal, because the version he truly missed *was* the version from his infancy. Of that short time from zero to eight; that time until Mitch Reynolds entered their lives. He'd spent his entire life being homesick for that mother, hoping to get her back.

Especially now, lying in his sister's spare room, his mind clear and free of booze.

Stephen had ticked off each day of his incarceration and yet, when he'd walked out on that crisp, blue-skied day in the November of 2004, he'd done so with £60 in his pocket and absolutely no plans. He had not expected Alicia to be waiting for him and she wasn't. Besides, she'd moved by that point, to start a new life 'up north' as she put in her letter – she wasn't specific. Tony was waiting for him, however, and Stephen had never been happier to see him, even if his father could not meet his eyes, and even though the only words he uttered on the first hour of the journey were: 'What's the nosh like inside, then? Not up to much by the looks of you.' A little later, he'd patted Stephen's thigh, looked across at his son – Stephen could have sworn there was a tear in his eye – and said, 'It's bloody good to see you.'

Stephen knew his dad to be a man of actions, not words anyway; a man who showed his love in his own quiet way. So, when Tony offered him a bed and a job at his butcher's shop, Stephen was filled with gratitude. Oh, how he wanted to be the prodigal son. But prison had changed him. How could it not? His moral compass had been skewed, his sense of what was normal. Addictions had blossomed too, inside, which felt cruel and ironic. As a result, he flitted between Canvey and London, taking every drug under the sun and lying through his teeth to his father.

Once his paradise, Stephen avoided the marshes after

arriving at his dad's. As a boy, he would gaze at them from his bedroom window; now he kept his boyhood curtains closed against them like a locked door, not daring to open it. The memories slipped through, regardless, though. One in particular . . .

When he was fourteen, a willow warbler flew into their patio doors. It hadn't died, though, and he'd rescued it, showing the tiny creature to Milly. The two of them had made it a comfy bed of moss and leaves in a shoebox, which Milly, for reasons Stephen still couldn't fathom, decided to show their mum – setting into motion a chain of events that haunted him to this day. Alicia had freaked out at the sight of the bird, and Milly had dropped the box, so the poor little thing fell onto the carpet. This had upset their mum even further, of course, which had in turn infuriated Mitch – not that it took much. Alicia had subsequently gone to bed with a stress headache, and Milly, who always hated it when Mum was ill or upset (which seemed to be getting more often), had gone too. Stephen had picked up the bird, checked it was still breathing – it was – and put it back in the box, which he then took to the garage. Not wanting to spend one more minute in a house where the only person conscious was his stepfather, he'd then gone down to the marshes, safe in the knowledge the warbler was out of harm's way.

It had been coming up to evening by this point, and

the air on the edgelands was soupy and thick with pollen. Stephen had gone to his favourite spot near the bird hide and had been leaning against it, the sun-warmed wood comforting against his back. He'd been happily watching the birds, immersed to the point of being unaware of his surroundings, when he heard a voice coming from the direction of the house, and looked up to see his stepfather striding towards him holding, to Stephen's horror, the shoebox under one arm. 'No,' he was saying. 'Oh no. You can't just run away out here. Your mother's had to go to bed you've traumatised her so much with your bloody birds. And your sister.'

An image flashed into Stephen's mind, of Milly asleep in the bedroom they shared: her long lashes on her cheeks, her blonde hair spread out on the pillow. Why hadn't he stayed with her?

'Bringing your revolting half-dead creatures into the house . . . Stand up when I'm talking to you,' Mitch had ordered, and Stephen had scrambled to his feet. 'You think you're special, don't you? You think you can just escape to your secret little hideout, you and your birds, like you do with Daddy. Well, let me tell you, you don't get away that easily with me.'

'You're not my dad!' Stephen shouted.

'No, but I can do a much better job than he does and I didn't even have a father myself. You want to know what the difference between me and your dad is? It's that

I know what it's really like out there. How tough it is. What you need to do to survive.'

Stephen looked at the shoebox on the ground, his mouth becoming dry as paper. The lid was on, his warbler wouldn't be able to breathe.

'I'm sure he thinks it's a tough job, cutting up those carcasses and hacking apart dead cows. But I've seen men butchered, Stephen, real men, lying with their legs and arms blown off, bits of their brains blown out, but still talking, still alive. Now what do you think is the kindest thing to do in that situation?'

Stephen eyeballed Mitch but didn't speak.

'Oh, you'd do nothing, would you? You'd leave them? To suffer, to die an agonisingly slow death?'

'No,' said Stephen.

'Good, so why would you do that to a bird then?' he'd said, at which point Stephen had realised where this was going and had begun to whimper. 'It's not the same. It's going to recover!'

'But he's not,' said Mitch. 'He's not, Stephen. So, the best thing you can do is be a man, and put it out of its damn misery.'

He took the top off the shoebox, at which point Stephen started really crying. Ignoring him, Mitch then took the bird out and dropped it onto the grass – which after several sweltering days was bone-dry, like straw – with a soft thud, as if it were nothing but a dog's chew toy.

Stephen saw the bird's head twitch. He covered his face with his hands. 'Now are you going to step up and be brave, or do I have to?' Mitch said, and Stephen's chest had heaved.

'No!' he'd sobbed, stamping his foot, as if that would make any difference. 'No, please. Please don't kill it!'

'Looks like I'll have to then,' Mitch had said, matter-of-factly as if he was talking about taking the bins out. 'It's the kindest thing, trust me.'

It happened so fast and yet in slow motion at the same time: Mitch lifting his steel-capped boot; then a noise like a crisp packet being stamped on, but slowly, heel first; the sound of tiny bones being crushed. And then another sound, one Stephen had never heard before, and, which he only realised later, was coming from him.

By the time Stephen was released from prison, it had been seven years since that night – but it might as well have been yesterday in terms of what Stephen saw in his mind's eye when he looked out of his childhood bedroom onto the marshes: him, fourteen years old and heart-broken. Of course, he'd been on the marshes since, taking his little sister when they were both still children. But somehow, during his time in prison, the marshes had come to represent something they never had before: not escape, not freedom, but the murder of that poor, defenceless bird.

One late afternoon, two weeks after he'd arrived, Tony

had appeared at his bedroom door, binoculars around his neck, and nodded his head towards the window. 'How about it?' Stephen had known this was coming and had felt the anxiety build accordingly. He'd fetched his coat and binoculars, though, because what else was he supposed to do? Then he'd followed his dad out, his heart beating in his chest like a trapped bird, knowing already this was a grave mistake.

Stephen had told himself to get a grip. He was with his father after all, not his stepfather. And these marshes – their familiar colour palette, the dark peat-greens and porridge hues of the sand and reeds – and, most importantly, the birds, they were theirs. For one glorious moment as he'd stood breathing in the briny air, he'd believed it too. He'd felt it was all going to be okay. Then they'd walked further out, the landscape bleak in the late autumn, and he'd seen the bird hide out of the corner of his eye, its blond wood luminous in the dusk, and everything had fallen apart for Stephen, it had all become horribly clear that this place was ruined for him now. It bore too many scars of his past. They were deep in the knots of the hide's timber, knitted in the sea purslane and reed beds. He could hear his stepfather's frightening voice in the wind, see his face reflected back at him in the pools. Hear the cracking of tiny birds' bones underfoot.

'I want to go back now,' he'd said, his voice laced with

panic, and his dad had stopped, turned around. 'Why?' he'd said, shocked. 'We've not even seen anything yet.'

'I just want to go back.'

That night, Stephen had scored cocaine from a dealer in Basildon, bought alcohol, gone down to Canvey prom and got so out of his head that he'd lost his house keys, broken a windowpane to get in and emptied his bladder in his wardrobe, thinking it was the toilet.

He'd disgraced himself, and, as his father had explained, it was three strikes and you're out.

The next two strikes came soon enough. After that, there was a short stay with Moose, his best mate from Canvey, who'd been a good friend to him, visiting several times in prison even though they'd lost touch a bit in his later school days. But Moose had moved on with his life – shacked up with a girl, a baby on the way – and they quickly came to a mutual agreement that this wasn't going to work out. Anyway, Stephen needed to get away from Canvey Island, which seemed to him now to be cut off from the rest of world, like a limb without blood supply, dead and yet festering with dark secrets.

So, he'd gone to stay with Hobbs – also released now – and several other reprobates in a squat in Marylebone, which turned out to be about as healthy and functional an environment as it sounds. Things had gone from bad to worse.

Despite his downward trajectory he had kept in contact – albeit with him as the instigator – with his mum that first year after release. It was sporadic: sometimes Alicia would answer the phone, sometimes she wouldn't. Often, he would write and she wouldn't write back for months. Eventually she would. Stephen had kept the bundle of letters that he would occasionally examine, forensically, for signs of love – and these gave him hope that she still felt the umbilical cord linking them, and couldn't quite bring herself to sever it.

Finally, Stephen had made that visit to his father, where he'd sat at the dining table and laid his soul bare. When his father had turned his back on him too, he'd embarked on a two-week bender, the one that had eventually spat him out on the doorstep of his sister's student digs only to find no room at the inn there either. At the time he'd felt abandoned and let down but the intervening years had changed his perspective. She was just a kid. It was a stupid idea to go there in the first place. That didn't detract from the fact that in his beaten state, Stephen had seen that night as his last chance of salvation. But it was not to be, and so had begun the helter-skelter to his rock bottom.

They say it takes a crisis to bring about an epiphany, however, and Stephen had had an epiphany of sorts. He had the birds. He might be homeless, but they could save him; they were all he needed. He would spend whole days walking, or catching a bus if he'd made a bit from his drawings, going from park to park: Regent's, Hyde, Battersea – St James's was his favourite. On dull winter days, he loved to go to the Wetland Centre in Barnes, hang out in the damp mist and watch the wintering fowl on the ponds and marshes, revelling in his melancholia. If the wanderlust was particularly tugging at him, he'd call Birdline, the recorded service telling twitchers which birds had been seen where, so they could follow.

Stephen sat up in bed now, the window wide open, so that he could feel the cool air on his bare shoulders. Just before bed tonight, Emily had given him back his copy of the Top Five list that she'd found in his rucksack pocket and Stephen was studying it, passing a finger along the sellotaped middle, which was raised like a scar. Despite himself, he remembered Mitch ripping it up when he'd found it in his bedroom one day following yet another argument between them: *You and your wimpy little hobby. It'll get you nowhere. I've tried to help you,* he'd said. *I've tried to toughen you up and be a role model because God knows your father hasn't done a good job. But you've just thrown it back in my face*. And he'd torn the list in two.

Two weeks passed for Stephen at Emily's. He'd arrived like a stray dog at the RSPCA: beaten, mangy, with only survival on his mind, just grateful for a bed for the night. One night had turned into two, into three, into several, and the best thing was that Emily was pleased to have him there. In fact, she couldn't do enough for him.

And so he relaxed. He made an effort to join the ranks of the civilised, if only out of politeness towards his sister. He registered with a doctor and a dentist, the latter being the worst: how did people cope with this? Being mauled by total strangers? Having someone rummage around their mouth as if it was the cupboard under their sink?

He and Milly had really *talked,* when, for years, he barely knew what talking was. Who had time to talk, to rake through the past or plan for the future when you didn't know where your next meal was coming from? But now Stephen felt like the earth itself, warming up after a long, cold winter, providing the conditions for hope to push through, like snowdrops in February. His parents had closed the door on him years ago. (Actually, he suspected his dad's door had been left ajar – Tony was a softie and he knew it. He'd never pushed it, though. Male pride. His father didn't need to know the depths to which his son had sunk. His mother, however, was another matter.) No, Stephen had shut the door on the idea of family and accepted it was just him and the birds. Yet this past fortnight, Emily had said things that had reopened that door. Things like the fact his parents still talked about him, that Emily was going to tell Mum she'd found him and he was staying with her. In fact, she probably had already. She was discreet, she probably didn't want to rub it in, but Stephen had clocked that she spoke to their mother often. And when he was lying in his warm bed in the mornings, or helping Seth in the garden that was becoming ever more beautiful by the day, the magnolia and cherry blossom putting on their best spring displays, Stephen thought about all this: perhaps it was not just serendipity that had brought him and Emily together. Perhaps something fundamental had changed, something with Mum, and that was why Milly had come looking for him. Perhaps after years leaving him out cold, on the outside, she was ready to let him back in.

'Green Sandpiper'

September 1994

'I told you not to bring those bloody things,' said Mitch, his voice competing with the high wind that undulated across the marshes. 'How are you supposed to run with those around your neck? You'll have two black eyes.'

Mitch had been about three metres ahead of Stephen since they'd set off on this ordeal half an hour ago. If Stephen hadn't been holding his binoculars to his chest so they *wouldn't* give him black eyes, or, worse still, break, he would have flashed the Vs to the back of his stupid bald head.

'That's why you can't keep up. How can you use your arms to power you along if you're clutching those to your chest like they're your comfort blanket?'

Things hadn't been too bad with his stepfather recently, but now Stephen felt the old resentment burning somewhere deep inside of him.

Mitch turned around to face him but continued jogging

backwards, knees up in his combat trousers, a souvenir from his days as a soldier, as Stephen was regularly reminded. 'What you got to say to that, eh? Do I speak sense or do I speak sense?'

Stephen didn't answer, so Mitch turned around again and carried on. He didn't seem to make any allowance for the fact Stephen's twelve-year-old legs were much shorter than his. Stephen, on the other hand, was concentrating on just keeping going, while also scanning the sky, a sheet of opaque white today but holding who knew what treasures? That was the best thing about it. You just never knew. September was a high point in the birdwatcher's calendar. Flocks of waders such as knots, redshanks and dunlins would be coming from their Arctic breeding grounds to spend winter on the estuary. If you were lucky (and Peter Trussell had made this point in his Top Five column in this month's *Young Ornithologist*), the warm westerly wind that arrived this time of year might also bring with it 'rarities' – birds blown slightly off their migration path, to make a celebrity appearance on England's coast: maybe a hoopoe or a yellow-browed warbler on its way from Siberia to Africa – and Stephen was missing all this for no man. Least of all the baldy slave driver in front of him. If he was going to come on one of these army-style runs, then his binoculars were coming too.

They carried on, a maze of creeks to their left,

gun-metal in the evening light, and the remains of the sea wall to their right. In between were mudflats, dry and cracked as a giant's heels, and Stephen found these easier to run on than the grassy parts, which seemed to require more concentration. He didn't know how much longer they had to go, and he didn't really want to. He just wanted to get home without damaging his binoculars; better still to get to use them. They were his first real pair (i.e. not kids' ones, although lightweight and compact), his dad's present to him on his twelfth birthday, which was only last month, and the most precious thing he'd ever owned. So, if it meant lagging behind Mitch to keep them safe, so be it.

Stephen tried to increase his stride to make all this end as quickly as possible, but it was fair to say he was not a natural long-distance runner, even without the binoculars.

'Don't you just love the feel of pushing yourself for a change? The blood pumping round your veins? This is what life's about, Stephen,' Mitch shouted over the wind. 'Moving forward, bettering yourself. You won't get anywhere in life standing still, you've got to *move*.' Stephen couldn't agree less. He had ants in his pants like the next twelve-year-old, but birdwatching was all about being still and it was where life was for him, where the thrills were, if you were patient enough to wait for them – not that Mitch was smart enough to understand that.

A minute or so later, and without warning, Mitch dropped down to the ground, onto the dry cord grass which was already yellowing – by November it would be brown – and launched into press-ups. This is how these runs went; Stephen had grown wise to it now. They ran for a while and then all of a sudden, Mitch would stop and start doing press-ups, or sit-ups or (the absolute worst) burpees, barking at him to do the same, like a frustrated sergeant major, which is what Stephen guessed he was, having only made it to the rank of colonel.

Anyway, Stephen definitely couldn't and wouldn't do burpees with his binoculars jumping about around his neck. He wasn't doing press-ups either and anyway, he'd already done some about ten minutes into this four-mile run. So, whilst Mitch grunted on the ground, he took the opportunity to have a little scan – just in case there was anything interesting. And it was as if the birds themselves had waited for him, waited for their biggest fan to pause and give them his gift of attention, because he heard a noise immediately, and he knew straight away it was a green sandpiper. Without missing a beat, he had those binoculars to his eyes, the world magnified, honing in, honing in . . . It didn't take long for him to be transported to that place where he was one hundred per cent absorbed, that trance-like bliss. He was so mesmerised, acutely focused, that he didn't even realise that Mitch was standing in front of him, red-faced and furious.

'Did you hear me?' he shouted.

Stephen jumped. 'Yes,' he said, even though he hadn't, and he lowered his binoculars.

'I said, do you think I'm doing this for the good of my own health?'

Stephen didn't know what possessed him but he dared to mumble, 'Well, it's not doing mine any good.' As Mitch stood back, Stephen thought for a second he might swing for him, but he just blinked, slowly. 'You're taking the bloody piss,' he said. 'Making an absolute mug of me.'

Stephen had the strong feeling that being taken for a mug would not sit well with his stepfather. He'd experienced his explosive wrath several times in the last two years. It was nearly always directed at him; occasionally Mum. (Never Milly, thank God, because if he was to do that, Stephen would murder him.)

'Has it not occurred to you that I might have much better things to do than to take an ungrateful little sod like you running, give up my evening, only for him to stand gawping at the sky, doing his wimpy little hobby?'

'It's not wimpy,' said Stephen, defiantly. 'It takes a lot of focus and knowledge. You have to be a good observer.'

Mitch laughed through his nose, and looked away, still out of breath from running, shaking his head. Then he looked back at Stephen and jabbed a finger in his face. 'Don't talk back to me. I'll show you what happens to silly little boys who talk back.'

When he got home from the run that evening, he burst straight into his and Milly's bedroom without so much as taking off his muddy running shoes.

'Milly, get your things,' he said. 'We're going camping.' And when she asked about his binoculars, he lied and said he, not Mitch, had broken them.

Chapter Fifteen
Emily

The swifts will be here soon.

For days after that conversation in the garden when Stephen first arrived, I replayed it in my head. What was his tone, exactly? Was he trying to bring up that terrible June day, all those years ago? Was it loaded or an innocent comment?

Either way, after so long banishing them from my mind, the swifts were back. It was as if a long-locked door had been opened, and the birds themselves had flown in and were talking to me. *Let's think of the good times,* they said. Those are the times to hold on to: the excitement I'd felt at their arrival every year; the sheer joy of looking skywards and seeing those black dots, knowing the epic journey they had braved to get there, like seeing Santa's sleigh, only this was no folklore, the source of wonder was real.

I thought about the hours Stephen and I had spent with them, transfixed, and the exhilaration I'd felt, cycling around Canvey with my brother, free as the birds we were on our way to see. And in my mind's eye, as we cycled to the memorial hall – mainly at dusk, but occasionally at dawn – the sky was always pink. It was always rose-tinted.

So, those were the good times. But with Stephen's arrival, the seabed of my childhood memories, left untouched for so long – through sheer force of will, I might add – had been disturbed, and, as well as oyster shells the colour of those rose-tinted skies, there was also the dark, tangled seaweed coming up to the surface.

As the days passed and the shock of Stephen's arrival faded, we fell into some semblance of a routine – albeit a routine the likes of which I had never known before, and one that involved me learning to turn a blind eye to the natural disaster that was Stephen cooking. The look of pride, though, on his face when he presented me with anything he'd cooked . . . Delicious, but I didn't have the heart to tell him I spent the next day scrubbing the tomato sauce splatters off my formerly pristine kitchen walls, or that I secretly followed him with a dustpan and brush, picking up the constant trail of tobacco left in his wake. And anyway, there was plenty to love about the new routine too.

Mostly, there were things to love.

For example, how we kept finding ourselves, in that hour just before bed, that came to be known as 'silly hour', lying on his bed or mine, laughing to the point of asphyxiation. At what? All manner of ridiculousness. Impressions of people from our childhood mostly. There were glorious memories that stuck out for us both – times at El Paradiso, our grandparents' house; endless days on the marshes; The Day of the Ducklings. We both remembered that event with total clarity and joy, and if we remembered what came after it – Mitch's wedding – we did not mention it; in fact, we did not mention our stepfather at all, come to think of it. All these stories made us remember how much of a team we were as kids, how we plotted, and laughed, how much fun we had. I'd forgotten some of that.

As well as the joys of silly hour, I was finding satisfaction from being able to help my brother at last and him accepting my help. I got him a pay-as-you-go phone and, despite major protestation, I got him to the dentist too. And to the doctor, where he got much needed treatment for a host of minor but nevertheless horrible ailments, including a throbbing, infected toenail, a rash, and that awful cough, which, thank God, turned out not to be tuberculosis, as the doctor feared – a disease which sounded Dickensian to me, but which was apparently rife among the homeless. It broke me to hear how much he'd suffered, or, more to the point, simply put up with. Because normal people didn't do that, I realised. If you were a 'normal' person – and by that, I mean not homeless – every toothache, rash, blister or cold would be attended to immediately, by popping a couple of Nurofen, applying a plaster, or having a duvet day in front of the telly. For people like my brother these simple acts of self-care were often impossible. Now I could make them possible. That made me very happy.

What didn't make me happy was the lying.

Every day I resolved to tell Mum that Stephen was here, and every day I failed.

I spoke to Mum most days, and usually she called me. But I had taken to calling her before she had the chance – she often called on the landline and that ran a high risk of Stephen picking up. So, I'd call her at work, on the bus, at lunchtime. She was delighted by her daughter's newfound attentiveness, but I felt increasingly wretched as another day went by and I lied again – albeit by omission.

It was the bare-faced lie, though, that really ate me up.

One afternoon, Stephen sauntered into the kitchen and, cocking his head, simply said, with a smile, 'So, have you told Mum yet?'

'Yeah,' I said, just like that – but the guilt spread in my stomach, like blood from a wound. 'Yeah, I did. And she's going to call, any day now.'

I invited people round. I wanted to introduce Stephen to people – to show him off; I was proud of him. Also, Seth's mum was going to stay with his sister, and he and

Stephen seemed to get on like a house on fire. I thought it would be nice for both of them to have some male company.

I decided on the Friday night three weeks after Stephen had arrived at mine, inviting not just Seth, but also Justine and her husband, Tim, who I love and who gets on with anyone, and a journalist friend of mine, Rachel, who's always good value. I was keeping it simple with lasagne: a meat one cooked by me and a veggie one by Stephen who was delighted to be asked. (He'd learnt to cook in prison but for obvious reasons had not had much chance to show off his skills.) It was clear from the offset that this had been a fine idea of mine. It was one of those nights when all the stars align and everyone's in a good mood.

Justine told the story of her and Tim's first date – how they'd shared an oyster platter then the toilet bowl of Justine's flat (she lived nearest) when a *Bridesmaids*-style food poisoning took hold. I'd heard it before but it really is the story that keeps on giving. 'It was like, move! Move! Get off the toilet!' Justine regaled us with the details with full, comic flamboyance, flinging her arms around. 'You'll have to take the sink.'

'A relationship butt-ism of fire, if you will,' added Tim, completely deadpan, and everyone fell about laughing, including Stephen.

'But hey, it'll take a bit more than scoring a number seven on the Bristol stool chart to put me off this girl.'

Tim put his arm around Justine and gave her a squeeze. 'I still married her.'

Everyone gathered themselves together and sighed and clutched their bellies and then Seth said, 'I take this ring . . .' And everyone was ruined again.

Seth was an interesting one. Without Joan he seemed different, younger perhaps, more relaxed. Very funny, I realised. And yet when Justine said, quite innocently, 'It must be nice to have a break from your mum, Seth?' he folded his arms and didn't answer immediately.

Then, eventually, he said, 'Yes and no. I mean, yes, obviously. But do you know what? She'd buzz off this. This is just the silly atmosphere she'd fit right into and not feel anxious.'

I was learning more about Seth and Joan. I'd always presumed, for example, that he'd had no choice but to give up his well-paid job to look after his mum; that it had been a great sacrifice. 'My sister offered, actually,' he said, when Rachel brought it up. 'But I wanted to. My ma's a star really, and to be honest, it beats the daily commute and sitting behind a desk every day. She's a lot less demanding a boss than some I've worked for, I'll tell you that for free.'

There was I presuming he felt wasted as a carer, trapped even, when all the time he felt the opposite.

More wine was opened. Stephen's lasagne went down a storm.

'That's probably the best veggie lasagne I've ever had,' said Rachel, arranging her cutlery on her empty plate and leaning back, stuffed and happy. 'And that's saying something, because my mum's a chef.'

If I could have bottled the look on Stephen's face . . .

It was spring, the sun had shone all day. I had all my favourite people in my home, around my table. Most importantly, I had my brother.

Chapter Sixteen

Stephen

Stephen was drumming his fingers on the dining table.

'Blur. Now they're a decent band,' said Seth. 'Good call, Em.'

'Too right,' said Stephen. 'Can't beat a bit of Blur, Mills.'

They were between main course and pudding now. The earlier hysteria and chattiness had passed to make way for the mellow stage of the evening that Stephen was enjoying even more. Justine laughed as she helped herself to more wine. 'Mills? How come you call her Mills?'

'It's 'cause he couldn't say Emily when he was little,' called Emily from the kitchen, where, bottom in the air, she was pulling some divine-smelling chocolate number out of the oven.

'It's true,' nodded Stephen, patting his already full stomach appreciatively. 'So, Emily became Milly, became Mills and . . . it just stuck. And, what did you call me, Mills?' he called. He was kind of holding court and he knew it. It felt really, really good. Emily stuck her head up above the kitchen worktop, and held her hands apart in their floral oven gloves. 'Deeby,' she said, pretend bashfully, fluttering her eyelashes, 'because I couldn't say Stevie.' There was a resounding 'aww'.

Stephen felt himself relax like sinking into a warm bath. To his delight, Justine and Seth were musos like him, and they'd been through a good portion of the Beatles discography, not to mention golden greats like Gladys Knight and the Pips, before discovering they shared a guilty pleasure: Justin Timberlake. So, this was what normal, functioning people did, he thought. They had food with friends and good conversation. And it felt wondrous. He felt a warmth envelop him, a sense of wellbeing and belonging.

The conversation moved on to The Clash.

'Gods,' said Justine, swinging her wine glass in the air. 'I mean, take *Sandinista*. That is a work of art.'

'Soundtrack to my adolescence,' said Stephen.

'Really?' said Justine. 'Wow, you had good taste.'

'Oh yeah, he did,' said Emily.

'I'll second that,' Tim cut in. 'I was listening to The Lighthouse Family.'

Everyone chuckled at that.

'My mate Moose got me into it,' Stephen continued. 'He had a much older sister who was really into her music and we just used to listen to all her records. I was hooked.'

'I've got it,' said Emily, suddenly, from her position standing behind the kitchen island, sorting out Spotify on her phone.

'Got what?' said Stephen.

'That record – *Sandinista*. I've got it on vinyl.'

'Really?'

Stephen felt goosebumps travel up his arms.

'Yeah, it's yours.' And up his neck for that matter. She must have got it from his bedroom at Dad's when he was in prison. Had she played it, and thought of him?

'I'll go and get it,' she said, standing up, and a hush descended, as if what they were about to listen to demanded respect.

Two minutes later, Emily came running downstairs with the LP. Just the sight of that moody black-and-white album cover shot triggered memories for Stephen: lying on his bed at his dad's house, eyes closed, hands behind his head, listening to it on the record player his dad had got him second-hand – he'd been thrilled. Losing himself in the music. So relieved to be at Dad's, not Mitch's house.

Stephen watched Emily slide the record out of its sleeve and put it on the turntable. The needle crackled, then came the slow, rising melt of the oboe.

They'd revelled in maybe a minute of the track when the landline rang. Emily had just come from the kitchen and was standing at the far end of the table, holding the hot chocolate pudding in oven-gloved hands, her cheeks flushed already from the wine, and Stephen noticed her look up quickly, towards the hallway where the phone was.

'I'll get it,' she said.

'No, it's all right,' said Stephen. His chair made a high-pitched shriek as he slid it backwards, and stood up. 'I will. You've got your hands full.'

He left everyone chatting, The Clash playing, like sweet medicine from another time, and walked the few steps to the far end of the hallway where the phone was in its cradle on the wall.

'Honestly, Stevie, I'll get it,' he heard Emily say, and when he thought about it later he would realise there was alarm in her voice but he hadn't clocked it by this point, and anyway, he had reached the phone. He cleared his throat and picked up. 'Hello?'

A pause and then a woman's voice – quite shrill, highly strung. Stephen's whole body felt charged. 'Who's that, is that James?' His neck tingled ice cold, then flushed hot. He needed to sit down but there was no chair. 'It's Alicia, love. Don't tell me, she's busy. That's fine, I was going to leave a message anyway, but since you're there . . .'

The receiver slid in Stephen's moist palm and he gripped it with the other hand to keep it steady. He said, 'It's not James.' There was silence at the other end of the phone, and then an almost imperceptible gasp, but Stephen heard it. 'Hello, Mum,' he said.

A long pause. 'Oh God,' she said. 'Oh God.' And then she hung up.

There was just the sound of his own blood pumping then, and the flatline tone of the telephone. Stephen held the receiver to his ear, his breath shallow. He tried to punch in 1471, but his fingers were trembling so violently, it was difficult.

The automated voice on the other end of the line gave him the number.

From the dining area, Stephen could hear Milly calling him, telling him to come and get some pudding before it went cold.

To press ring back, dial 3.

He pressed three. Then, his mother's voice again. A needle twisting in his heart and a bedtime story from some other time, some other life.

'This is Alicia. I'm afraid I can't get to the phone right now. Leave a message and I'll call you back.'

Stephen sank against the wall.

There was a beep indicating that he should begin his message. In the other room, he was aware of chatter. Seth was saying something funny about Emily and he could hear his sister laughing. And despite the shock he was feeling (or perhaps because of the shock he was feeling, as if his mind was trying to save him from thinking), a thought floated into his head about Seth: he liked Emily. And yet she seemed completely oblivious.

He stood up just as Emily poked her head around the door.

'You all right?' she said.

'Yeah, coming.'

Only in hindsight would Stephen realise how blanched her face had been.

'Who was it?'

'Oh,' said Stephen. 'Nobody.'

'Nobody?'

'No, just a sales call.'

Chapter Seventeen

In the September of 2005, nearly two years after his release, Stephen managed to persuade his mum to meet him in a motorway service station near Birmingham, equidistant from each of their homes. (Not that Stephen had one of those by that point, but he wasn't going to tell his mum that.) He was going to tell her about Mitch, though. He was going to tell her the truth about how it had been for him – not sensationalising anything, just giving her the hard facts about how Mitch had humiliated him as a child; how he'd drip-fed darkness into their lives and brought Stephen to the brink.

He'd realised his mum probably had no idea about many of these things, these events that had scarred his childhood. If she did, she'd understand. Everything would make sense. Even if she couldn't forgive him, she would at least understand.

A mate gave Stephen a lift and he arrived early that gleaming September morning, wearing the most presentable clothes he owned, having had a bath and a shave.

He was a bag of nerves, twitchy and hyper, and so he strode straight to the gents' where he locked himself in a cubicle to rehearse his speech, to literally speak out loud the words he knew would blow his mum's world apart but that he had to get off his chest. He could not hold these secrets, these scenes in his mind any longer.

He was sitting at a table in the Burger King area, hands cupped around his coffee, knees jiggling madly under the table, when he saw her come through the revolving doors of the entrance and towards him. She looked thin and tired, that glamorous sparkle she'd always had about her gone, but she was still his mum and he had missed her, viscerally. He stood up.

'Hello, Mum,' he said. He ached to hug her, or, if he were honest, to be hugged by her. But she stood at the other side of the table, adjusting her handbag on her shoulder, looking as awkward as if he were a stranger. Stephen saw that there was anger in her eyes, and pain too. So he held out his hand across the table to her instead, and she took it, briefly squeezed it, thanked Stephen for the coffee he'd taken the liberty of buying her, and sat down. She removed a packet of cigarettes from her bag, took two out, offering him one, which he declined. He'd been chain-smoking all morning and now felt quite sick.

As his mother lit her menthol cigarette across the Formica table and sipped her black coffee, Stephen felt the cold shiver of déjà vu. 'Thanks for coming,' he said.

'That's all right.'

'How are you?'

'Well, let's just say this isn't exactly how I expected life to pan out.' She gave a nervous smile. 'But I'm here, I'm surviving.'

'It's good to see you.'

'And you,' she said. 'Although you look terrible.' She gave a mirthless laugh, but Stephen saw the tears in her eyes. 'Jesus, Stephen, you look worse than me.'

'I thought about you a lot in prison,' he said, changing the subject. 'Thank you for the letters, they really helped.'

'I enjoyed writing them,' she said. 'Not that I ever had anything to tell you, but it was something to do, something to distract me. God knows I've needed that.'

'I loved getting them. It was the highlight of my week.'

Alicia gave a small smile in response, but Stephen knew every word, every expression was loaded.

Eager to lighten the mood, Stephen said, 'I thought a lot about Dukes Avenue too, when I was inside. I hadn't thought about that house, that time, for years.' Dukes Avenue was where they had lived before Milly was born, before they moved to Merlin Drive.

'Gosh, I'm surprised you even remember it,' said his mum, flicking her ash. 'You can't have been older than four and a half when we left.'

'Oh no, I remember a lot now. When you've so much time on your hands . . .'

'Yeah, well, I wouldn't really know about that.'

'All sorts of memories and thoughts start coming out of the woodwork,' Stephen said, ignoring her dig.

'Such as?' said Alicia. Stephen had been hoping she would.

'I dunno, like, nice stuff, happy stuff.' He looked up at her, searching her face for some 'in' here, some acknowledgement that they hadn't seen one another for five years, that she'd missed him too. He'd thought about the good stuff. And he needed to talk about it for his own sanity, but also for hers, to soften what he was about to say. 'Like, do you remember I had that yellow paddling pool and a little plastic slide that went into it in the back garden?' He leant forward. He knew it was a random memory, that he was somewhat clutching at straws, but he wanted to create an intimacy between them but her body language was stiff and closed.

'Vaguely,' she said.

'I kept having this dream about that, this memory about it being a boiling hot day and me being in that paddling pool and Grandma and Grandad Paradiso turning up to visit, and Grandad pouring water over my head with a watering can, and everyone laughing, and me loving it and being so excited . . .'

'Oh, you were always excited,' said Alicia, rolling her eyes, but Stephen lit up inside from this scrap of intimacy. She remembered stuff about him, her little boy.

'And happy,' Stephen added, pointedly. 'I do remember being happy then. And when Milly came along. Loads of happy times.'

He paused, watched Alicia as she drank her coffee. Stephen knew she was uncomfortable but he was going to persist. 'I remember the living room in that house. It had a fireplace with dark red tiles around it, didn't it?'

'Yes,' she smiled with recognition. 'It did, come to think of it.'

'And a huge, squishy couch in nineteen-seventies mustard and that wallpaper, that mad wallpaper – I think it made me more hyper.'

That raised a small laugh.

'It was so comfy, that couch.'

'Blimey, you've got some memory. Your Aunty Diane gave us that when we got married.'

'I broke my arm at school once, d'you remember that?' said Stephen, knowing he was getting carried away now, seeking her attention, but not wanting to stop. 'Fell out of a tree. I was only in reception.'

'Yes, well, you were forever falling out of trees.'

'And you picked me up and brought me home and lay me on that couch and then you made me chips in the fat fryer, but put them in newspaper, like they were from the chippy. Never been so delighted in all my life.' He grinned, and a smile spread across his mother's face, and Stephen thought it as lovely as sunshine, making a brief appearance from behind a cloud. 'I did used to do that, didn't I?' she said. 'I did. You're right.'

'And then when we moved to Merlin Drive and Milly was really little, Dad would spend Sunday afternoons with us watching birds in the garden, teaching us what they all were and their calls whilst you made the Sunday roast. I remember those times like they were yesterday. I remember . . .' His mother's mouth twitched, and warmth, love even, flashed in her eyes, but then died, like a fire not quite catching light, and she cast them down to study her coffee.

'They were good times, Mum. We did have good times.'

She sighed. 'Yes, we did.' Stephen noticed something change in her face, something shut down. She put her cigarette out and seemed to survey him for a second. Then she unfastened her handbag. 'But it feels like another lifetime ago,' she said. 'Today, life is very different.' She brought out a photograph and handed it across the table to Stephen. He took it and looked at it, fighting the impulse to gasp or convey his shock. It was a picture of Mitch, but he only knew so because his mother had given him the picture. The man he knew as Mitch Reynolds, who had blighted his childhood, who had been the cuckoo in his family's nest and murdered his warbler in cold blood, was nowhere to be seen. Gone was the imposing military stance, the strong jawline and defined muscles. Gone were the hard eyes, which could light up, like a TV personality, with charisma and charm when Alicia or anyone else he wanted to fool was around. No, this was the shell of that man, a totally incapacitated figure. He was in a wheelchair, head stiff and pushed against a headrest, feet and hands at an awkward angle, and Stephen was disappointed to find that all he felt was pity. He could feel his mother's eyes on him. 'I'm very happy you're out of prison,' she said. 'But that's my life, every day, Stephen. That's my prison sentence. My prison sentence carries on.'

Stephen handed her the photograph back and she put it in her handbag, closing the clasp with a soft click. He had a dawning realisation that this was not the best time to say what he had come to say, but it was too late now. He cleared his throat. 'Mum,' he said, 'I wanted to meet you today because I wanted to see you, but also because I have things I need to tell you. Things that happened between Mitch and me. I tried to tell you some of it years ago but I didn't have the words. And there was never the right time . . .'

'Jesus Christ, Stephen.' She was staring at him, cigarette poised, eyes wide in alarm. 'Just spit it out, you're scaring me.'

Her face darkened further then, and a firework of thoughts exploded in Stephen's head. There was no turning back now. Had she known about what had gone on? Because if she had, and she hadn't protected him or intervened, he wasn't sure he could cope. If she hadn't, though, would she believe him now? Because if not, he didn't know how he'd cope then either. He'd really not thought this through. He stood at the cliff edge and felt a burning sensation in his throat. He jumped.

'Mitch, he . . .' He was suddenly aware of the noise of the general public around them, of the clanking of cutlery and the crying of a baby somewhere. Why the fuck had he decided to meet somewhere like this? To talk about things like *this*? He was struck by his tendency to make terrible decisions. 'He bullied me, Mum.'

Alicia didn't move or make a sound for a good five seconds. Just the cry of that baby, the cutlery, lives going on just as before. Then she drew her chin back. She made a noise that was part cough, sob and laugh. 'What do you mean, "bullied"?' She was breathless and white, as if he'd winded her. 'What are you talking about?'

Stephen jiggled his legs beneath the table again. He knew what she was thinking: she was relieved he hadn't accused Mitch of molesting him.

'He had to discipline you, Stephen.' She was fiddling with her St Christopher again; her throat flushed red. 'He had to pull you into line now and again, give you structure; you were always such a wayward thing.'

Stephen shook his head quickly at that. Free spirit, yes, but wayward? Malicious in any way?

'Mitchell risked his life at war, Stephen. Showed

courage you wouldn't understand, saw things you couldn't imagine. He worked every hour that God sent to give you a lifestyle and opportunities that your own father couldn't have dreamt of being able to give you.' This wasn't true and she knew it, and anyway, Dad had given him the birds, nature, something Mitch could never have given him and had even tried to take from him. There was panic in her dark eyes; she was a wood-land animal caught in headlights. 'And you weren't an easy child,' she continued. 'You were a bloody night-mare, in fact, running around those filthy marshes all day instead of concentrating on school work, dragging your sister behind, you two and your little club.' Stephen smarted at that. She'd never said anything like that before. 'Mitch is – was – just a man. A man doing what he thought was right. You needed some toughening up, you were always too sensitive. So, if you're talking about a bit of discipline now and again, some tough love . . .' The harshness of her tone did not match her face, which had crumpled. The tragedy of it all. He knew how she felt.

Silence. Just the sound of that baby crying. Stephen had the awful sinking feeling he was losing this.

'It was more than that. It was bullying . . .'

He didn't have the vocabulary to express what it actu-ally was. Bullying sounded too trivial, but abuse?

'Well, did he . . . ? Did he . . . you know what I

mean . . . interfere with you?' said his mother, a sob catching in her throat. Now Stephen felt bad for bringing her here, putting her through this.

'No,' he said firmly.

His mother glared at him. 'Well, maybe it's a matter of how you perceived it.' There was a long silence and when she eventually spoke again it was no more than a whisper. 'He just wanted to make a man out of you.'

'There are different ways of being a man, Mum.' The words had come out louder than he'd intended.

Stephen looked to the ceiling. His heart thudded slow and strong. He'd been going to tell her about Mitch stamping on the warbler, breaking his binoculars, but somehow these things sounded petty, trivial, even though they'd destroyed him at the time.

'Also, you've never said anything before. Why have you never said anything all this time?'

'Because . . .' began Stephen, but Alicia was putting her cigarettes and her purse in her bag.

'Mum don't go. Jesus . . .'

'Don't you think I've been through enough?' She was tearful, her whole body trembling as she stood up. 'I don't need to sit and listen to this. How awful life was for you. You did what you did to Mitch, Stephen, and we've all had to live with the consequences. You can't start changing your story now.'

'Mum,' said Stephen. She pushed back the red plastic

chair as if she thought it was moveable and then swore under her breath when she found it was not. 'Don't go, please, I know this is hard to hear but it's true. Why the hell would I lie about something like that?'

She didn't answer. She just waved her hands in front of her face as if she couldn't cope, because she couldn't. Ever. With anything.

And then she left.

Chapter Eighteen

Emily

The note was sitting there, propped up against the kettle when I got back from a flat viewing with a client. I had a raging hangover. Dehydrated, I'd gone to the sink, filled up a pint of water and begun to gulp it down when I'd seen it and my heart had stopped.

Milly,

You've been amazing, but I think it's time I got going now. I don't want to outstay my welcome. The wild is calling me! A million thanks for getting me back on my feet. I would have said goodbye but you were sleeping, and anyway, I hate goodbyes.

Love, Stevie xx

I'd run straight upstairs to his bedroom to find it empty, except for his slightly fusty, faggy smell lingering that made me yearn for him immediately.

I had let Stephen slip through my fingers again. I had failed him.

I went downstairs. I pulled up the blinds in the lounge, feeling a leadenness as grey as the sky fall on me. I tried Stephen's phone only to be told by the automated voice that his number was currently unavailable, which I hoped to God meant he had no credit rather than he didn't want to be contacted but it still felt like he'd died or ceased to exist; as if he'd disappeared in a puff of smoke, as suddenly as he'd appeared – and, worse, that I'd let it happen.

The place was still a tip from the night before, when I'd been having far too much fun to bother clearing up. What was I thinking of, getting so drunk? With my brother here, not drinking? Perhaps that was even why he'd gone, I thought, in a panic.

I couldn't bear the quiet – the flat already felt so lonely – and so I put on the radio then grabbed a bin bag from under the sink and began clearing up, scraping the left-over food from plates, throwing away empty cans and napkins. We'd had several candles going, and there were great lumps of melted wax stuck on saucers and the tablecloth where they'd burnt right down, and I pictured Stephen's face last night, glowing in the candlelight across from me. He'd been happy, hadn't he?

I thought back: he'd seemed fine when he came back

from taking the call in the hallway. It had crossed my mind it might be Mum, so I was so relieved when he said it was a sales call. He'd stayed up chatting and listening to music for at least another hour after that. Then he'd gone to bed before anyone left, before I'd gone to bed, but I thought that was just because he was the only one not drinking and things had got a bit rowdy by then. Had I missed something? I'd been drunk and giddy last night. It felt like the first time I'd properly let my hair down since he'd arrived. Him being here had started to feel normal.

I strung out the clearing up so I didn't have to face the rest of the day, the question of how long before I saw my brother again. The thought it might be never made me want to curl up and die.

I tried his phone, wanting to hurl my own across the room when an inane voice told me his number was still 'unavailable'. I had a shower, forced some toast down, and then went back into Stephen's room. An image flashed into my head of him on the marshes as a kid, binoculars to his eyes, scanning the sky. Sometimes he'd go out there first thing, still in his pyjamas. Never wanting to miss the 'best part of the day', as he called it, and that comforted me. Perhaps he did genuinely just prefer to be outdoors, in the wild. I changed his sheets then began sweeping the floor, getting under furniture with the dustpan and brush. This revealed mugs with entire biospheres in them;

green furry islands floating on beige seas. Countless dirty socks were under there too; pants and bits of notepaper, with scribbled lists of birds and lyrics. I began to feel a bit better. Perhaps a tiny bit of me was relieved and, in time, I'd come to think this was for the best. I wouldn't miss the mess smell of cigarettes, that was for sure. (Stephen seemed to think that simply leaving the door open constituted as 'smoking outside'.)

I carried on and the relief grew. Then, it was like déjà vu. I became aware that this feeling was familiar, and not only that, but that I shouldn't trust it. As I was polishing the bedside table – the photo of me outside my student house on it – it came to me: Glasgow. I'd felt like this when he'd left Glasgow, when I'd gone back to the hostel the day after he showed up and the lady at reception had told me he'd checked out. What was that feeling? Relief. Relief that I'd been let off the hook, that I didn't have to face responsibility, or deal with my brother upsetting the lovely little life I'd built. I did not have to face the shame I felt all the time. But I was eighteen then and I had – it could be argued – the excuse of youth. Now, I was thirty-one, a grown woman. Was I really going to let my brother slip away again?

After finishing his room, I moved on to mine. Then, I lit some candles and made a coffee downstairs. Then I lay down on my bed. It was 2.30 p.m. and the day felt like a yawning black hole in front of me. Here was my beautiful, now spotless, flat, all of it returned to order – and yet, without my brother. I wanted to be anywhere but here.

I rolled onto my side and stared into the candlelit dimness. That's when I saw it. Sitting atop a pile of books on the bedside table. *The Garden Birds Guide* – and inside it, our Top Five list, sticking out in its plastic slip. An idea began to form. Perhaps I didn't know my brother as much as I thought I did. Why would I know him at all? Since that day and the ladder incident he'd lived a hundred lifetimes more than me. The Top Five list – our 'passport to freedom' – was something we had in common. It was a pact we'd made. If I could persuade him to complete it with me, that would give me a chance to make things right.

All I needed to do now was find him.

Chapter Nineteen

Stephen

The light was dying, and through Stephen's binoculars, the sky was a piece of smoky-blue dusk, streaked with wisps of blush-pink clouds. There was the mournful squawk of geese from the River Colne that snaked through the moor, the constant low rumble of planes coming in to land at Heathrow behind him. Stephen adjusted his focus and felt his feet sink into the boggy, squelching earth. He'd been here all afternoon, on these edgelands, this landscape more familiar to him than his own face, just waiting, waiting . . . And oh, the relief of it. The simplicity. The knowledge there was nowhere else on earth he'd rather be, nothing he'd rather be doing. This was where he would channel his hopes and his faith from now on. Here was his life.

And yet, try as he did to stop them, the events of the last twenty-four hours wouldn't leave him alone. He wanted to surrender himself to this vigil, to think only of the wide-open sky, and what wonder might appear in it if he were patient and kept the faith. But the images kept coming at him, playing on a loop in his mind's eye: him answering the phone in the hallway, the way the lamplight had fallen on the parquet floor. Him speaking those words for the first time in thirteen years: 'Hello, Mum.' And then that gasp of horror and the rejection, the simple but devastating, 'Oh God.' The flatline of the ringtone when she'd hung up. Worse, the fact she'd not answered when he'd rung back. The pain he'd felt had been immediate and physical: he'd sunk against the wall like he'd been shot. He knew in that instant that whatever happened, he could not afford to feel pain like that again. He was not strong enough to feel that vulnerable. And to think that earlier that evening he'd sat at his sister's dining table and dared to feel happy, to think this was how it could be for him: friends, company, laughter, his family back in his life.

After he'd gone back, announcing it had been a sales call, he'd sat down at the dining table where Emily was holding court, and everyone was merry and laughing while The Clash played on, and it had dawned on him: there were no photos of him anywhere; no evidence he existed, even. It was as if he'd been whitewashed from her life. The penny had dropped then: nothing had changed. Nothing at all. Mum still wanted nothing to do with him. Dad? Who knew what was going on in his dad's head? Stephen just missed him, that's all he knew. But Emily? He'd hoped for more from her, he realised.

She hadn't told Mum he was at her house, which was one blow. This suggested she'd told her nothing else, either, over the past nineteen years. And that hurt. He wished it didn't but it did, and he feared what would happen if he left that hurt to fester; what it would make him say, what it would make him do.

All this on his shoulders, he'd woken up this morning feeling more wretched and hopeless than he had in years. More, even, than the day he'd arrived at Milly's, after that awful bender. His only hopes then had been about survival, after all; about warmth, shelter and not going off the rails. Then, like a fool, he'd allowed bigger hopes to grow; hopes for living, not just surviving. How wondrous that had felt – to be given a whole new go at life. Then the elements had turned on him and he hadn't been prepared, had he? He'd been as exposed as a sapling on a hillside in a storm.

Stephen felt his soles firmly planted in God's sweet earth, took in the beauty around him and felt a wave of deep gratitude that this morning, he'd come downstairs and the first thing he'd thought of was his and Milly's bucket birding list. Drawing it out, he'd looked at the sellotape holding it together and heard that voice: *You and your wimpy little hobby, your silly little dreams. You're going to come to nothing.*

Number one on the list was to spot two rare birds in twenty-four hours. He'd circled that instruction, twice in black marker pen, pressing down hard on the nib as if it were a weapon. Then, on the same phone that twelve hours earlier had allowed him to hear his mother's voice for the first time in thirteen years, only for her to take it away again, Stephen called Birdline. Birds had always been his salvation; now his list could give him purpose when he badly needed it.

So, he'd called Birdline. He'd wanted fate to take over: if there was a bird he longed to see out there, right now, a little miracle waiting to reveal itself, then it would be an *actual* miracle, a sign from God or Mother Nature that he must keep going because there were things to fight for. The recorded voice on the other line was as soothing as the shipping forecast. And then there it was – a ring ouzel seen on Staines Moor, at dawn today circa 5 a.m. GMT. And so, he was here instead of the gutter and he was thankful, oh, he was. For he may not have had a house, or even a family, but he had this and he would be okay; he would be as undaunted as a swift flying over the desert.

There was a rustle in the reeds that bordered the river. Binoculars and telescopes were swung, soundlessly, to the left. A communal intake of breath . . . Was it? No, it was just a pair of egrets, nonetheless beautiful beyond words to Stephen, and anyway, he felt relieved. Once they'd seen the bird after all, and everyone had packed away their tripods and telescopes and gone home, where would he go? It didn't matter how long he'd been at this game, the fear of not knowing where he would lay his head come nightfall never left him.

He was contemplating this when there was another noise: high-pitched, a kind of squawky *weeear weeear*, and Stephen thought it was a crow at first, but then realised it was a human voice, and that it sounded like someone shouting 'Stevie'. That was because, he realised, it *was* someone shouting Stevie and then it clicked who that someone was and Stephen swore to the sky, because he could not believe it.

'Stevie!' she screamed again across the moor, and he turned around but not before the whole bloody anoraked massive had too, expressing their disgust at this atrocious lack of respect, with a wave of muffled oaths, tuts and sighs.

'Steeeephen!' Christ alive, people had made less noise running for their lives in a war zone, and to make matters worse, the egret took off then, along with every single other bird and creature known to man on that moor, no doubt. Stephen imagined the ants scarpering, the worms wriggling down a layer, but could do nothing but stand, helplessly, and watch his sister running towards him over the moor, scattering molehills and sending ditchwater flying with that funny knock-kneed run she'd had since she was a kid.

He held up a hand and gave a tight-lipped smile to

the rest of the group by way of apology, then began walking the twenty or so metres to meet her, which was when he noticed she was wearing a tightish skirt, for crying out loud, and some kind of heeled boots.

'What the hell?' he said when he reached her. 'What are you doing here?'

She was standing with her hands on her hips, feet astride a boggy patch, trying to get her breath back.

'I came for you,' she said, her chest heaving, mud up her legs. 'I wanted to find you.'

Stephen looked at the ground, kicked at a bit of dirt and shook his head. 'Well, you shouldn't have,' he said quietly. He felt mad for reasons that ran deeper than he wanted to feel, to acknowledge even, but mainly he felt irritated with her for coming after him like this. 'You should have just let me go.'

'But I only just found you!' Emily's light blue eyes were full of hurt and Stephen felt bad, then annoyed he felt bad. 'We were just getting to know each other again and then you just . . . took off,' she said, with a flick of her hand.

'I'm sorry,' he said, 'I had to.' A pause, then he added, 'I wanted to.'

Emily looked at him for a moment, as if she were completely baffled by him, as if she had no idea who he was – *and you don't*, he thought to himself, sadly. *You don't, not anymore*. Then she looked past him, towards the line of twitchers, who were standing, perched forward, looking through cameras on tripods, like men at the front line, waiting for battle. 'How do you know about this place anyway?' she said.

'Never mind that, how did you know I was here?'

'There was a bit of paper,' she said. 'On the table by the phone.'

Stephen kicked himself inwardly.

'It had the Birdline number on and information about a ring—'

'Right,' he snapped. 'But still, how did you find this place?'

'With great difficulty! I was beginning to think it was just a mirage, that it didn't actually exist, that it was a secret or something.'

'It is,' said Stephen, sharper than he'd intended. 'Or it was, anyway.' It had taken two trains and a fairly long walk from the station to get here, and he'd had to ask various locals for directions on the way.

They were both silent then. Another plane rumbled above, and a nearby swan gave a loud echoing honk. Stephen watched it glide along the river and was instantly mesmerised, thinking it looked as glorious as a Viking ship.

'Please come back,' said Emily suddenly, and Stephen saw that her eyes were filling with tears and he felt a tightness in his chest because he never could stand it when she cried. 'Please. I got used to you. I loved you being there. I don't think I want to even be there, in that horrible flat, without you.'

'Emily, it's a bloody beautiful flat.'

'Oh, I know,' she said crossly, and she covered her mouth with her hands as if she understood how that might have come across and wanted to take it straight back. 'I know. I didn't mean that. Sorry.'

'Come on,' said Stephen, stepping towards her, placing his hand on her shoulder. 'Don't do this, Mills. Go back home – back to your life. You've got a really good life, you don't need me coming and messing everything up.'

'You don't mess everything up. Well, you do, you're literally the messiest cook I have ever known but also, you made my place feel like home.'

Stephen sighed and rubbed his forehead; he didn't want to be dealing with this.

'Listen,' he said, after a pause. 'The flat is beautiful – you've made it so nice, it's a palace! You've got a great job . . .'

'So what? It's all meaningless without you, I realise that now. I don't want to do anything if I lose you again.'

'I want to be on my own, Milly. I want to go off and just birdwatch on my own, like I have for most of my life, like I've been perfectly happy doing for the last fifteen years.'

Emily almost laughed at that. 'You've been homeless!'

she said, incredulously and so loudly that Stephen had to shush her. 'Sleeping on the streets, barely surviving. Have you forgotten the state you were in when you turned up at mine? Don't you know what happens to homeless people?'

Stephen felt this was pretty arrogant, not to mention stupid, of her. 'I might have some idea,' he said.

'They succumb to addiction just to cope, and they die early deaths from drugs or hypothermia or suicide. And you're my brother and I love you and I just can't let that happen to you. I want to help you.'

Stephen sighed, blowing his cheeks out, and looked to his left where, on the other side of the moor, the M25 roared like a stormy sea. Why now? Where had she been all that time? Had she really tried to look for him as hard as she said she had? 'I think it's a bit too late for that,' he said, quietly. 'It's all a bit too little, too late . . .'

Just then, there was a shrill whistle from one of the other birders. Stephen swung around immediately, his pulse racing, because he knew exactly what that meant, and he began striding towards them before breaking into a jog, but softly-softly, keeping low, like a commando. *Please don't fly off. Please, please* . . . Lenses were extended and focused with utmost precision, eyes down them. He heard the distinctive *tuk-tuk* sound before he saw the bird. Then he *did* see it, and he lifted up his binoculars so he could see every detail of it, as adrenaline coursed through his body, making his heart pump, sending tingles up the back of his neck and all over his skull.

The ring ouzel was perched midway down the still-bare branches of a pine tree about ten metres in front of him. Worth the wait and then some, she was, with her perfect proportions, her sharp, elegant beak and her creamy white bib on velvety brown plumage. And she was all the more magnificent for being completely oblivious to their worship of her or the fuss her presence had created. Stephen focused right in to watch her, completely enthralled. And he entered another plane of consciousness, then: one where he was not aware of anything else, not the fact the mud had begun to seep into his trainers and he hadn't eaten all day, or how life was relentless sometimes, and could break your heart again and again, or the fact he had nowhere to sleep tonight, or that he was mad with his sister in a way that scared him. It was just him and the view through his binoculars and it was all he needed – although at some point, he became aware that Emily had crept up behind him, and, without thinking, he put his arm around her, bringing her in, so that she was standing right in front of him, the back of her head on his chest. He put the binoculars around her neck and held them to her eyes. 'See it?' he said. 'Up there, in that tree to the right; about four branches from the top.'

She was silent. He could feel her heartbeat, fast and

strong. 'There!' he whispered, when the bird moved its head, pointing towards it. 'She's looking at us.'

There was a pause, then Emily nodded, excitedly. 'I see it,' she said, and she gave a muted squeal of delight. 'I see it.'

They watched it, spellbound, along with the rest of the group, and there was not a word, a sigh or cough among them until, after ten minutes or so, the bird flew off west and it was as if everyone had been holding their breath and could now exhale. There was euphoric chatter – *Wow, beautiful, hey? Well, that's made my month!* – and high fives exchanged, including between Stephen and Emily. Then everyone began to pack up their things: telescopes were taken down, tripods folded away, and Stephen felt the coolness and anxiety towards his sister creep back in, as well as the worry about where the hell he would sleep tonight. He was grateful then when a man in a proper sou'wester beside him struck up conversation, asking what else he'd seen recently, where he was from. He glanced over at Emily as they chatted; she was looking awkward in her work clothes, her arms wrapped around her body. *Just go,* thought Stephen. *Don't make this harder than it needs to be.* Then Sou'wester touched his arm and said, 'Well, listen, myself and these guys are all going to Norfolk next. There's a citril finch along the River Waveney, apparently – near the border between Norfolk and Suffolk – on what they call the Angles Way.'

'Wow, really?' said Stephen. He felt a stab of envy. He'd read about the citril finch and he wanted to see one, badly. 'I'd love to see one of those.'

'You don't fancy it?'

'Oh yeah, I do,' said Stephen, when he realised what the man was getting at, 'but I'm not really a twitcher. I don't have the transport and the resources for it, sadly . . .'

The man offered a regretful smile. 'I'd gladly give you a lift,' he said. 'But there are already four of us in my Fiesta.'

'I've got a car,' Emily piped up, brightly, and Stephen swung around to her. He'd momentarily forgotten she was there. 'I'll drive you to Norfolk to see this bird, if you like.'

Sou'wester laughed as he bent down to zip up his tripod case. 'There you are,' he said, 'an offer you can't refuse.'

Stephen looked at Emily, who shrugged and smiled, her hair about her face, as if to say, *What are you waiting for?* But Stephen was torn: he wanted to be on his own, badly. He wanted to slip back into that wild, as if through the gate of a secret garden, where nobody knew where he was, and nothing or nobody could touch him. And yet . . . he also wanted to see a citril finch. He imagined the thrill – that delicious tingle all over his skull and the feeling of achievement that he so rarely had. Here was an opportunity – as if straight from the sky, almost literally – and it seemed ungrateful not to take it. Foolish too. His sister had transport – and, okay, he didn't want to be with her right now, was scared of the feelings she was bringing up – but equally, she owed him. She owed him big time.

Sou'wester stood up. He looked from Stephen to Emily and back to Stephen, hands on his hips, a grin on his face as if trying to work out exactly what this guy's problem was – was he a true birder or not? 'Well then?' he said. 'Aren't you going to take her up on it? You'd be mad to miss this, mate.'

'Er, yeah,' Stephen said, looking sideways at Emily. She nodded encouragingly at him, grinning. 'Okay, if you don't mind.'

'Cockatoo'

February 1996

'Oh, hello, Alicia.'

Emily was in Canvey Island Stores with her mum, when they were stopped in the freezer aisle by Joyce Fields. Joyce Fields was one of Mum and Mitch's friends from Canvey Island Golf Club where, along with Canvey Island Social Club, Mitch was held up like a local hero, a god. Joyce Fields had short blonde hair that was spiky on top, which Emily thought made her look like a cockatoo, and a small, yapping dog that always tried to lick Emily's ankles. After her mother and Joyce's lengthy gossip-fest, which Emily spent hiding behind her mother's skirt to avoid the dog's tongue, Joyce Fields put her hand on Alicia's shoulder. 'And . . . your Stephen?' she said, as if Stephen were a dirty word. 'Mitchell has, well . . . he's filled me in a little – I mean, dare I ask?'

Alicia gave a defeated sigh, that pained expression she seemed to wear when talking about Stephen. 'I worry he's a lost cause, Joyce,' she said, bleakly. 'I swear he's got the devil in him sometimes.'

Joyce Fields nodded and smiled sympathetically. 'Well, at least you've got this one,' she said, indicating Emily.

Outside, Emily and Alicia sat down on a bench, Alicia lighting a cigarette, while a pigeon pecked around their feet. 'Mum?' said Emily. 'Has Stevie really got the devil inside of him?' This – even at nine – felt like a shocking damnation, and, more to the point, there was no evidence for it that she could see.

Mum took a drag, tipping her head right back, and exhaled into the blank, February sky. 'No, love,' she said. 'No, it's just a thing people say.' Then she sighed. 'But there has to be some explanation as to why he puts your stepfather and me through the things he does.'

Emily was confused. She'd been feeling like that a lot recently. There seemed to be two versions of her brother: the one Mitch and Mum knew, and the one she did, and they were nothing like each other. She'd begun to notice too how Mum often complained about Stephen to the neighbours, Ron and Penny Callaghan, and to friends, but was rarely angry with him herself. Her complaints were always second-hand: *Mitch says . . . ; his stepfather has had enough; Mitch doesn't know what to do about that boy*. Of course, sometimes she lost her temper with Stephen, just as she did with Emily, but it was normally about little things, like getting in the way of the hoovering (she would blow her top about that!). Yet to hear their mum talk, Emily was an *angel, a good girl* and *sweet pea*. With Stephen, however, it was *trouble* and *nightmare* and *soft in the head*. (That was Mitch's favourite at the moment.)

Emily didn't understand it. She knew their mum suffered with her nerves, and sometimes found Stephen too much, but before Mitch, she'd never talked about him as if she didn't even like him.

Chapter Twenty

Emily

'Look, Stevie, look at this,' I said, pulling the box out from the shelf, with some difficulty, I had to admit. It was longer than I expected and just kept coming and coming. 'This is perfect.' I pushed it up with both arms like a weightlifter, so I could read from the product description on the underside. 'Three-man, one-room tent with front porch, grey and orange, taped seams, blue hydrostatic head, outer fly, internal storage pockets . . .'

Stephen began to laugh.

'What?' I said, affronted. We were in the 'outdoor living' area of a twenty-four-hour Asda superstore just outside Staines – the type of mega-branch that sold everything from food to footwear to, thankfully, tents. It just so happened you could also buy an inflatable watermelon, should you need one.

'Nothing, it's just the way you said grey and orange. As well as everything else on that list, to be honest – like that would make any difference whatsoever.'

'What do you mean?' I could feel myself blushing.

Despite my efforts to convince otherwise, tents, and the outdoors generally, were not my domain, not anymore, and I sensed Stephen knew this. I hardly ever left the city these days, unless to visit Mum.

'What I mean is, that the fact it's grey and orange or has seams or storage pockets, or whatever other gubbins is listed on there, has no bearing whatsoever on how good an actual shelter it will be . . .' said Stephen. 'How good a tent it is.'

I huffed a bit. 'Well, what do you think then?'

'You know what I think. I think we'd be much better sleeping in a doorway, or a disused building, or frankly under the stars if it's dry, than trying to put that thing up, or lugging it around. I do have quite a bit of experience of this kind of thing.'

Stephen yawned, for so long and so wide I could see his tonsils. He looked destroyed, suddenly, pasty under the harsh supermarket strip lights, and I felt a flood of relief – and pride. Yes, I don't mind admitting I felt proud of myself – for persevering today and tracking him down. After all, if this was what he looked like after only one day back out 'in the wild' as he so romantically put it, how would he be after a week? We'd be back to that wreckage that washed up on my doorstep, three weeks ago now.

I slid the tent box back in its place like a body in a mortuary freezer, somewhat petulantly. The truth was, although I wanted to go with Stephen to find this bird, the reason had nothing to do with some wilderness experience. I wanted to make things right, once and for all. Even if it meant hours spent standing in the freezing cold just waiting for a bloody bird to show up.

Don't get me wrong, I like birds. I really like birds. But I've always understood that Stephen loves them – possibly more than humans; I suspect because he feels he can trust them more than humans. So, I was one hundred per cent committed to taking him to see this bird if that's what he wanted, if that's what it took not to lose him again. But I was not sleeping in a doorway. No chance. I'd done that once as a teenager in the Lake District, in June I might add, when me and some friends got locked out of our youth hostel, and it was not an experience I intended to repeat. Not if I didn't have to.

I said as much to Stephen. 'I'm sorry, but if I'm coming, we're getting a tent.'

Stephen drew his chin into his neck and frowned, a dismissive expression I'd never seen before and certainly didn't like.

'Right,' he said. 'Even though I didn't actually ask you to come. In fact, with all due respect,' he mumbled into his armpit, 'I didn't *want* you to come.'

I was hurt by that but I did not show it.

'Well, you need me, so there, because I have the transport.'

He mumbled something else that I chose to ignore.

What was the matter with him? I'd basically rescued him from homelessness and this was how he behaved? And yes, it was painful. But underpinning that pain – I knew, deep down – was terror that, having finally found him, he might take off again, like a bird, and I couldn't cope with that.

I decided to put his mood down to exhaustion and hunger after a day spent on a wild and windy moor. When he got back into my warm, dry car and had a good sleep in the warm, dry tent I was going to buy us, he'd be grateful; he'd appreciate me.

I sighed at him. 'You're being a bit mean. I am offering to buy the tent for us.'

'Man, you are so extravagant. You've got a car!'

'There's no way we'll get any sleep in my Clio, you're too tall for starters. Also, I wouldn't call thirty-five pounds particularly extravagant if it's going to mean we're dry and safe. I'll put the tent up,' I said, immediately regretting it. 'I'll buy us a mat too, and a sleeping bag for me so we don't have to share yours. Also, I'm going to get me some warm clothes, actually, and alternative footwear, so I won't be tottering around Suffolk in these boots, like the embarrassing little sister I clearly am.'

'We're only going to be there for one night – two at the most.'

Too right, I thought. *And then, I'm bringing you home.*

*

I compromised, getting a two-man, not the three-man tent, a cheap sleeping bag for me and a mat, and put them all in a trolley. We then wheeled around to the clothing section, where I picked out some thermal leggings, jogging bottoms, a fleece jumper and cagoule. Stephen stood there, a mix of bewilderment and disgust on his face. 'It's not a fashion show,' he said.

'I know,' I said, sifting through a rail for a suitable anorak or waterproof of some description. 'In no world would I call a pair of George jogging pants "fashion". Now, do they sell wellies?' I said, before remembering I had some in the boot of the car that hadn't seen the light of day in years.

Stephen went outside to smoke. Whilst he was gone, I rang Justine.

'This is a nice surprise,' she said. 'To what do I owe this pleasure?'

I could hear water splashing in the background; she was bathing the kids.

'Sorry, is this a bad time?'

'No, that was fifteen minutes ago when I had to fish out Olivia's turd. We're all refilled and good to go now,' she said and I laughed, despite being appalled. The world of kids (and fishing out turds from baths, come to that) still felt some way away for me. If I were honest, it felt like some mystical world that I just couldn't see myself being part of, nor where I belonged. It's not that I didn't want children – I loved babies. When it came to seeing cute babies in cafes and parks I was a baby-botherer of the highest order. It was just that when I tried to imagine that easy, unconditional, uncomplicated love that Justine seemed to have with her kids and husband – and, most importantly, with her mother – I couldn't.

A voice over the tannoy called, 'Maureen Jewson to the deli section, please. That's Maureen Jewson to the deli section.'

'Where are you?' said Justine.

'A twenty-four-hour Asda, just outside Staines.'

'Wow, aren't you the lucky one. What are you doing there, you nutter?'

I looked up then from where I was standing in the middle of the footwear section to find my reflection in a long mirror. I did look somewhat nutterish, there was no denying it. Actually, with the mud splashed up my flesh-coloured tights and over my suede ankle boots, I looked as if I'd just been viciously attacked down a dark, country lane.

'It's a long story, involving a tent and my brother, which is why I'm calling . . .' I sighed heavily. 'He left this morning.'

'What? But he was only there last night, what do you mean he left?'

'I mean, he just went.'

From the revolving door exit, I could just see the back

of Stephen, in his orange puffa jacket, puffing away. He'd been so pleased with himself finding that in a charity shop on Lordship Lane. I didn't have the heart to tell him that it was probably a woman's jacket and had gold lettering on the back, spelling out the words 'Hello, you'. For someone so observant, he didn't seem to notice these sorts of things.

'I got back from showing a client a flat this morning to find a note he'd left, saying it was time he went, that he didn't want to outstay his welcome. That was it.'

'Oh, Em.'

'But it's okay, 'cause I found him again!'

'Oh,' she said, surprised and confused. 'I see.'

'I won't bore you with the details, but I tracked him down this afternoon. He'd gone to see some bird on Staines Moor – the feathery variety,' I added for clarification. 'You know, like twitchers do.' I realised this all might sound a little salacious. 'You know what twitching is, right?'

'Uhh . . .'

'It's like hitch-hiking the length of the country – obsessively – to find a rare bird. The thrill is in finding them, then ticking them off the list.'

'O-kay . . .'

'Bear with me . . . Basically he wants to go and find this other bird now – it's like his life depends on it.' This was exaggerating somewhat but it had dawned on me

Justine might say no and I couldn't risk that. 'But the thing is, he needs transport to get there and also, I just really need to go with him, to keep an eye on him. I really need him not to disappear again, Juss, because it might be another nineteen years. But the thing is, this trip might run into Monday. . .'

'Emily, just go.'

I stopped, not expecting that. 'What? Really?'

'Yes, we can manage. Just take it as holiday. He's your brother. I know how much him turning up means to you.'

I realised I'd been holding my breath and exhaled. 'God, thank you – thanks so much. I just really want to help him, you know, after so many years when I haven't been able to?'

'Sure, sure.'

'He deserves my support,' I said, and I heard Justine say something to one of the kids, but she didn't respond to me. 'I mean, obviously he's had issues.'

'Yeah, I know,' said Justine. 'Actually, I was going to say something about that. Now, I know he's your brother and you love him, and I've met him and I can totally see why, but I think it's important to remember – and forgive me if I sound prejudiced or bigoted here . . .'

You do, I thought, the smile slipping from my face. *You do, stop it.*

'But you don't know what sort of people he's got involved with on the streets, what kind of connections he might have. I mean, he's been in prison and for a serious offence, you said.' I felt a sensation like my scalp was being stretched. 'And I'm not saying he's not totally rehabilitated, or that it was even his fault . . .'

'It absolutely wasn't,' I snapped. The anger reared up so quickly and uncontrollably that it surprised even me. 'He was driven to it.'

Silence. I squeezed my eyes shut and swore to myself under my breath.

'Emily, I'm really sorry.' Justine, when she spoke, sounded mortified but mainly shocked – this kind of outburst was out of character for me. 'God, sorry, I didn't mean to . . . I shouldn't have . . .'

I clenched my jaw together and could feel the blood pulsing in my ears. 'It's okay,' I lied, tears springing to my eyes.

Neither of us spoke. I could hear water splashing and her son, Finley, laughing with delight, then Justine said, 'Look, darling, I'm sorry if I upset you. I know you just want to help Stephen, course you do.' Her voice was extra gentle and I felt bad for snapping. 'In fact, I was thinking, have you considered the local connection thing?' I ran through the minefield that is the housing priority system in my head. 'Applying to another local authority?' Justine said, reading my silence. 'You know how, if a client can't get accommodation in the area they're in, but have close relatives living in another area of the country, how they can apply there for council housing? I was wondering, what about your mum or your dad?'

It rang a distant bell. 'You mean housing people on the cheap by exiling them hundreds of miles away where they don't know anyone – hundreds of miles from London?'

'Well, just think about it. It just might be a way of getting a roof over his head.'

I could see my brother coming back in and waved at him so he knew where I was.

'It's a good idea, I'll think about it,' I said, closing the conversation down. I didn't want Stephen to know we were discussing him, but Justine had planted a seed of an idea. 'My brother's coming back from his cigarette now, so I best go, but I'll definitely think about it. Thanks, Juss. And for letting me take this time as holiday. You're a legend.'

Asda was like a vortex, sucking us in against our will, because by the time we were out of there, packing up the car, it was gone 8 p.m. and pitch black. I'd bought us both a sandwich, which Stephen didn't protest about – probably because, judging by the way he inhaled it, it was the first thing he'd eaten all day.

We'd sought information from the guy wearing the sou'wester and other twitchers before we'd left the moor and were headed for a town called Harleston, which was next to the River Waveney (or rather, for a place to pitch the tent around there). The plan was, tomorrow we'd get onto the footpath along the river, following it to the area where the citril finch was said to be.

We put Harleston in the satnav. The M25 was oddly quiet. Stephen soon fell asleep, head lolling in seconds, so it was just me, the road and my thoughts, a situation I generally try to avoid.

I'd not spoken to her since Wednesday and it was now Saturday. This was a worry in itself, because normally I speak to Mum most days, and if I don't call her – as I'd got into the habit of doing – I would have thought she'd almost definitely call me. She likes to download every single detail of what is undeniably her sad and limited life to me; how every mealtime and toilet visit has gone with Mitch; what he's eaten, what they've watched on TV. She likes to voice every single disappointment. These are constant and without scale, so she'll seem as disappointed about a new cereal she's bought to try, as she does about not getting more funding for respite care for Mitch. It's as if she expects to be disappointed by every single thing in her life, and so she is. Not that I blame her: her life has certainly not turned out as she'd hoped. As anyone would hope.

Throughout *my* life, though, it feels that she's always been this way, to a greater or lesser extent, and sometimes I feel I've been a disappointment to her too. I've not been able to make her happy, after all. Me, the daughter she always wanted. Was she disappointed with me even when I was little? I'd never wear the dresses she bought for me. I always preferred to go out on the marshes with Stevie than shopping with her, or have a girly afternoon painting our nails. She was forever painting her nails, her face, putting her mask on, as if it was the only bit of control she had. Why couldn't I have done that with her? Just once? Just to make her happy?

Saying all this, after the last few conversations we've had, I've dared to think things might be improving, that progress is being made in terms of my mother's happiness levels. She's socialising with friends like Sheena who seem to be having a positive influence; she's talking about putting Mitch in a home and getting her life back. 'You're my angel, my lifeline,' she said to me often since Mitch became paralysed and Stephen went to prison, the subtext being, *Unlike your brother who ruined my life*. But could that be changing? Was it just wishful thinking, or could my mother putting Mitch in a home and closing the door on him mean another could open for my brother?

Could she forgive him?

Justine's idea about the local connection thing was great except for one, major spanner in the works: the rules were that someone would only be eligible if they'd had regular contact with that relative who was based in the area in the last five years. Mum hadn't even spoken to Stephen for thirteen years, never mind had regular contact. Looking across at my brother, fast asleep, vulnerable, I had a moment of clarity: this situation could not go on. This was crazy. I could not stand another visit to my mother's where Stephen's name was unspeakable. I could not choose between my mother and my brother like a child of warring divorced parents. Moreover, I would not. My brother, her son, needed somewhere to live and he needed the help of both of us. What happened with Mitch was years ago, and it was high time my mother put the past behind her and got behind her son. Tomorrow, I would find a time Stephen wasn't around and I would call her, and I would tell her this in no uncertain terms. I'd tell her too that I was with Stephen and had been for weeks. It had been awful lying, but sometimes you just have to, don't you? Or you have to play with the truth for everybody's sakes. But now I realised, what if something happened to Mum? What if the cancer returned and she died without ever seeing Stephen again, or vice versa – and I could have done something about it? I was struck, like a punch in the stomach, by the awfulness of this possibility; the knowledge I'd not be able to live with myself.

I thought back to the April of 2011 – so, seven years ago now – when Mum had just finished her last round of chemotherapy. Mitch had been in respite care while she had her treatment and, despite looking physically diminished, her head covered with a scarf, Mum was more cheerful than I'd ever seen her. I was with her in the kitchen. 'I can't tell you what a joy it's been to have a break from him,' she'd said, despite Mitch being in earshot in the lounge. It was the first time I'd heard her speak about him like that: dismissively, disdainfully, even, with no air of martyrdom, and it was kind of encouraging. Physically, however, she was frail, which is why I'd gone up to Yorkshire to help her. One particular day, I was feeding Mitch his lunch in the lounge while Mum was washing up in the kitchen. The electric fire was lit despite it being April and sunny outside, and the TV was on extra loud, as if Mitch were deaf as well as paralysed. He was watching as I fed him – it was *A Place in the Sun*, I remember it clearly. I say watching it, but you couldn't tell, because his eyes stared straight ahead all the time, fixed and unfocused. 'Open,' I said, gently, and he duly opened his mouth and I put the next spoonful in, wiping his lips with a napkin afterwards.

The woman on *A Place in the Sun* was waxing lyrical about a dilapidated French farmhouse. 'I'd never take something like that on,' Mum said from the kitchen. 'Not if you paid me.'

'Open again for me, please?' I said again to Mitch, after he'd finished the painfully slow job of chewing and swallowing the previous spoonful, and his jaw dropped robotically and in went another spoonful of mush.

'Now, Emily has come all the way from London to help,' Mum called from the kitchen where she was still washing up, 'so, behave yourself, please. She's taken this as holiday from work – not much of a holiday, is it? She's an angel, that girl, never forget it.'

'Finished?' I said to Mitch, and then his dead eyes came to life in the most awful way and locked with mine – he was looking straight at me, or so it felt, straight into me. Then his eyes began to bulge, the veins in his temples swelled and he began to cough then choke, then actually fight for breath. 'Oh my God! Oh my God!' Mum ran from the kitchen, a tea towel in her hand.

I don't remember what happened next, although obviously Mitch was okay. In that moment, though, I was sure he knew who I was. He knew who I was and he hated me.

Chapter Twenty-One

Stephen

What's with all the orange? was Stephen's first thought on waking. The bright, glaring orange everywhere? Also, he was damp – that was his second thought. He tentatively patted around and under himself and this – accompanied by an awful rolling sensation in his stomach, like seasickness – brought on his third thought: he'd wet himself. He'd got obliterated last night, and he'd wet himself.

He closed his eyes again in self-disgust, not wanting to face this reality, when he became aware of a voice – it was faint, but not so faint that he couldn't recognise it as his sister's – and this brought him round enough to remember what was actually going on, which was that he and Milly had spent the night in an (orange) tent somewhere in the Waveney Valley, in Norfolk, because they'd come to see a bird, and that the damp beneath him – thank the Lord – was simply morning dew. Stephen eased himself up in his sleeping bag, leant forward and unzipped the tent. A glorious filmy light met him; reeds along a riverbank and, through them, glimpses of the silver water, morning mist rising off it like a thermal lagoon.

Stephen shuffled forward in his sleeping bag. If he craned his neck to the right, he could see Milly, some way down the riverbank in her Asda joggers (everything was slotting into place now) on the phone. She was too far away for him to hear exactly what she was saying, but he caught a few words and her tone, which was agitated.

'I just . . . I didn't know how to . . .'

Then, 'A week, just over a week.'

'Mum, please. I'm sorry, okay?'

Anxiety squeezed Stephen's stomach and he found himself instantly reaching for his tobacco tin, feeling around the side pockets of the tent for it. He retrieved the tin, opened it, glancing at Emily while he rolled his cigarette. She was standing holding the phone in one hand, the other hand on top of her head, the call obviously over. But rather than walk back to the tent then, she stayed where she was, her back to him, perfectly still – as if she was thinking deeply. (*You bet she is*, thought Stephen. *She has plenty to think about*.) Stephen was halfway through his cigarette when she dipped her head forward, passed her right hand around the back of her neck, held it for a moment, then turned swiftly on her heel.

'Hey,' she said as she approached him, like butter

wouldn't melt, but he saw alarm flash in in her eyes – the realisation he'd probably heard her.

'Morning,' said Stephen, somewhat moodily, squinting up at her. 'Sleep well?'

'Gosh, like a baby,' she said, with irritatingly fake breeziness, turning to look across the river. 'You?'

He shrugged and put out his cigarette. 'Not too bad, bit damp.'

'I was fine,' she lied, and Stephen frowned at the back of her navy fleece as he remembered her, last night, erecting the tent in the copse of white ash trees they'd found to camp in, lit only by his torch. It had been like a scene from a horror film, her burying a body at night, and he'd offered help but she'd stubbornly refused. 'I said I'd put it up on my own, and I will.' She'd not grown out of that, he'd thought – that stubborn streak. *I do it myself, Deeby! I come to the marshes with you, Deeby.*

Immediately after Stephen put out his cigarette, he began rolling another. The only noise was the birds – the chiffchaffs and wrens chirruping sweetly, completely unaware of any tension in the atmosphere. How he envied them – because he was feeling increasingly tense. He dragged enthusiastically on his roll-up. *This was a mistake,* he thought, *I should never have come.* At least not with his sister, not with his head the way it was. He didn't want to feel this, this bitterness towards her and this disappointment; he'd done so well at burying all that. He'd nailed it and yet, now? He should never have gone to her house in the first place – a can of worms was an understatement. Yet, he'd missed her, he'd missed her so much. He didn't even know how much until he had her in his life again.

He glanced up at her now, her head turned away from him – almost as if she couldn't look at him. Totally as if she couldn't look at him. She still had the same blonde hair she'd had as a kid, although it was chin-length now and comically knotty, Stephen noticed, like a bird's nest, after only twenty-four hours on the road, just as it always was when she was little and she'd spend the whole day on the marshes with him, the estuary winds whipping it up. And just this connection, this memory, brought on an unbearable pang of longing for what was, but also what could have been; how their lives, their relationship, might have gone if their childhood had not combusted, sending them both in opposite directions.

He heard Emily take a deep breath. 'Stevie, look,' she said, turning around, rubbing her forehead, obviously about to say something important, but at the same time, there was a cacophony; an explosion of feathers and a noise like a small, yappy dog barking. Emily gave a small shriek and covered her head and Stephen looked up as a pheasant flew out of the copse, a squawking mass of tawny-brown with that shot of bottle-green. 'Jesus,' said

Emily, hand clutched to her chest. 'Christ, that gave me a shock.'

'Calm down,' said Stephen, unable to hide the irritation in his voice. 'It's just a pheasant.'

They watched as it flew downstream and out across the valley, which was brightening now, the mist lifting. Then Emily sat down next to him, tucked her hair behind her ears and plucked a blade of grass that she began studying, hard. Stephen had an idea of what was coming next.

'Listen, I know why you left,' she said, looking up at him with those intense blue eyes she'd got from Dad – he'd got Mum's murky hazel ones. 'I know about Mum calling and putting the phone down on you on Friday night and I know that you know I was just on the phone to her . . . and I'm sorry I didn't tell her you were at mine, like I said I would. I'm sorry I lied. I feel shit about it. But she called back, Stevie. She called back yesterday, but we'd both left. Now, I don't know what this means for sure – she was too angry that I'd not told her about you to talk about anything else – but I reckon it's a sign she's coming round, that she wants—'

Stephen was feeling darker by the second. He squashed his cigarette butt into the earth, then put it into his tin. 'Milly, just don't.'

'She's going to put Mitch in a home,' Emily blurted, desperately. 'Things are changing, *she's* changing, she'll come round, I know she will.'

'I said don't,' said Stephen wearily. His stepfather going into a home would mean he was out of sight, sure, but out of mind? He doubted it would make that much of a difference to his mother, and it certainly wouldn't mean she'd forgive him. It wouldn't change the past. The fact her life had been destroyed. He lay back down, his upper body inside the tent, his legs outside, and put his arms behind his head. He'd been all right these past few years. He'd survived, he was a survivor. And now this again. He did not want to deal with this. 'Just don't bother, okay?' He felt resentful and angry and he hated that feeling more than anything. 'It is what it is.'

There was a long silence, except for the chatter of birds, the call of a wood pigeon. Somewhere far to their left, a man shouted after his dog. After a good few minutes, Stephen sat up again, slowly. Everything ached already – he'd got used to that comfy bed. 'Right,' he said, trying his best to sound enthusiastic and cheerful. 'Are we going to find this bird, or what?'

Stephen had taken Sou'wester's mobile number and now sent him a text, asking for the latest on the bird, his phone pinging with a reply almost immediately, telling him where, vaguely, on the Angles Way it had last been seen.

The location was a little way west of where they were now, but the bird was on the move, apparently, and so Stephen and Emily packed up the tent and loaded the car. They found a layby to park in, and proceeded on foot, following the Angles Way footpath signs, staying in contact with Sou'wester and his friends as much as they could.

The mist had cleared, and the day sang with spring. Stephen loved the way the countryside seemed to split open, like it was rebelling after the confines of winter. England looked sensational all year round, as far as he was concerned, but especially in spring. Take where they were right now, walking down your ordinary country lane that was anything but ordinary: the blue sky a vault above them, on either side, hedged in by the blackthorn – that exquisite white flower; at their feet were buttercups and primroses. When they got to the end, the land opened up to a patchwork of green corn and acid-yellow rapeseed fields. They saw three wild rabbits in half an hour, darting to the safety of hedgerows, slinking under fences. They chatted as they walked, easily at first. Emily had not lost her curiosity, and Stephen was in his element, explaining things to her, answering her questions, his attention outside of himself, where he liked it best: why were the fields ploughed in this particular fashion? What kind of tree was that again? How did trees' branches know how to grow like that, so that none stuck out more than the others and their sides were symmetrical? Stephen began to list for her which migratory birds would have arrived in England already, and which were on their way, before remembering that the swifts (due in two weeks or less) were unmentionable because of the memories he knew they could trigger.

Just be in the moment, he told himself. *Just be grateful for now and the chance to see this bird. Don't think, don't remember, because all that makes you is mad and sad, and you can't afford to feel either.* And he did, truly, want to simply drink in all this beauty around him; to be wrapped up in it and let it take him away from things, as it had always done. And yet something had changed – he felt it. The wild – the countryside or the wild inside of him – had always been a sanctuary, but coming back to it now was not like it used to be, not after being cossetted at Milly's for three weeks. He could not count on it to numb his pain anymore. When he'd been at Milly's, he'd been not just in the present, but allowed himself to think of the future too, and somehow a wound had been opened, and the past could now bleed out.

Before Stephen could think too much more, they approached a series of fields – Stephen counted three of them – linked by kissing gates. The ground was saturated, sodden as to feel like sinking sand in places, and they had to concentrate on striding quickly, so as not to get stuck. It was in the second of these fields that they came across a rusting combine, which looked to Stephen like a carcass of a prehistoric beast, and, at the foot of it, a dead wheatear. It was not long dead by the looks of it and the absence – as yet – of flies; probably killed by the sheer exhaustion of migration.

Emily stopped when she saw it. 'They always make me so sad,' she said, in that slightly melodramatic way she still had, and yet Stephen knew she meant it, and this touched him. 'Dead birds – they make me so sad.' A sudden feeling of doom descended upon him, although he wasn't sure why. 'Do you know the first thing I thought when I heard your voice in the room next to me in the council offices?' said Emily. 'I thought of that little injured warbler we once found on Mitch's patio, do you remember?'

Now Stephen fully understood what the feeling was about and inwardly willed her to change the subject.

'I was convinced it was dead, but then you got hold of my hand and put it where its heart was, and I was so happy when I felt it was alive.' She smiled, her face reliving the relief. 'And then we put the bird in a shoebox and we took it inside the house, do you remember?'

Stephen smiled, thinly, his jaw throbbing. 'I do. Now, come on, let's go and find this live bird.'

'And Mum started freaking out and I dropped the bird,' Emily continued, oblivious to his building distress, the scenes that were flashing through his mind: a quivering bird on dry earth, a steel-capped boot coming down hard. 'But you were the one Mitch went crazy at, yelling his head off. That happened a lot, didn't it? I never understood that.'

Stephen placed his hand on the small of her back. 'Yeah, well, I never understood a lot of things either,' he said, giving her a gentle push. 'Anyway, come on.'

'God, I cried so hard when Mitch told me the warbler hadn't made it, but you were so sweet.' They'd started walking again now at least, but Stephen found he was breathless, that he was having trouble slowing his heart rate. 'You buried it on the marshes, you told me so we could go and visit its grave.'

'I know, I remember.'

'We never went, though.'

No, thought Stephen, *we never did*. But the grave would still be there if they went back now, even if the little wooden cross he'd made to mark it had rotted away long ago. If he got down on his knees and dug into that patch of earth on the marshes, the one next to the bird hide, they'd still be there – those tiny bones. A skeleton from his childhood.

They walked on, any signs of civilisation far behind them. It was nearing 11 a.m. and the countryside had grown more luminous, the day gathering energy, opening out before them in all its natural glory. They passed through woodland, the sunlight winking through the pine trees, scattering a host of diamond rings on the river that ran to their right. And Stephen was vaguely aware of Emily mumbling now and then.

*

'Stevie?' Emily had stopped walking and was standing, staring at him. 'Are you okay? Because I was just saying that here's where the bird's meant to be, according to the sou'wester guy; somewhere around here.'

They were in a valley now, hills rising to their left, the sound of running water to their right, beyond the shade of trees. And Stephen looked around at England flaunting herself, dripping in beauty, and yet he couldn't feel it, couldn't connect to it; his drug of choice had stopped working. Then he looked at Emily. She had her hoodie tied around her waist, her head tilted to the sun, pleasure on her face, and he felt resentment. Wasn't she haunted? Wasn't she ever tormented? Did she even remember *anything*?

'I think we should stop,' Stephen said, suddenly.

'What?' said Emily. 'What do you mean, stop? You mean, for a rest?'

No, Stephen wanted to say, *not for a rest, you idiot, but because I can't go on with this. With you. Because I can't be near* you. But then he happened to look to his right where, like a guardian angel, a bird dropped from the trees and hopped onto the floor – and Stephen knew straight away, from its yellow breast, as bright as the rapeseed fields they'd just crossed, that it was the citril finch. The citril finch!

It was only afterwards – the buzz still coursing through his veins, them lying in the shade of the pines, drinking water and eating the nuts that Stephen had brought with them – that Emily said, to the sky, 'It's like the list.'

And Stephen's blood thumped because he knew that she knew.

She turned her head to face him. 'That's why you're doing this, isn't it? It's the first thing on the list: see two rare birds in twenty-four hours.'

Stephen was silent.

'We could carry on,' she said, more urgently. 'We *should* carry on, do the rest of the list. We made a pact to, after all. We made a pact that when we were old enough and free—'

Stephen swallowed. 'Or *I* could just carry on,' he said. Because they weren't free, were they? How could she say that? He could feel her looking at him but he did not look at her.

'Oh, right.' He could hear her attempt and failure to conceal the hurt in her voice but he didn't care. 'I'd hate to just leave you now, though, and not know how you are.'

Hasn't been a problem for the past nineteen years, thought Stephen.

Milly turned on her side, propped up by her elbow. 'Come on,' she said. 'We've already ticked off number one, we may as well try and see how many more we can do.'

Stephen thought again of Mitch tearing the list in two. *You and your wimpy dreams, your stupid little hobby.*

'Also, we did make that pact, Stevie – that we'd both do the list, not just one of us – and since you're here now and we've missed out on so much time, it's just, like' – she shrugged – 'something cool to do. You did say when we made it that it was like our . . . what was it?' She tapped her finger on the grass trying to remember.

'Passport to freedom,' he said.

'Yeah.' He heard her smile. 'That was it.'

If only you knew, he thought. *How much I'd needed that passport, and to fly away.*

Then selfishness kicked in, or something – the love of the birds overriding every other pull – it was that simple.

'All right,' he said, finally turning to her too. 'Fine, let's carry on with the list and see where we get to.'

Chapter Twenty-Two

Emily

When I was little, too little to go out birdwatching with Dad and Stephen (or later, when he was old enough to go on his own, with Stephen), I used to hang on to Stephen's trouser legs as he tried to leave the house. 'Deeby!' I would cry, lying at his feet on the doormat, clutching his ankles, Stephen trying to shake me off like a puppy. 'I go with Deeby to see the birds.' I was quite prepared to graze my entire underside being dragged the length of our front path, rather than let go. I once held my breath for so long in protestation that I passed out. 'Now, that's what I call headstrong,' I later overheard Mum saying to a friend. I think she was quietly proud of me.

Yesterday, after Stephen and I had seen the citril finch – in fact, ever since he'd left my house – that's how I'd felt: as if I was four years old again and hanging on to his trouser leg, desperately trying to get him to take me with him. I knew something fundamental had changed in him, and therefore between us, since he'd left mine;

I'd seen it in his eyes on the moor. The shutters had come down, and he'd retreated back to his old life where I wasn't welcome, much less wanted, and although I knew he was angry with me about Mum and not telling her he was at mine, it didn't take away from how much it hurt, how much I'd wanted to scream into the fields, *But I'm here now, aren't I? Does that not count for something? Am I* such *a bad person?*

His moodiness was a challenge. It felt so foreign and unsettling. I don't remember one cross word from him when we were kids, not one time I felt he didn't want me around, and yet here he was being snappy and distant and I did not know how to deal with it. My *Hey, how about we do this list thing together, rather than you do it on your own?* might have come across as a sweet and sentimental off-the-cuff suggestion, but inside, believe me, it felt anything but. My brother was starting to look as if he couldn't get away from me fast enough, and my suggestion was a last-ditch attempt to keep him with me.

I did not, for one second, think he'd actually agree to it – so when he did, I was so relieved, so happy. It felt like I'd hung on to that trouser leg, and now he was snoring in the sleeping bag next to me, and I couldn't quite believe it.

It was mid-afternoon by the time we got back to the car after seeing the bird. It would have made sense to pitch the tent in the same place by the river again, but we both had this need to drive somewhere else. Perhaps it was that achieving the first item on the list felt like a full-stop, the end of a chapter, and we were excited to begin another. Or maybe we both suspected that being stuck together in the same place for too long was not a good idea.

'Let's drive to the Fens. I want to go to the Fens,' Stephen announced, still with an undercurrent of sullenness and irritation, after we'd been sitting in silence in the layby for far longer than felt natural.

All I knew about the Fens was that they were marshlands around the coast of the Wash, the great bay where Norfolk meets Lincolnshire; a mythical-sounding place much like The Wolds or the Forest of Bowland, which I remembered from looking at Dad's *Road Map of Great Britain*. Stephen told me he'd read an article about the Fens that said they were Europe's most important wetlands, a birding heaven, and so, although it seemed random to drive there, as if I were jumping to his every whim, I was just so delighted he wanted to go anywhere, and with me, that that's exactly what we did.

We decided to head for a place called Reffley Wood. Stevie had spent a lot of time in public libraries – libraries being one of the few dry, free places to go when you're homeless – and one of his favourite nature writers had written about the magical birding there, so it seemed as good a spot as any. The satnav said it would take an hour and a half, which didn't seem long considering we were coming inland from the edges of Suffolk, then curling back on ourselves to the northernmost tip of Norfolk, at the very top of East Anglia.

After stopping on the way – we found a Little Chef on the A134 where we overdosed on hash browns – we arrived in the early evening and set up our tent. 'You sure it's okay to camp here?' I said, my girl-guide side kicking in. I wasn't the natural rebel Stephen was.

'As long as all we leave is our thanks,' said Stephen.

By 7 p.m., we were shattered and, everything set up, crawled in to sleep.

'Have you seen outside?'

I was woken, at 10 p.m. by Stephen whispering next to me. In the gloom, I could just about make out his figure, hunched at the entrance to the tent. I sat up beside him and gazed out to find a bed of moonlit bluebells – glowing like phosphorescence – that in our exhaustion, and in the daylight, we hadn't appreciated earlier.

We were silent, in wonder. Clearly our thinking had synched too, because as I opened my mouth to speak, so did Stephen, both of us saying the same thing. 'You know what we should do? Let's go!'

2. Go on a night birding woodland walk

Enchanted and with a second wind, it was the perfect opportunity. And so, Stephen wearing the headtorch he kept in his rucksack, we ventured into the woods. Twigs snapped and bracken crunched underfoot and we rolled logs and tossed branches onto the leaf-strewn ground, like Hansel and Gretel, so we could find our way back home.

We wandered between the ash and maple trees, their trunks marble pillars in the spotlight of the moon, the bluebells and foliage at their feet seeming stage-lit. We must have set up camp at the edges of the woods since, just beyond the trees, fields rolled out. 'Right, stand still and close your eyes,' whispered Stephen, which made me smile because he used to say that when I was little and we were out on the marshes or the beach, or in the woods. 'Your other four senses will become super powerful if you shut one down,' he would explain and I'd do it, and find he was right, and it used to feel like magic to me: if you held your nose, you could hear so much more! If you shut your eyes, the wind didn't just whisper, it moaned.

Now, when I closed my eyes, the air smelt gloriously pungent with earthiness, like nature itself, devoid of anything synthetic. And perhaps we expected an eerie silence, only to find a symphony being played amid those trees; a ballet or night circus was underway and we were honoured guests: there was the distinctive trill then quack-like call of a nightjar; we thought we heard a bittern boom among the wetlands not far away; there was a background percussion of unidentifiable scurrying and fluttering. And then, just as we were about to walk back into the dense woodland, feeling as if we'd spent an hour or so in another world – which in a way we had – something happened that I'll never forget. A screech like someone being attacked pierced the air, making me shriek myself. Stephen pointed, open-mouthed towards the fields, an expression of sheer wonder on his face, at the ghostly shape of a barn owl flying past, silent now, Almost as if it were floating across the air. In my delight, and without thinking, I threw my arms around Stephen and he didn't flinch; in fact, he hugged me in closer and we walked back to the tent like that, sharing our elated disbelief about what we'd just witnessed.

It was half past midnight when we got back to camp, armed with wood with which to make a fire. We put on every layer we had, got into our sleeping bags and sat in the glow of the flames; they spat and crackled; soothing voices drifted from the radio, the midnight news winding down. I looked over at Stephen. He was lying against his rucksack, gangly legs pulled up, cheeks flushed with the heat of the fire. *Maybe everything will be okay*, I thought. Maybe there *was* a different life waiting for us, one where we were a family again. Mum might come round, Dad might reinstate himself in our lives, play a bigger part; might remember he had two of his own kids, as well as his stepchildren. Flawed and complex, but his kids all the same.

Mum was going to take some working on, it was true. During our conversation this morning – which already felt like a week ago – she'd been upset I hadn't told her Stephen was back in my life. And although upset was an improvement on what I'd expected, which was appalled, it was still hard to hear her say, 'I felt betrayed, Emily, and sad, really sad, because I didn't think we had secrets between us.' That had cut deep. I'd felt guilt creep up my neck and snake around so it was facing me, looking right at me, because I am the only person in the world my mother trusts. To think she felt betrayed by me was hard to stomach. Very hard.

Stephen had his eyes closed but I knew he was awake. 'Doesn't this remind you of our camping trips when we were little?' I said, watching the fire. 'What I loved most about them is that you'd just decide we were going – and then . . . we'd go! I'd even be in the middle of something like homework or watching TV but we'd take off, we'd just go.'

Stephen didn't reply. I turned my head to look at him. Was he just sleepy or had his mood cooled again? I found I was constantly taking the temperature of his moods, like touching a child's brow.

Then he cleared his throat abruptly: 'So, Mills, what

vas the deal with James?' he said, completely out of the lue.

I frowned. 'The deal with James?'

'Well, no, actually, with men in general,' he said luntly, rolling a cigarette. 'You said yourself it's like a ne in, one out policy with you and men.'

Actually, Justine had said that and I'd relayed it, that ight we'd had our first heart-to-heart when I was talking bout my past boyfriends (the never-ending procession f them), because I thought it was kind of funny. Also, nfortunately, it was painfully true.

'I've told you,' I said. 'My problem with James was is problem with you.'

Stephen said nothing, just concentrated on rolling his ag and raised one eyebrow, gave an infuriating little oise – half laugh, half cough.

'But it's true!' I said, giving his sleeping bag a push.

'So, what about the other long line of guys you dumped efore him? Who never made it past go. All the guys ou went out with before I turned up, they can't all have een duds.'

'Why not? Maybe they were. Maybe I'm just unlucky n love.'

'Do you know what I think?'

I sat up properly then in my sleeping bag, hugging ny knees. I felt annoyed by his unwavering confidence bout matters to do with my life, and yet intrigued to hear his observations. I was beginning to see that you didn't watch life from street level, the world magnified through binoculars for fifteen years, and not have powerful observations to make.

There was a crack of a twig. Beyond our fire, the woods seemed frighteningly dark all of a sudden, as if even the stars had been switched off.

'Go on. I'm sure you're going to tell me anyway.'

'I think you purposefully go for guys who aren't right for you, so it won't work out and you never have to commit,' he said, licking his cigarette paper, sticking it down. 'And you don't want to commit, or you can't because you're restless, you feel uneasy in your own skin. You're not settled. Inside here.' He hit the centre of his chest with his fist, as well as the nail on the bloody head.

Silence. Stephen smoked his cigarette then spoke again. 'Also, not only do you go for men who are wrong for you, you're also completely oblivious to the ones who are right for you.'

'Such as?'

'Seth.'

'Seth?' It came out as a yelp.

'Yes, Seth! He's totally into you, you dingbat.'

'He is not! And anyway, he's already got one woman in his life keeping him busy; he doesn't need another,' I said, but I was glad it was dark, because I didn't seem to be able to stop myself from smiling. I remembered what Seth had said, one evening when I'd gone round for a chat; his face as he'd looked up from his coffee and said, 'Well, I think you're amazing, it's not everyone who would do what you're doing,' and while it was a lovely compliment, the feeling I'd had then, the same as now, was that I was a fraud.

We woke in the morning to a forest shot through with sunlight. I felt full of hope and purpose, although a little ruffled by what Stephen had said about me and men, about Seth. It had hit a nerve, that much was true. But I was putting it to one side for now because we had a mission to complete.

'You see, I bet you're glad your lil sis came now, aren't you?' I said as I laid out a breakfast of cereal bars and bananas – part of the supplies I'd thought to get. Stephen mumbled agreement. His mood, which had lifted after the two-for-the-price-of-one last night (the night walk and the incredible sighting of the owl) seemed to have dipped again. He'd retreated and I was trying to claw him back once more, to hold on to that trouser leg.

After eating, we took a walk under the sun-dappled canopy of elms, field maples and birch – I hoped that would help. Nature always helped.

The air smelt of greenness, the wild, and there was a distinctive bird call – like running your finger along a wooden xylophone.

'What's that?' I said to Stephen and he stopped and tuned in, passing a hand over his stubble that was fast becoming more of a beard.

'It's a long-tailed tit,' he said, after not more than five seconds. 'Calling for his bird – in the most literal sense.'

Spalding was about thirty miles north, in the next county of Lincolnshire. I hadn't overtly discussed it with Stephen, but I'd mulled over Justine's idea about finding him a flat through local connection and I'd decided it was my best bet if I was going to get a roof over his head anytime soon. It didn't have to be forever. My plan, then, was to head north-east towards Yorkshire, a birding heaven of a county, and home to Bempton Cliffs, one of England's biggest seabird colonies (number four on our list), as well as, crucially, our mother's house.

I would use the local connection to our mother and get him a house in Yorkshire, there being fat chance of getting him one in London. If I could just get Stevie a roof over his head, I figured, I'd have done my job as a sister. After all, that's what siblings are meant to do, right? Rescue their brothers and sisters when they fall through the net. Be there for them – as he always had for me. But I hadn't been there for Stephen, and that had eaten me up for almost twenty years. So as much as this was for him, it was for me too: my chance to put things right.

The only problem with the local connection thing,

however, was that our mother had to be on board. The 'I disowned him for almost killing my husband and haven't seen him for thirteen years' line . . . was, well, problematic to say the least. She may have been recovering from the shock of what she saw as my betrayal, but I still believed things were shifting with her, that I just needed to work on her, knead her, like a piece of dough, into something softer.

The journey to Spalding took us through picturesque villages, electric-green fields and vast skies – England in all its supercharged spring glory. Stephen was lost in a book called *The Genius of Birds* from which he would occasionally quote:

'Now we know that bird navigation involves . . . a remarkable ability to build a map in the mind, one far bigger than we ever imagined.'

Like the map of our marshes was etched into ours.

I was thinking about what he had said the night before around the campfire about Seth. Could there be some truth in it? Did he like me – like *that*?

We'd discussed it further on our walk in the woods that morning.

'Look, take it from me, he's into you,' said Stephen, slightly impatiently, I noted. 'All the signs are there.'

'Signs? What signs?' If there had been signs, it was true I'd been oblivious to all of them.

'The way he looks at you,' said Stephen. 'And he mentions you all the time to me. Like, even when it's not natural.'

This seemed ridiculous. 'What do you mean, not natural?'

'Well, it doesn't matter if he's talking about golf, or the benefits of secondary glazing, he'll find a way to crowbar you in.'

Now I was laughing. 'When has Seth ever spoken to you about golf?' I said. 'Or secondary glazing for that matter? And anyway, how come you know so much about this stuff?'

That led on to a general conversation about relationships and I told Stephen I'd never been in love and he told me that he had – twice – and I had to pretend not to be surprised. Surprised at what, that homeless people fell in love like anyone else? Perhaps I had preconceptions I wasn't even aware of.

I thought about it as we drove, though, and, in fact, it made total sense. Of course Stephen had fallen in love: he had nothing to hide, no barriers to falling in love. He just didn't have bricks and mortar and somewhere to call home. But I was going to fix that.

About ten miles into our journey from the woods to Spalding, we suddenly came to a huddle of ramshackle houses, composed, it seemed, primarily of corrugated iron, clapboard, chicken wire and felt.

'Look!' we said in unison as I slowed to a stop. 'They're like El Paradiso. They're like Grandma and Grandad Paradiso's house!'

As children, we'd both loved our maternal grandparents' house, on the marshes, and, more importantly, the people who lived there. 'El Paradiso is Spanish for heaven,' Grandad was always telling us. 'And we called this house that, because to us, it is our little heaven on earth.' We loved the story of how El Paradiso came to be, as much as we loved the house itself. The story went that during the war, when the East End of London (where Grandad Paradiso, Mum's dad, lived with his parents, and later his wife, and where our mother was born) was bombed in the Blitz, East Enders came to Canvey Island and nearby Jaywick Sands to build second homes – bolt-holes, really – for themselves on patches of unused ground. These little Shangri-Las were made with anything they could find, and the builders of these communities were called 'plot-landers'.

El Paradiso, then, was the house our plot-lander great-grandparents had built in 1940 as a holiday home, the house that Grandad Paradiso loved so much as a kid that after he met Grandma Paradiso and they had our mum and Aunty Diane, they made it their permanent home. Obviously, the plumbing, insulation and so on was improved, but apart from that El Paradiso remains the same today as it was in 1940 – a house not just on the marshes, but part of them. And just as it was a sanctuary from war for my great-grandparents, it felt like a sanctuary for me and Stephen too.

Sadly, the developers had come in and got rid of most of the plot-landers' homes on Canvey now. El Paradiso was one of only two left. Legend has it that my brother loved that house so much that when asked, in Year 3, when he was seven, to draw his fantasy house, other kids had drawn castles and stately homes and Stephen had drawn – to our mother's mordant shame – the ramshackle, clapboard bungalow, with its felt roof and chicken-wire front yard, which was Grandma and Grandad's El Paradiso, and her childhood home. A home that was not good enough for her, even then. But then that's always been my mother's problem with everything.

We got out of the car to have a proper look at them, splendid against cloudless blue sky.

'That is my perfect kind of house,' Stephen said, dreamily. 'Nothing fancy, but made with love, like Grandma and Grandad's El Paradiso.'

I put my arm around him. He did not reciprocate.

'And I'm gonna get you your own paradiso. We're going to sort this out. I promise you.'

During the rest of the journey I introduced him to my idea – just to seed it in his mind – that he'd have far more chance of getting a flat in Bridlington, given Mum lived there, and that this could be his ticket to his own keys, his own front door, a new life.

Spalding was perfect for what we wanted: a one-stop high street with everything – chemist, supermarket, clothes shops, barber's – next to one another. A pretty river ran through it, with weeping willows lining the banks, and clusters of white daffodils.

'So,' I said, turning to Stephen as we were crossing the bridge over the water that led from the small church car park to the town centre, 'where do you want to go first?'

He wrinkled his nose. 'Pub?'

I made a not-amused face.

'I'm only kidding; it's just I don't know what you're meant to do in places like these.' He did look kind of lost, and even more a fish out of water than usual, all of a sudden.

'Well, get organised,' I said, trying to sound cheery. 'Pick up supplies, you know, toiletries . . .'

'Now you mention it, I'm desperate for a wee.'

I rolled my eyes. 'Actually, I meant like going into Boots and getting some deodorant and facial wash and wet wipes, you know . . . things we actually need.'

'Right, I might pick myself up a carrot face mask in that case.' The words were light, but his tone wasn't.

'What's wrong?' I said, gently, but inside I was

terrified, panicking like a little frightened bird that he was about to take off like one at any moment.

'Nothing's wrong.'

'You're being . . . flippant.'

'Sorry, I didn't realise facial wash was such a serious business.'

I made an executive decision, that no matter how hard it was, I would ignore Stephen's mood. I gave him some cash and told him to go and get a haircut, a sandwich and to top up his phone. Then we'd have a rummage in some of the charity shops for new clothes – it would be *fun*.

I got supplies from Boots, then wandered into the charity shop to find him already rifling through some jeans, looking quite happy, and felt immediately bolstered. 'Try some on,' I said, trying to sound casual. 'And some shirts, go on.' But he gave me a look that said *Please leave; you're not my mum*.

I decided this was a good time to slip out and call Justine; she and I had already had a conversation and exchanged a few texts okaying my extended holiday so I could help my brother. She had also agreed to do some research for me on the local connection policy.

I found a seat in the market square, where they were selling handbags and candles and from where I could see Stephen when he came out of the charity shop.

She answered on the second ring: 'Justine Goulding, homeless department, can I help?'

'Hi, look, I've really gone off my husband recently. He's put on an awful lot of weight and the beard is just intolerable. I'm in priority need of a two-bedroomed flat now, please.'

There was a second, then Justine gave a snort of laughter. 'Oh Em, I do miss you.'

I smiled. I missed her too, although I couldn't say I was missing the job – the constant feeling of powerlessness, of making people's days worse, not better. At least I felt I could do something for Stephen, *was* doing something for Stephen. Hopefully.

'How's it going, Juss? Place falling down without me yet?'

'Crumbled, mate. The waiting list has doubled.'

'Well, I did try and tell you I was single-handedly solving the London housing crisis – people just don't appreciate me.'

'Ah, how are you, Em?' Justine sounded pleased to hear from me.

'I'm good, I'm okay.'

'Oooh, did you find the bird?'

'We did! And we saw a barn owl last night. Oh my God, it was amazing. We were at the edges of these beautiful woods and it was all moonlit, and this barn owl just came out of nowhere. It was totally otherworldly, like a ghost . . .'

'Wow,' she said, generously. (I'd long known that birding was very much a 'you had to be there' kind of experience.)

'And how's Stephen?'

'Better. He was thrilled to see the bird – it was so lovely to see him excited like that, like I remember him. He doesn't seem quite as irritated with me for coming to find him now,' I fibbed, my chest tightening.

'I should think not,' said Justine. 'He should be bloody grateful.'

'Yeah, he is. Anyway, that's why I'm calling . . . I've been kind of trying to warm him up to the possibility of a place in Bridlington but I don't want to get his hopes up, only for them to be dashed again, so I just wanted to sound you out: how possible do you think it's going to be?'

Justine sighed. 'Well, pretty possible. I mean, obviously, when you look into the ins and outs of the rules for local connection and applying to different local authorities, then it's about as clear as mud . . .'

'I can imagine.'

'I spent two hours reading the info last night.'

'Two hours? I didn't expect—'

'No, I want to help. I know how much this means to you, but I have to say, it was like reading the manual for the lawnmower for all the sense it made to me, and I've got a degree in housing management. The number of exceptions to the rules makes it a waste of time having any rules, but I will say one thing . . .'

'Go on . . .' I was feeling a tad deflated at being

reminded what an utter minefield housing policy is. There was a joke at work that you had to be a recently deceased mother-of-seven whose house had burnt down before you'd be eligible for council housing, which didn't seem that funny when you were dealing with your own brother.

'Well, as you can imagine,' Justine carried on, 'it all comes down to eligibility and priority. We have to decide if he's eligible in the first place and then we make the referral to Bridlington. There may be an issue with the fact that he was staying at yours and then left of his own accord – that makes him "intentionally homeless", I guess.'

I sighed.

'Nobody need know he was with you, though, I suppose,' said Justine. 'And it was only three weeks.' She cleared her throat. 'I'm sure we can gloss over that.'

I smiled. 'Thanks, Juss.'

'Does he have a serious mental or physical health condition?'

'Not really.'

There was a moment's silence where we both surely knew what the other was thinking, what this was about, the fact we were basically conspiring to swerve the system; to jump the waiting list. I saw Stephen coming out of the charity shop armed with two bags, blinking in the sunlight, into this normal high street, full of normal families, normal society. And I suddenly saw him as other people might: vulnerable, on the fringes. Not included. And I thought, in what world would you not help your own flesh and blood if you could? Even if it meant some bending of the rules? It's not like the big guys don't rig the system all the time.

Then Justine said, 'Anyway, the government are gagging to get people to move up north, to free up properties here, so, you know . . . they should be thanking us.'

Stephen's expression had darkened. I tried to smile at him but the muscles in my face wouldn't let me. A sense of dread and panic was building within me. It felt as if the molten lava that I'd feared would come bubbling up with my brother's arrival had now risen to the lip of the volcano and was about to cascade down – and there was nothing I could do to stop it. There was nowhere left to run.

'Exactly,' I said.

'Crow'

April 1997

It was a month before the swifts were due to arrive and an unusually warm April. Stevie and Emily had already come back from the marshes with terrible sunburn, warranting a telling-off from Tony, largely because he knew Alicia would invariably use this as ammunition against him, to ease her own guilt.

'Maybe they'll come early this year,' Stephen said one day on the walk home from school. 'In fact, let's go down now.' He did not need to elaborate for Emily knew where 'go down' meant.

She grinned at him. 'I'll race you!'

He always let her win.

They heard the bulldozer before they saw it: a thunderous, ghostly sound, like wind howling down a tunnel. Stephen's face turned white, then puce, as he opened his mouth to let out a roar as loud as the bulldozer itself. 'Nooooo!'

He bolted towards the high fencing that surrounded what was now a demolition site. A high-vis jacket and hard hat strode angrily towards him, hands in the air, yelling over the racket, 'What the hell are you doing? Can't you read? It says KEEP OUT!' Beyond the fences, the memorial hall was no more, its insides hanging out, guts on show. That was how brutal it felt. And the wall that had housed the swifts' nest was now a pile of rubble, a single crow atop, like an undertaker in hat and tails.

'You bastards! That's our swifts' home! You've made them homeless, you bastards!'

Stephen's voice was hoarse with heartbreak as he fell to his knees and even though Emily was only ten, her heart broke too, to see him like that. The air was foggy with dust and smelt of it too. She ran over and cradled him, her tears spilling onto the back of his school shirt. 'Don't cry, Stevie. Don't cry. It's going to be all right.'

'It won't! It's not.' It was the only time he'd ever raised his voice at her. The only time she'd seen him rage like that.

Three weeks or so later, Emily woke up in their bedroom at Mum and Mitch's to find Stephen dressed and sitting on the carpet surrounded by copies of *Young Ornithologist*, flicking frantically through their pages.

She sat up in bed. 'What are you doing?'

'We're going to make a new nest for them,' said Stephen, without looking up. Emily heard the newfound letermination in his voice, his lifeforce returned, and vas flooded with relief. 'There was an article about how o make a swift box in one of these magazines. I just have o find it. Can you help me?'

She slid straight out of bed and onto the floor where he began, with ardent concentration, helping him go hrough the magazines, even though she didn't fully nderstand what she was looking for – what a 'swift box' ven was. All she knew was that since the hall had been nocked down, and their swifts' nest with it, Stephen ad been sadder than she'd ever known him. Part of her eared it was her fault – just as she feared it was her fault hat Mum always seemed to be sad. The other part realised he loved the swifts but, to Stephen, they were everything. nd Emily was willing to do anything to bring them back nd make him happy again. Anything at all.

The magazine article, when they found it, said that he difficulty level for making the swift box was 'hard' vhich only added to the thrill of the challenge. They vaited for an afternoon when they knew Mum and Mitch vould be out for some time – not difficult, since Mitch's ole as treasurer for Canvey Island Social Club meant their ocial life was thriving, even if it had not escaped Emily's otice that Mum seemed to plaster on a mask for all those unches and drinks parties they went to. A mask that ame off as soon as she was home.

They took a list of the things the article said they'd

need – glue and plywood, a saw and screws – and ventured into the garage, where, Emily acting as Stephen's eager assistant as he drilled and sawed, they made the finest home they could for their swifts – in the absence, perhaps, of their own.

When it was done, they carried the big ladder, one of them at either side of it, from the garage. 'The box needs to be fifteen feet up,' said Stephen, his voice straining with the effort and seeming extra clear in the quiet of dusk. Emily's arms felt like they were about to give way but she wasn't going to let them for the world.

They carried the ladder around to the east side of the house.

'Put it against the wall here,' said Stephen, explaining that he wanted to mount the box in the eaves, like the nest at the memorial hall. But it was so high! So much higher than the nest at the hall. Stephen was almost fifteen, fit and tall for his age – six foot already – but still, Emily's insides swilled with dread as she stood watching him climb the ladder, the power drill in one hand, as blithely as if he were going upstairs to bed.

'Stevie, I don't like it, you're going to fall!' said Emily.

'I'm not gonna fall,' he said, laughing (laughing!). 'God wouldn't let that happen. Not when we're doing something so good – saving the swifts' lives. Plus, you're going to hold the ladder really steady now, okay?' he called down to Emily. 'Absolutely no wobbling.'

Unfortunately, their swifts didn't find the nest that year – or the next. During that entire time, Emily worried about them, imagining them flying all the way from Africa, only to find, when they arrived, a building site where their nesting place had been and then, come the second year, an estate of new-builds. She knew that if she was worrying about them, then Stephen would be too – and worse – and the matter became taboo, unsayable. She didn't dare bring it up for fear of upsetting Stephen and presumably, for similar reasons, he didn't say anything to her either.

And then one day in 1999, Stephen burst into the kitchen and shouted, 'They're back!' There were tears of actual joy in his eyes, and it had felt like a miracle. Better still than meeting them for the first time with his dad all those years ago, because it felt like they'd come home to him, to *them* – to him and Milly. They'd chosen the home *they* had built for them and that meant the world to Stephen.

And so, when, just weeks later and in a towering rage, Mitch marched from the garage, dragging the ladder behind him, shouting he was going to *murder the fucking things*, he had to be stopped.

Chapter Twenty-Three

Stephen

The plan, Emily said (and she very much had a plan, it turned out), was to make their way up to East Yorkshire, to Bempton Cliffs and that seabird colony – and that's all Stephen tried to think about, to concentrate on. As they left Spalding, however, he could feel his annoyance growing. If he were honest, it had never gone away. He'd merely been distracted by ouzels and finches and barn owls; now the cracks were *really* beginning to show.

When he'd overheard Emily on the phone to Mum outside the tent and she'd tried to apologise for lying to him, he'd brushed it away. 'Just leave it,' he'd said. But he'd found that *he* couldn't leave it – how could he? He'd allowed himself to build up hopes of a reconciliation. Worse, he'd realised just how much he wanted that.

Emily had lied to their mum. She had lied to him. And now she would not drop this flat in Bridlington idea. She was delusional if she thought getting a house in Bridlington was going to work. Why was she pushing for all of this? Well, he knew why, and he suspected she did too, deep down – but nobody could say it, least of all him. He was between a rock and a hard place: the truth had to be spoken, or there was nowhere further to go – and yet what would it do to Emily when it was? It might destroy her and it was his job to protect her from destruction, from pain. He'd made that vow, the day he'd met her. The day he'd held her, his tiny baby sister, in his arms.

For some reason, Stephen couldn't stop brooding about one conversation in particular, when he'd asked specifically if Mum ever talked about him and she'd lied through her teeth. 'All the time,' she'd said. In reality, Mum didn't just not talk about him, she wanted nothing at all to do with him. Dad did at least talk to him on the phone now and again. Why the hell would he want to live in the same vicinity as Mum? So they could bump into one another in the local Tesco?

Milly kept saying Mum was turning a corner and that she was 'working on' her. But Stephen had spent so long yearning for his mum, for her love and forgiveness, that now, even if she was to forgive him, he was starting to wonder if he could forgive her.

Being with Emily had dislodged something for Stephen. And not just concerning his mother. More and more memories of his stepfather were surfacing too. He couldn't predict when something would trigger him.

Take now, for example. They were driving out of Spalding past a trickle of houses much like their childhood home on Merlin Drive, and just the sight of these sparked a memory: Mum's thirtieth birthday barbecue, the first time he'd realised there was something going on between her and Mitch Reynolds. The shock of seeing his hand on the blue silk of his mother's dress at the kitchen sink. It had given him a horrid fizzing feeling at the back of his throat, the same feeling Stephen was getting now, sitting in the passenger seat of his sister's car, watching Spalding's edges give way to country roads.

Stephen watched the Lincolnshire landscape slide past – the endless flat fields, arrow-straight dykes slicing through them, flickering by like a deck of cards being shuffled. They entered the Lincolnshire Wolds – the soft hills revealing themselves at either side; the land folding into itself, like a crumpled duvet hastily thrown over a bed.

Sometimes Stephen thought about what life was like before Mitch Reynolds, about his parents' marriage in the early days. Did he really remember a time when his dad would kiss his mum when he came in from work and she would kiss him back? Or was that just a scenario he'd conjured over the years because he'd learnt that was what loving couples did?

He certainly remembers feeling happiness and love when Emily was born. His mother's face in the back of the ambulance. His dad beside himself with pride when Emily came home from the hospital.

Stephen thought of his father now and felt a swell of affection: he'd been through more than some. Divorce. His so-called friend stealing his wife. A son in prison then on the streets. All the shame and sadness these things must have brought him.

He had a sudden urge to call him.

'Oh bollocks,' said Emily, next to him. Stephen had been so lost in thought he'd not noticed they were at the end of a long tailback – and also that the sun had gone in, the day had clouded over. 'Probably a bloody tractor.'

'Well, it's all right,' said Stephen, impatiently, feeling increasingly not all right at all. 'Just be patient, it'll clear in a minute.'

'Nyeah . . .' said Emily, shifting on her seat. Her tone worried him. 'We kind of need petrol.' And without checking there was anything behind her – thankfully the woman in the red Nissan had seen her reverse lights go on and backed up, anyway – Emily turned around and drove at some speed back along the country lane.

Stephen glanced at the petrol gauge and baulked – they were running on fumes – then Milly gave him a sheepish grimace and they drove in silence, Stephen gripping the seat, biting his tongue, hard: why the hell hadn't she filled up in Spalding? By some miracle, within two miles or so they reached a village with a petrol station – a tiny toy-town petrol station, but it was petrol all the same. Close bloody call.

'Aaaah,' said Emily as she put the handbrake on. Stephen's jaw was still pulsing, her attempts to jolly things along making him more cross. 'Want any sweets or water while I'm in there?'

'No.' He couldn't look at her; he was seething. 'I think I'll get out and stretch my legs.' He opened the car door. 'Besides, I feel like calling Dad.'

'Oh?' said Emily, surprised but encouraging. 'Sure, you go for it. Take as long as you like.'

Stephen walked away from the garage muttering expletives, rolling a cigarette. He found a bus stop and sat down.

Tony answered after the fourth ring, giving his number by way of a greeting, the old-fashioned way, in that thick, dour voice that Stephen knew so well.

Stephen had a deep, deep longing all of a sudden to hear that voice in person.

'Hi, Dad, it's me.'

A long silence, then: 'Oh, Steve. Hello.'

He sounded surprised but also pleased to hear from his son, and Stephen was buoyed.

'How are you, Dad?'

'Us?' *Well, no, you,* thought Stephen but didn't say so. 'We're fine, good. Keeping busy, you know.'

Stephen nodded.

'How are you? It's good to hear from you,' Tony said with an exhalation that sounded like relief. 'Finally. You know, it would be good to know you're alive at least.'

Stephen winced, realising the last time he'd called his dad had been six months ago or more.

'I'm okay, Dad. Good actually. I'm kinda on the road, seeing lots of good birds.'

'Oh yeah?' He'd really got his dad's interest now.

'I saw a citril finch.'

A little laugh of surprised delight. 'You never did?'

'No word of a lie, on the Angles Way – have you heard of it? It follows the River Waveney along the Norfolk–Suffolk border, absolutely stunning . . .'

'Really, well, I'll have to look that up,' said his dad, with another chuckle of pleasure. Stephen gripped the phone to his ear and felt warm inside.

'I'd give my right arm to see a citril finch.' In the background Stephen could hear Sandra calling, *Tony*.

'Yeah, you'd love the Angles Way – that part of the country,' said Stephen. 'Hey, maybe we could meet there one time?'

'Yeah,' his dad said, warmly. 'Yeah, I'd like that.'

'Be nice to see you, Dad.' He could hear other voices now in the background, a male and a female. 'Maybe I could come and visit?'

Tony, Stephen heard Sandra call again. *Who is that?*

'Let me have a word with Sandra,' his dad said. Stephen

felt deflated. 'And I'll get back to you. If it's okay to call you on this number, that is.'

'Yeah, sure,' said Stephen. 'Or I'll just call you back in a few days.'

There was a non-committal pause from his dad.

'It's just until things have calmed down, you know?' Tony said eventually. 'Until things are less hectic.'

'I miss you, Dad.'

'I miss you too,' said his dad after another pause. Stephen could have cried. Then, 'Listen, I'd better go, Steve, we're just about to have some cake and stuff to celebrate.'

'Oh, celebrate?' said Stephen.

His father hesitated. 'Sandra's Matthew's here with his wife and new baby.'

'Oh, right,' said Stephen, noticing it had begun to spit. 'Lovely, well, congrats to them, that's great. What type of baby?'

He could hear his dad smile. 'It's a little girl, Stephen,' he said. 'She's absolutely perfect.'

Stephen had a vivid memory of that day his dad had opened Stephen's curtains and announced the same thing about Milly. His dad had always loved babies.

'Anyway, bye, Dad. Let's get a date in, yeah? For an actual visit? Maybe we could meet for a birdwatch somewhere . . .'

Stephen stopped, maybe he'd gone too far, but then his dad said, 'I'd like that Steve. I'd like that very much.'

'How was Dad?' said Emily, with more of that forced brightness when he arrived back at the car and got in. 'Did you tell him you were with me?'

'Yeah,' Stephen lied.

'So how was he?'

'Good,' said Stephen. 'Happy.' He paused. 'They've got a new grandchild – Sandra's boy has had a baby girl.'

'I know,' said Emily, patting his leg. 'I know.'

Stephen had only just regained his composure after the close shave of the fuel when, twenty miles down the road, halfway between Louth and a small village called Binbrook, the tyre blew. And, of course, Emily hadn't replaced the tyre repair kit from a previous calamity – meaning he blew too.

'So you think about facial wash and frigging wet-wipes, but not if you can repair a blown tyre? Jesus, Emily,' he yelled, with such anger that even he was shocked. Emily looked shocked too; actually, she looked close to tears.

Stephen could understand it. He'd never shouted at her. Ever.

'I hate this,' she said. 'Why are you being like this? It's not just the spare tyre, I know it's not. So just tell me. I want you to tell me.'

Chapter Twenty-Four

Emily

With no phone reception and in worsening weather conditions, we had no choice but to leave the car in a layby and walk to find help. Stephen was infuriated with me – for deeper reasons than petrol and the blown tyre, I knew that much. But, after pleading with him to tell me the truth in the car, I was now terrified he might take me at my word, and so I was desperately trying to distract him, to stop things completely collapsing, which was feeling increasingly inevitable. I knew the handbrake had gone, we were rolling off the cliff and there was only one way down. But I was clinging on to that last thread of possibility that I could right things, make things good.

'But there's every chance there will be a house for you,' I shouted, to his back sloped forward against the wind. I was having to shout because of the heavy rain and wind that was now blowing in erratic gusts from the east, making my hood stick to my face. 'Me and Justine have been looking into the local connection thing. I do work in the housing department, you know. I do have some idea what I'm talking about.' My attempts at being authoritative and compelling were undermined by the fact I was having to concentrate hard on dodging huge puddles.

'Stephen!' I called again to the back of the orange puffa. It felt as though I'd seen a lot of that coat these past twenty-four hours, a lot of my brother's back. I knew he could hear me, and this infuriated me.

'Stevie?'

'Yeah, I can hear you, Emily.' He didn't turn around.

'Well, what do you think? I mean, don't you think it's worth at least trying to get on the list? Going to see a few houses, even? Just think, your own front door, your own set of keys. You might even—' Stephen said something but another gust of wind hit me from my right and so I didn't hear. 'Sorry?'

'I said . . .'

God, would he just look at me when he was talking to me at least? I sounded desperate. I felt desperate.

'Stop trying to fix me in the way you think is right. I don't even know if I want a house, Milly. I like being outdoors in nature, in the wild.'

'Surely to God you can't like being in this?' I said, as driving rain needled my cheek. 'Surely you want somewhere to go to at night. A home? You did when you came to the council looking for a flat. I'm bending rules to sort this out. There are thousands of people out there who would cut off their right arm for a flat in Bridlington, or to have a relative working in the council willing to pull some strings for them, at least understand the ins and outs of housing policy . . .'

Stephen stopped, his back to me, and did not move for a few seconds. Then he turned around. 'Please stop treating me like I'm one of your cases at work.' He said it calmly but his face was dark and strained with anger. 'I'm your brother, not one of your clients. Stop trying to sort me out; trying to get me a house, and new trainers and a job and bloody facial wash . . .' He flicked a hand at me before striding on.

I stood there, hurt. I had only ever wanted to help him. I had an awful, plummeting notion that the wheels were coming off. And, beneath that, a feeling I could not even bear to name, thick, dark and coming for me like a storm rolling in over the marshes, or an oil spill on a beach.

I limped on. Neither of us spoke. The cold was seeping into my bones. 'Stephen!' I yelled. 'Can we just have a rest, please?'

'No, come on, there's not much light left,' he said, marching on grumpily. 'We need to find help before it's dark.'

'But surely a five-minute stop won't make much difference?' I sounded whiny but I didn't care. 'Please, I'm so tired . . .'

He did slow down a little so I could catch up. 'I did warn you this is what it would be like, that this is what the "great outdoors"' – he made speech marks in the air with his fingers – 'is like. I did tell you when you were busy buying tents and mats and thermals. It's all the gear, no idea with you . . .' I gave Vs to the back of that orange bloody puffa jacket. I could not bear this. I wanted this to stop.

We stomped on in silence again until Stephen did stop, abruptly. I quickly realised why: the lane in front of us was completed flooded. What were once grass verges were now mudbanks, mini-landslides into filthy brown water that was ankle, possibly knee, deep and at least five metres across. I stared at it. The rain drove down mercilessly. I could feel a blister forming on the arch of my foot. I wanted to cry. 'I'm not crossing that,' I said, and Stephen looked at me with annoyance – no, worse: disdain – in his eyes, the likes of which I have never seen before.

'Right, so what do you suggest we do?' he said. 'Because I, for one, am not turning back. There are no houses for miles that way, no way of getting help. We're just going to have to wade through it. What's the worst that can happen?'

'Well, we get soaking and then have to walk for ages in wet clothes then it gets dark and still doesn't stop raining and we have to sleep in a field and catch pneumonia and eventually die.' Fear and shame again, they made me petulant.

He wiped the rain off his nose with his sleeve and eyed me coldly.

'Take it from me, you'll survive. Believe it or not, this is not a life or death situation, Emily.' And with that, he took three huge strides across the lake-sized puddle and I followed.

'Urgh, I hate this!' I shouted at his back. I didn't just mean the flood. 'This is just . . . hideous.'

'Well, I never asked you to come.' He mumbled it but I heard, and anger rose uncontrollably up my throat, anger that, I knew, was masking fear.

'How dare you?' I said, my eyes filling with hot tears. 'Just how dare you? I'm trying to help you here – I've only ever tried to help you, using my car to take you to see birds you want to see, risking my job to get a house for you.'

Stephen laughed, bitterly. 'What, a nice house in a town where I know nobody except for the mother who hates me? Who blames me for ruining her life? You reckon that's going to be a home for me?'

I was standing shin-deep in water. 'She doesn't hate you,' I said, and despite the fact I believed those words wholeheartedly, I knew I sounded unconvincing. 'I told you, I'm talking to her – all the time. reminding her that you've changed, that you're not sixteen anymore . . .'

Stephen shook his head, quickly, once. 'What?' he said, so bitterly that it made me jump. 'What did you just say? Oh my God . . .' And he half laughed mirthlessly and stumbled back as if he'd been pushed.

I could hear my own breath inside my hood and the endless patter of rain outside of it. I had the dreadful feeling of not understanding what I'd said wrong, but knowing it was very, *very* wrong, and that it had broken a seal, so that the very thing I was afraid of – had always been afraid of – would escape, and the worst of it was I still didn't know exactly what it would be. Or I did, I did, but I had pushed it down so far that it had become fainter and fainter until it didn't exist anymore. It had been completed erased.

'Jesus Christ, Milly.' Stephen was beginning to look agitated and upset in a way I'd only seen previously when the bulldozers arrived to knock down the memorial hall, and our swifts' nest with it, all those years ago. 'You don't get it, do you?'

'What? Stephen . . .' My voice sounded meek and pleading. My heart was pounding. 'Stop it, you're scaring me.'

'You don't fucking get it, do you?' he said again, eyes full of hurt. 'You just don't get it.'

I watched in horror as he sat – no, collapsed – on one of the mudbanks and mud splattered immediately up the side of his jeans, like blood.

'I knew this would happen. This is exactly what I wanted to avoid,' he said, his voice croaky with emotion. 'This, us – me having to feel like this.' He looked at me and pressed his lips together, as if he might cry, but instead he hit the ground next to him with the palm of his hand. 'To feel like this towards *you*. That's why I left your house, because I wanted to be on my own and not have all this come up – for me, but mostly for you. I wanted to protect you. But you had to come after me, didn't you? Bringing the list and dredging up the past. You couldn't just leave me be like you've been quite happy to do for the last nineteen years.'

'Is this because I lied about telling Mum you were at mine?' I said, desperately clutching at straws because I knew absolutely it was not that. 'Because if it is, I've said I'm sorry and I don't really know what else I can say, except that I've told you I'm talking to Mum. I'm working on her.'

'God, Emily.'

'Stephen, please,' I said, as if I wanted him to stop talking, but really, I was pleading with him to say it finally, to say out loud this terrible truth.

'It's not about Mum!' Stephen shouted and something fizzed at the back of my neck, like an electric charge. 'It's about you.' He thumped the mud again. 'About you and what you did and what I did for you.'

'But you haven't once mentioned it in three weeks! In

fact, ever.' He punched the bank again, harder. Then he completely lost it, pummelling the mud with his fists, sods of earth flying everywhere, dirt all over his coat. All the time, making this awful hoarse cry, that was half little boy, half animal. I just wanted to run, to bolt, but I could only stand there in the water, and watch him, until finally he stopped and, breathless, looked at me, his gaunt, pale face streaked with muddy tears.

'You pushed the ladder, Milly,' he said. 'You. You did it, not me. I spent four years in jail for a crime you committed. Don't you remember?'

'Swift 2'

Emily

June 1999

I became aware, around the age of eight of nine, that Mitch never had one good word to say about my brother. I don't remember him ever uttering one kind or supportive comment. And because I loved my brother so much, I hated Mitch for this. We never 'got on' as such anyway. It was just the case that because I'd been so young when Mum got together with him, I accepted him, as you accept other misfortunes in life as a kid. Like your parents having really bad taste in home decor – only, this was bad taste in men and with much worse consequences. I didn't know any different is what I'm trying to say. As I became more aware, however, I began to see the truth of the situation, which was that Mitch fed Mum propaganda about her son and, because she was besotted with him, at first, anyway, she believed it.

It didn't make sense: how could this boy, this thorn in their side, be the same person that I knew and adored?

Where Mitch saw someone *feral and soft in the head*, I only saw someone wise and brave and passionate about the things he cared about. Whereas Mum saw a bull in a china shop, I saw someone calm and gentle, especially with living things – including me.

My brother was particularly calm in a crisis, I found. Even when he was at the centre of that crisis, and even when it was the biggest crisis of his life – the day he got arrested for pushing our stepfather off a ladder. Mind you, anyone would have looked calm next to me that day, the worst day of my life.

Stephen

It was a hot, hot Saturday. The sky was so blue, so kind of taut with it, that Stephen felt it might crack, like a pot in a kiln. Alicia was out shopping, no doubt to escape Mitch who'd been in a vile temper all morning, prowling around the house in his white vest, muscles bulging, looking for his next victim to take out his anger on. He needed help, that man. He was like a bad case of appendicitis: started off grumbling, then always, always burst. He was heading for a heart attack – sooner rather than later, if Stephen had his way.

That morning, Alicia had accidentally shrunk one of his woollen jumpers in the wash and you'd have thought she'd cut off his balls, the rage he was in, screaming at her, calling her an idiot. 'Don't speak to my mum like that,' Stephen had said, calm as anything but defiant, looking straight at him, at those black, shark eyes he had.

Of course, Stephen had got the whole *keep out of it* from Alicia, which drove him crazy, but he didn't care; he was almost seventeen now and he wasn't having it anymore. He was not having this man filling the place with his toxic energy.

Still, he was keeping out of Mitch's way – it wasn't as though they had anything to say to one another – and had spent the hour since lunch playing swingball with Emily in the garden, then lolling on the patio furniture eating ice pops, watching the comings and goings of their swifts – pretty much how they'd spent most weekends for the past six weeks since the birds had arrived.

Emily had gone back in the house, hot and bothered, and Stephen was looking through his binoculars, watching the entrance to the swift box intently. Eggs had been laid a few days ago – he could tell by the way some of the birds were spending longer inside the box. He could feel the sun burning the back of his neck and knew he should probably get some shade now, but, as ever, he couldn't tear himself away from the birds. He wondered how old these ones were; at least three, when swifts began breeding, but they could be much older – could live up to twenty years.

From somewhere around the side of the house, the driveway, he heard Mitch swear. He was after a fight – Stephen knew it. He'd known from the moment he'd got up this morning and Mum and Milly had tiptoed as if on eggshells around him, as he'd cursed about his shrunken jumper, the heat, the fact Alicia was going out shopping, *spending* his *money again*. But Stephen had stood up to him – and there was nothing that enraged Mitch more than someone standing up to him. Least of all his stepson, who at six foot two was now four inches taller than him (that growth spurt had arrived all right). No, Mitch hadn't finished with him today, but then the feeling was kind of mutual.

'Stephen,' he roared. 'Get round here now.'

Stephen rolled his eyes and didn't move. Then came the crunch of Mitch's army boots on gravel as he appeared around the side of the house; that stance he always adopted, with his enormous arms held away from his sides, chest pumped, ready for attack. 'Your fucking birds have shat all over my car, I only had it valeted yesterday.'

Stephen couldn't help but let a little laugh escape.

'Oh, you think it's funny, do you?'

'Not particularly, I just wonder what you want me to do about it,' said Stephen, as casually as he could.

'You're going to dispose of them, that's what you're going to do about it.' Mitch was shouting again. He was incapable of saying anything in a normal voice. 'Disgusting vermin, disease-carriers, shitting all over my car and my house. I never said you could build that thing in my roof in the first place, you did it without asking, so you can damn well take it down. Then you can clean my car.'

'What's going on?' Stephen looked up to see Emily leaning out the bathroom window, face still flushed from the sun, wondering what all the noise was about.

'Why don't you clean your mouth out first?' quipped Stephen. 'All the disgusting language you use. I thought you were meant to be a pillar of society. Emily's just here, she can hear you effing and blinding.'

Mitch had been about to walk off, having delivered his orders, but at that, stopped in his tracks, so angry he seemed to have lost the power of speech. There it was, thought Stephen, the appendix about to burst. 'I said, get rid of it,' said Mitch, jabbing a finger in Stephen's direction, his lips retracting, baring his cigar-stained teeth. 'Now.'

'Not happening, mate. Not over my dead body.'

Out the corner of his eye, Stephen could see two figures at the far side of next-door's large, sweeping garden. The neighbours, Ron and Penny Callaghan.

'Oh, I see.' Mitch was incandescent. 'I see. That's how you want to play it, is it? Then I shall do it myself.' Stephen watched then in horror and disbelief as Mitch strode off around the front of the house.

'What's happening?' called Milly, tearful. 'I don't like it.'

'Don't you worry,' said Stephen. 'Everything's okay.' But in truth, he felt sick and pale. His mouth had become sticky, all the moisture evaporated, as he watched Mitch stomp back around dragging the ladder under one arm, face puce, eyes wild and bulging.

He had a sledgehammer in the other.

Stephen stood helpless, as Mitch extended the ladder in one move, as easy as if it were a flick-knife, and almost threw it against the wall of the house. Then he began to climb it.

Emily was still leaning out of the bathroom window, screaming now: 'No!! Stevie. He can't kill our swifts, no!' Normally Stephen would have reassured her. But he knew what his stepfather was capable of.

'Mitch,' he shouted, walking over to him, his voice full of panic. He felt utterly powerless. 'Please, come down. Please don't hurt the swifts. Please . . .' He'd started to cry now. Then, as Mitch raised his sledgehammer, he saw red. 'You'll pay for it, you bastard!' he screamed, holding the sides of the bottom of the ladder with wringing wet palms that couldn't have gripped it enough to shake Mitch down, even if he'd wanted to. Which he did. He was grappling with this thought, this desire, when he realised the ladder *was* shaking, because Emily was shaking it. She was at the open bathroom window, holding it on both sides and rocking it, from side to side, sobbing, beside herself.

'Stop it, you're going to kill him,' shouted Stephen. 'You're going to kill him!' Then, suddenly – so suddenly he could hardly process it – he realised Milly wasn't holding anything anymore. That her hands were up by the sides of her head. That the ladder was falling, Mitch on it. There was a scream, truly, a blood-curdling, primal roar. Then came the slap, almost like a whipping of a wet sheet, as Mitch's body hit the ground, the clatter of metal like a hundred bin lids crashing, as the ladder piled on top of him.

It was very quiet then, except for a single blackbird's fluting.

'Stephen?' Ron Callaghan was shouting from over the hedge. 'Stephen? What's happened? What the hell have you done?'

Emily

After it happened and Mitch lay on the patio floor, the blood pooling around his head, I hid around the side of the house, cowering against the pebbledash, hyperventilating, sobbing, totally out of control.

Stephen on the other hand had already called the ambulance and done what he could with Mitch. Then he came around the side of the house and held me by the shoulders. 'Breathe with me, Mills,' he said, calmly – he was worried about me, even then. 'In through the nose, out through the mouth.'

Stephen was still trying to calm me down when we heard the ambulance siren wail down the close. I knew Mitch was on the patio, I'd seen him – but I could not, would not, go and look at him now. No matter that Stephen told me over and over that he was alive and still breathing, I was convinced he was dead.

I thought it was murder. It turned out to be nearly as bad. Possibly worse.

The ambulance arrived, then the police: a man and a

woman. I watched them walk along the side path of the house towards us. Later, I found out that the neighbours, Ron and Penny Callaghan, had called them; they'd been gardening and had seen Stephen at the bottom of the ladder, heard him shout, 'You'll pay for it, you bastard!' And then they'd heard Mitch's scream as he fell.

Both the policeman and policewoman were in uniform and seemed so much bigger than normal adults to me. I felt myself about to lose it again, then thought about what Stephen had said: *Keep calm, let me take care of this, this is not your problem.* They taped off the patio – this was a potential crime scene now – and the policeman took Stephen inside the house. Then the police-woman crouched down opposite me. Her name was Paula and she had a large, dark mole on her cheek; I'll never forget it. She told me she had a niece called Emily, and she thought it was a really pretty name. Then she asked me to come with her inside the house too, and she took me into the dining room. I said I wanted my mum, when would my mum be back? And Paula said there were police out looking for her now, in Basildon, and that she'd be here any minute, which might have sent me over the edge but I stayed calm as Stephen had told me to and said *I can't remember* to everything she asked – again, just as Stephen had instructed.

Everything was so quiet in the dining room – the only sound our voices and the crackle of Paula's walkie-talkie.

There was a vase of sweet peas on the table, not that I can stand the smell of them to this day. Then, after half an hour or so of being interviewed, I saw the policeman walk past the dining room window with my brother in handcuffs.

That was when I really lost it. Where were they taking him? Was Mitch dead? Would my brother get done for murder and go to prison for life?! Because if that were to happen, I didn't think I could endure it.

I went to the window, my palms up against it, and watched, helplessly, as the policeman opened the back door of the car, put his hand on my brother's head and gently yet firmly pushed him inside. Just before he did, however, Stephen turned around and smiled at me and that smile, although regretful, was also reassuring: *It's going to be all right*, it said, *everything's going to be okay.*

Stephen always made everything okay.

Chapter Twenty-Five

Stephen stood up slowly from the grass verge, covered in mud. He lifted his hands in the air. 'I can't do this,' he said. Then he turned and he walked away and I watched him go, the blood thundering like rapids in my ears, down the lane, hands in the pockets of his coat. I watched him as he got smaller and smaller, until he was just an orange dot, blurred through the rain, and yet all the time, it felt as though I was the one getting smaller, and when he disappeared into nothing at the vanishing point of the lane, it felt as if I had vanished too.

I stood there for a few moments, the only sound the relentless rain, and then I turned around and began walking in the direction of the car, feeling as if I was leaving landmines in my wake; bombs that were catching up with me, that any minute now would detonate my entire world. And the sky was a heavy stone lid closing over me. The hedgerows seemed to be closing in on me too, and the chapters of my life played themselves over in my head, but in reverse, the most recent first – a life played backwards: me, only days ago, running across the moor to Stephen, desperate not to lose him again. Then me serving lasagne at the table to him and my friends, who don't know me, really, at all; moving into my flat three years ago, knowing that somewhere else in the city, my brother was sleeping on the streets and somewhere deep, deep inside me, that this was because of me. At work now, handing someone their keys to a new home, feeling as though I've done something good for once, something I hope will ease my conscience, but it never, ever will do. I picture myself at university in Glasgow, telling my new friends about the brother I have who lives in Kenya and is building a school. And then finally, in Mum's lounge in Yorkshire, spoon-feeding Mitch, his eyes fixed on me, then beginning to bulge as he starts to cough, and knowing, in that hidden place inside of me, where the dormant volcano lies, that he isn't choking on what I'm feeding him at all, but on the deceit I have fed everyone for years – starting with myself. And as each chapter, each scene ended, it was as if it erased itself before the next one began, until it was like rubbing out an entire book, an entire life. After all, whose was this life I had lived? Who was I?

It was dark by the time I made it back to the car. I opened the boot – I was wailing like a little girl, but if anyone was to hear me, I wouldn't have cared. I yanked out every item of clothing I could find from both rucksacks, took both sleeping bags then crawled onto the back seat pulling them over me and sobbing until my throat hurt and my eyes felt like slits.

The knowledge of that terrible day, 12 June 1999, and the truth of what I had done, had been there all the time – of course it had. It had just been locked in a room along a passageway down which I chose never to venture. Occasionally, a storm would arrive with no warning and blow open the door to the passageway, but I'd slam it shut again, standing with my back against it if needs be, holding it tight against the high winds. But today, the storm to end all storms had arrived, and I didn't have the strength to hold the door anymore.

I was the reason Mitch was paralysed. *I* was the reason my mother's life was ruined. *I* was the reason my brother went to prison and ended up homeless. He sacrificed his life for me and I could not even bring myself to thank him? I remembered how I hadn't even been able to face visiting him in prison – after that first, awful time, when I cried until Mum took me home – and I wanted to die.

Stop it, you're going to kill him!

Those words flashed into my head as I faced what I had secretly known all along: I had not shouted those words that day. Stephen had. He had shouted them at me.

You did it, Emily. You pushed it. You were the explosion

in everyone's lives, and yet you walked away from the blast, leaving a trail of shrapnel, everyone's lives in pieces, as if you were nothing to do with it, entirely innocent. How could you have done that? How could you be a good person, and do something like that?

Eventually, I guess I must have cried myself out, but that's when things got worse, because that's when the silence settled and my thoughts had nowhere to go but the pitch black of the inside of that car. I wanted to sleep, to fall into unconsciousness, but no matter how I arranged my limbs, I could not get comfortable. I put on the engine, which for a while made things warmer, but I know nothing about cars and was worried something might blow or I might poison myself with carbon monoxide. So, I turned it off, and then, no matter what socks and towels I put up against the doors and windows, the cold seemed to find me, like groping, icy fingers.

But, of course, it wasn't really the cold that stopped me from sleeping; it was the fact I could not escape the very thing I wanted to – which was myself. Stephen had done time for me, four years of his life. He had lost his family, his dignity, ended up on the streets. He had lost everything, basically, because of me, because he wanted to protect me and I thought it could all be solved and I could pay him back by getting him a flat? I'd made out I was being the heroic sister helping him, scooping him up, taking him in, fixing him, bit by bit, when all the time, it was me I was trying to fix. I was trying to make *myself* feel better.

The night seemed endless. I'd look at my watch after what felt like two hours to see that five minutes had passed, and all the time I was thinking, *this is horrible and yet it's only one night*. Stephen had dealt with night after night like this, while I'd been tucked up in my huge sleigh bed with my White Company linen. My God, all the things I'd bought to make my house feel like a home, when *nowhere* was going to feel like home, because I was the person living there, and I couldn't even live in my own skin. I could not live my truth. And when I began to think like that, it dawned on me that Stephen might not come back and I wouldn't blame him, that I might have lost my brother again – and for good this time.

I must have dropped off eventually, because the next thing, I was aware of birdsong. Just one, single note, so sharp and pure, that it seemed to cut the day open. And I lay there until, eventually, the blue dawn bled in through the windows of the car, misted with condensation, not daring to face this new day for what it might hold, yet knowing I had to.

Chapter Twenty-Six

Stephen

As Stephen walked he watched the sun rise over the wheat fields; he saw how it began as red wisps on the horizon, became a strip of orange and then a shiny new penny, shimmering with promise. He watched the changing light turn the hills from bruise-coloured, to tan, to revealing them in all their green, undulating splendour, in the space of half an hour. He was thirty-five years old and could not imagine a time when the sheer beauty of the natural world would not blow his mind on a daily basis, and yet this morning he could not enjoy it for the anxiety churning up his stomach.

He'd spent a terrible, sleepless night in a farm outbuilding that he'd come across about a mile after leaving Emily, and the last nine hours or so had seen him go through every emotion. Initially it had been pure relief, the catharsis of getting the truth out in the open; to say those words out loud: YOU DID IT, NOT ME. For a while then, he'd felt high on self-righteousness, triumphant almost: did she know what he'd been though for her? How long was she going to carry on this ridiculous charade, as if everything could be solved by her getting him a flat, new clothes, ticking birds off a list for that matter? Because even that had begun to lose its appeal under the circumstances, namely Emily's insistence on utter denial. The list itself, with its sellotaped scar down the middle, had begun to open up old scars in him. But then night had fallen and Stephen's righteousness and anger had ebbed away to make way for a whole array of bleak fears and self-doubt. The ghouls of 4 a.m. had come out in full force. Yes, in the end he had needed to speak the truth in order to survive. But should he have done it in the way he had? Detonating this emotional nuke, which he knew would blow her world apart. Then he'd left her alone, on a country lane at dusk. His baby sister.

After he'd begun to think like that, he'd given up all hope of sleep. He'd sat bolt upright, in fact, against the wall of the outbuilding, feverish with a creeping horror: what if she hadn't been able to find the car? Or open it? He'd pictured her struggling with the door, the wind howling, the rain relentless, and felt sick to the stomach. What if her fears, which had seemed irritatingly over-dramatic yesterday, had come true, and she was dying of hypothermia in wet clothes somewhere right now? Or something had happened to her like she'd been knocked down by a car – she was wearing practically all black, they wouldn't have been able to see her – or attacked?

Or simply – and this was almost as bad in Stephen's head – she was scared witless and freezing cold. Stephen knew all about that.

And so eventually, he'd hauled himself up and, whereas yesterday he'd only wanted to get away from Emily, he now found himself retracing his steps. Heading back towards his little sister. He walked quickly, his hands deep in his pockets because the dawn air was cold, his head all over the place, but his main thought was just, *Please, let her be okay. I'll deal with anything after that, just let her be okay.*

This stretch of the lane, the hawthorn thick at the side, went on endlessly, the dawn chorus seeming to amplify with Stephen's stress, like a kettle whistling at the boil. Finally, then, there it was: Emily's blue Clio in the layby, its windows misted up – surely that had to be a good sign, didn't it? He quickened his pace, almost breaking into a jog – but then he thought that might scare her, so he slowed to a stop, took a moment to gather himself, then walked calmly over instead, crouched so he was face level with the passenger seat and knocked twice, softly, on the window. 'Milly? It's me, it's Steve.' At first, he couldn't hear or see anything through the windows and his chest thumped horribly, but then there was movement from the back seat. She wiped the condensation from the window and, suddenly, Emily's face appeared, and Stephen hung his head between his knees and swore under his breath with relief. When he looked up again, he noticed her eyes were swollen from crying and no doubt being awake all night. He opened the door and whispered, 'I'm sorry.' Then he crawled into the space beside her as Emily sat up on her knees and folded into him. 'I'm so sorry,' he said, holding her. 'I'm so sorry I left you.'

'I thought you might not come back,' she said, her voice thick with snot and tears. 'I thought that was it and I wouldn't have blamed you, because I ruined your life and all you ever did was try and protect me.' Her voice gave way to gut-wrenching sobs and all Stephen could do was hold her until they subsided. When they had, she sat up, the morning sun bleaching her tear-stained face, and pulled her sleeves over her hands.

'I am so sorry,' she said. 'And I don't expect you to forgive me, I really don't. I just want to understand, like, how could I have blocked it out like that? How could I have deluded myself and lied to everyone for so long? How could I have done that? I must be bad, I must be really, really bad . . .'

Stephen shushed her. 'Listen,' he said, 'I know what you must be thinking, how fucking huge this must feel, and I know I was so angry at you last night and God knows what went through your head, what you thought was going through mine . . .'

She made a little noise as if to say, *you don't want to know*.

'But I want you to listen, okay? Because this is important. It was *my* lie. *I* chose to say I pushed the ladder. *I* chose to take the blame. Then I asked you to go along with it – and that's what you did. You just believed it and accepted that as the truth, like I asked you to do.'

Emily frowned, then sniffed loudly. 'But it wasn't the truth, was it? I pushed it,' she said, hugging her knees. 'I stood in the bathroom, holding the top of that ladder, and I shook it, then pushed it. I put Mitch in a wheelchair, Stephen. I was scared he was going kill the swifts, that's why, but that doesn't make it okay. I still did it.' A tear fell. She wiped it away with the corner of the sleeping bag, and all Stephen saw was twelve-year-old Milly again, scared out of her wits and cowering by the side of the house while Mitch lay on the patio.

'Yes, but you didn't ask me to take the blame,' said Stephen. 'I looked at you that day, twelve years old and petrified. How could I, as your big brother, let you have that on your conscience? Carry that around with you when you were just a little girl? It was too big, it would have ruined your entire childhood, and that's without the fact that at twelve, you were criminally responsible and might have had to go away for it. That would have crushed you, not to mention me. Also, I'd whipped you up into a frenzy about Mitch killing those birds, I was the one who was yelling, "You'll pay for it, you bastard," and, Emily, if he'd have killed those swifts – and there's no doubt in my mind that he would have, if you hadn't stopped him – then who knows? Perhaps I would have killed him; I certainly wouldn't have been responsible for my actions.'

Milly was picking at a bit of loose thread on the sleeping bag, trying to take all this in.

'Do you see what I'm saying, Mills?' Stephen said, scanning her face, making her look at him. 'I'm saying, it was right I took the blame because I was the one having those thoughts. If it hadn't been that day, then I probably would have ended up snapping and doing Mitch in another day, for the way he'd bullied me all those years.'

Stephen thought about the list Mitch had ripped up; the binoculars he'd smashed. The willow warbler. He could tell Milly about them, but what would be the point, now? 'It was a long time ago and he can't hurt me anymore. I'm just telling you because I want you to know, that in a way, I was already screwed. I was already a mess. And I already hated him, not just for what he'd done to me, but to Mum and our family. And even though you pushed the ladder, I wanted to hurt him, very, very badly, preferably with a blunt instrument in his sleep.'

Emily squeezed him tighter and laughed through her tears.

Just then, Stephen became aware of the sound of an engine, and he sat up and looked through the front seats to see a Land Rover approaching. 'Oh Christ,' he said, realising suddenly how their set-up might look. He flipped back the sleeping bag and got out of the car, hoisting his jeans up, an action that he immediately regretted. The driver, a slim-faced man with strawberry blond hair, wound his window down and stuck his elbow out, grinning.

'You all right there, mate?'

'Yeah,' said Stephen, clearing his throat. 'Fine. Just er . . . me and my sister in there.' Inside the car, he heard Emily give a little snort. 'We've got a flat tyre.'

'So I see,' said the man. 'You've got a right dead'un there. No spare? Or, er, have you been otherwise engaged and not had time to change it yet?'

Stephen laughed, blushing. 'I promise you, it is my sister!'

'Sorry,' chuckled the guy. 'I'm only teasing you. Do you want a tow to the next village? I can take you to my mate Franco's garage if you like. He'll sort you out with a new one.'

The tow to the garage took about ten minutes, then, of course, they had to wait for a new tyre to be fitted. It felt surreal, in a way, after their night of recriminations and revelations, to be somewhere as mundane as a garage; around normal people going about their normal activities. Stephen was chatting to Franco when he heard Emily's phone ring. He was aware of her answering it, looking over at him, then wandering off to the other side of the road to talk to whoever it was. She was still on the phone when Franco finished up with the new tyre and, eventually, Stephen walked over to her.

'Milly,' he said, to her back. 'Is everything okay?'

'It's Mum,' she said, turning around. 'She wants to talk to you.'

Whatever lightness Stephen had briefly enjoyed evaporated in a heartbeat but he reached out to take the phone. Emily didn't take her eyes off him as she said, 'Mum, he's here. I'm going to hand you over now. But also, I want you to know that when we see you, I've got something I have to talk to you about too.'

Chapter Twenty-Seven

Stephen walked across the car park in the midday sun. Then he went around the revolving doors, coming out onto the food concourse of the service station. It was the tail end of the lunchtime rush, and modest queues were still stretching back from the till points of Burger King, Chozen Noodle, KFC and Dunkin' Donuts; much of the seating area was taken up with people eating, or clearing their trays, and there was loud, echoing chatter to contend with. Yet Stephen spotted his mother after all of three seconds (and thirteen years). His eye honed in on her like a lamb to its mother across fields. She was sitting in a booth at Costa Coffee, ash-blonde hair clipped up, sleeveless blue blouse, rummaging in her handbag on the table in front of her. And what Stephen noticed in particular were her arms, which were slightly crêpey and pale, and how this did something to his heart, something he could not control. It was like sadness, pity and love rolled into one. They'd missed out on so much, the two of them.

He watched as she took something out of her bag – a mint or gum – put it in her mouth, then closed the bag, put it down on the seat next to her and subtly scanned the concourse, her fingers to her painted lips. Eventually, her small, dark eyes found his. Stephen swallowed and lifted a hand. He gave a little wave and she returned it with a hesitant smile. Then he walked over – his legs felt too light, like rolls of foam – and he pulled the chair out with a squeak and sat down opposite her. 'Hi,' he said, pulling in the chair which was too small for him so his knees were up high, jarring with the edge of the table.

'Hi, thanks for coming.' Her eyes were searching his face, her lips still smiling.

Stephen simply nodded.

'I got you a coffee,' she said, sliding the steaming mug over to him; Stephen noticed her hands were shaking. 'I hope that's okay?'

'Yeah, thank you.' Stephen cupped his hands around the mug, grateful for something to do with them.

'I presume you still have it black?' his mum said with a nervous half-laugh and Stephen said he did. 'I wasn't sure about the sugar, though, so I got some of that too,' she said, pushing two sachets over. Stephen tore the top off both and poured them in. Stirred.

His mum sighed, then she looked back at him and smiled thinly. 'You look well, Stephen. Healthier than the last time I—'

'Mum, it's been thirteen years since the last time.' Stephen made sure he looked directly at her when he said this.

She looked down at her coffee; even though she still had that prettiness she'd always had, neat, symmetrical features, and perfectly applied make-up, there were deep furrows on her forehead. They were the lines of someone who had lived a hard life. *It was a hard life you just let happen, though,* Stephen couldn't help thinking. *A life that was so unnecessary, all those bad choices you didn't have to make.*

'Stephen, I'm sorry I put the phone down,' said Alicia, still not looking up. 'I felt so terrible about that.'

Stephen looked out of the window again and had to stop himself giving a little puff of derision – was that all she felt bad about? Because there was plenty more to choose from. Then he remembered that she did have a reason – even if it wasn't a reason he agreed with, or indeed one that had any truth in it – for hating him still. Emily hadn't told her yet, after all, and there were no guarantees she would. He wasn't even sure he wanted her to.

'I was just shocked,' she said. 'So shocked and unprepared. I rang you back the next day but you'd left. I had no idea you were at Emily's. I don't know why she didn't tell me. Well, I do,' she corrected herself. 'But oh, Stephen, I wish she had.' There was a pause while they both took another sip of their coffee. Stephen could not bring himself to look at his mother. He didn't trust what might come out of her mouth yet and he was protecting himself, keeping some distance. 'The most important thing is, I didn't mean to put the phone down on you, you have to believe me. I was about to set about finding you, making contact. I'd been thinking about it for months. I was just plucking up the courage.'

'I thought you still hated me, that's why you put the phone down,' said Stephen, his voice flat. He was tearing up a receipt into tiny pieces. His mum closed her eyes and sighed so deeply, it was more like a groan. Then she leant forward. She still wore the St Christopher she'd worn since he was little, although the skin it lay on now was sun-aged – and it dangled over the table. 'Stephen, I never hated you,' she said. 'You're my son. I've never stopped loving you.'

Stephen felt a lump the size of an orange in his throat. How he'd longed to hear those words. How he'd fantasised about them, dreamt about them even. What if it was too little too late now? If that was true, it felt too sad to bear.

He put his elbows on the table and pressed the heels of his hands into his eye sockets, partly to stem the tears that he knew were on their way. 'Mum, why did you come here today?' he said. 'Why did you ask me here?' He could hardly bear to hear the answer, to look at her, for her to see his vulnerability, his need for her. His love.

She didn't say anything for some time and he feared she might not. Then, her voice choked, she said, 'Because you're my child. I can't go on any longer without you in my life. What happened was so long ago – I've had many years to think about what happened – and yes, it made my life very difficult, I can't deny that.'

'I don't think anyone could deny that,' said Stephen.

'But I am so full of guilt and regret . . .' – she closed her eyes and when she opened them, a tear fell down her cheek and off her lip – 'that I think it's slowly killing me.'

Stephen watched it land on the Formica table.

She quickly wiped both cheeks with her fingers. Her nails were painted the same blood-red that Stephen remembered from childhood. 'You know, I was going through some old photos the other day, and I came across one of you and Dad in the garden. You couldn't have been more than five. Dad's holding you up and you're both pointing at the new bird feeder we got, because you were so bleeding obsessed with them.' She laughed. 'As soon as you could open your eyes, practically. There are a couple of birds already on there – I couldn't tell you what they are. But the look on your faces . . .' She bit her lip and shook her head. 'It might as well have been a spaceship that had landed in the garden.'

Stephen did look up at her now and they were both smiling.

'I so envy you that, Stephen. I so admire you – the way you've always seen beauty. The way the simplest things have made you happy. Because all my wanting, wanting, wanting . . .' She squeezed her eyes shut as she said this, as if she could wish the 'wanting' away. 'It's only ever brought me misery. It only ever brought all of us misery.'

Stephen opened his mouth to say something but she put her hand gently on his. 'When I met you that day and you told me what Mitch had done, how he had made you feel, I already knew that. I already knew that my grass is greener attitude had brought that man into our lives and that what had happened was my fault. But I couldn't say it then. I couldn't admit it, even to myself, because it was too painful and I was a coward. So, I'm saying it now. If I could have my time again, none of this would have happened because I would have been able to see what I had already, I would have seen what was right in front of me, which was a good man and two beautiful children – both you and your sister already much better people than I ever was. But I didn't say it, did I? I've never said it in all these years. So, even though I forgive you wholeheartedly for what happened, I understand if you can't forgive me. I had to come and try, though.'

Stephen couldn't speak for the surge of emotion making its way from his chest to his throat, suffocating him, rendering him mute.

'Stephen, please say something,' his mother said then.

He could fight it no longer. He let *his* tears come. Then his mother stood up from her chair, she came around his side of the table, and she sat down next to him and put her arms around him. She smelt so good.

'Please forgive me,' she whispered. 'Can you forgive me?'

And Stephen laughed, even though he was crying. 'That's the second person who's asked my forgiveness in twenty-four hours,' he said.

'Why?' she said. 'Who's the other one?'

Chapter Twenty-Eight

Emily

I sat in the service station car park waiting for Stephen. It was quiet, save for a wood pigeon cooing somewhere like a lullaby, doors slamming and muffled kids' voices: families glad to break free of the claustrophobia of the car; to have a rest after hours on the road. I watched as one particular family – mum, dad, older boy and younger girl, the little girl skipping, holding her dad's hand – made their way towards the entrance and remembered with a smile how Stevie and I used to think service stations were the very epitome of thrilling, how they filled us with the excitement of the journey ahead and, of course, the destination.

I was so caught up in nostalgia that I lost sight of the present moment, why I was here at this service station today. Then I watched as the same family – the skipping little girl in her pink striped dress – went through the revolving doors inside and my heart rippled with nerves. How was it going in there? How long would he be?

Just before Stephen had got out of the car, he'd turned

to me and said, 'Milly, do this if you need to do it for yourself, but don't do it for me.'

And I'd thought about my mum in there – as I had for the past twenty-four hours since she'd called asking to meet us, asking to talk to her son for the first time in thirteen years. I thought about her face when I told her, what her reaction might be and, of course, of the myriad consequences, although to dwell too much on the latter, I knew, would be to drive myself mad, when right now I needed to be calm.

I remembered sitting in Mum's car in the prison car park all those years ago after that one and only visit to see Stephen. How she'd glared across at me, a wreck in the passenger seat. 'Well, I don't know why you're so upset, why you feel so sorry for him, it's not as if he hasn't ruined my life,' she'd said. And I cried because I knew it was me who had ruined her life.

The truth of what happened that June day had always been there, but I chose to believe another version – one I could cope with. The real version was far too awful, after all, and I had this other version readily at hand, a version that everyone kept telling me was *The One*: he did it, he was trouble, he had always clashed with his stepfather, something was bound to happen. And the more I heard and told this version, the more real it became to me until I had erased the real one, like painting over old wallpaper you don't like, with enough layers that you don't see it anymore.

Now I had to face it, to confess. The fact was, I had just found my brother, and was probably about to lose my mother. But I'd decided that a relationship built on truth with my brother meant more than a relationship built on a lie with her, and this was the right thing to do, the only thing to do. What was done was done and the only thing I could change, was this – the present. I could see that now. For nineteen years, this secret had lived inside me, so deep that it caused a constant dull ache. Now, it was a searing, insistent pain but I had a feeling that, like childbirth, it was a pain I had to go through to get to the beautiful thing on other side, which was the truth – my truth – and the only thing worth having.

Chapter Twenty-Nine

Stephen

Stephen unzipped the tent as slowly as he could so as not to wake Emily. It was just after 4 a.m. – pre-dawn – and the world was blue-washed and cool, the only source of light a lemon glow on the horizon, like a door left ajar.

Stephen stepped into his muddy walking boots, which he'd left outside the tent, rolled a cigarette and then began walking across the small campsite, the seagulls squawking exuberantly overhead, heralding the new day. By the time he'd finished, the sky was already two shades lighter, and he could just make out the curving spit of land in the distance, laid across the water like the tail of a sleeping dragon, the famous lighthouse halfway down.

He wound around the end of the field, out of the gate and onto the pathway that led to that lighthouse, some two miles in the distance. Either side of him the yellow gorse shone, and underfoot, the sand was fine as flour.

They'd come to Spurn – the peninsula that jutted out from the coast of East Yorkshire at a right angle, then dropped, as thin as an olive oil drizzle, into the North Sea.

Every summer, birders from all over the world came to see the spectacle that had earnt Spurn the title of 'Britain's swift capital' as flocks passed through on their way south to spend winter in Africa. Stephen had spoken to other birders about it; he'd watched the videos at the library and read the blogs. He knew how the swifts would come first in their tens, then hundreds, then finally in their thousands; great clouds of them wheeling down the peninsula, skimming over the sea. This north to south odyssey – or 'vis mig' (visible migration) as it was called in the birding community – passing off Spurn every year was an ornithological mystery: nobody could be really sure where these swifts had come from and where they were going. The general consensus was that most of them were young birds, just fledged that year from their nests in the highlands of Scotland and Scandinavia, and that they were making their first southerly trip of their lives, heading undaunted towards the warmth and the light.

Seeing this spectacle was the finale of their Top Five.

5. Watch the swifts' migration from the Spurn Peninsula.

Stephen could have gone any number of times in his life, he realised now. Hitch-hiked up to Spurn, one July. But he'd waited. Why? Because he'd wanted to do this with Milly, he'd wanted to keep their pact, just as he'd kept the physical list all these years. He must have had hope, always, that one day it would happen.

Wearing just his pyjama bottoms and hoodie, Stephen followed the pathway onto the strip of beach that led to Spurn Point – the far tip of the peninsula. To his right, the Humber Estuary was calm, but to his left, the North Sea crashed and churned. He stood for a while watching the sun rise over the sea. He'd watched a thousand sunrises in his life and yet now, he realised, he felt completely different.

Two and a half months had passed since the day they'd met Alicia in the service station, and in some ways that felt like yesterday – when the memory of his mother's smell came to him, for example, stopping him in his tracks – yet in others, a lifetime ago.

And in too many ways to count, it was. There was certainly a lifetime of healing to be done between the three of them. But work was already underway there. Work that could never have begun without the truth first.

Stephen waited until the sun was a fully fledged glowing orb, revealing the white caps of the waves, and the paleness of the sand. Then he turned, scrambled up the dunes and walked back to the tent where Emily was just emerging, befuddled with sleep and with a serious case of camping hair. Whilst she dressed, Stephen got a kettle going on the camping stove and they sat on the grass, still damp with dew, to drink their tea, Stephen marvelling at the vista before them: the way the sun was bleeding orange into the silver sea; the birds overhead already – gulls and terns and heavens knew what.

Emily sighed.

'Best part of the day, hey?' said Stephen pre-empting some deep and profound comment from his sister.

'Stephen Nelson,' she said in a mock 'serious reporter' tone. 'Been waking his sister up before dawn since 1987.'

Stephen snorted. 'It is dawn!' he said. 'Look at it, woman!'

'It's half past effing five,' she said, laughing too. 'This better be worth it.'

'Oh,' he said. 'It will. It's all going to be worth it.'

'El Paradiso'

Stephen stood at his kitchen window and set about preparing the salad: rocket and tomatoes and cucumber from his garden – the garden round the back of his house, El Paradiso. It had been the first thing he'd tended to when he'd moved in five months ago now, and the salads he'd made these last two weeks were the fruits of his first harvest. They tasted like heaven on a plate.

It was six o'clock on a still warm July evening and his guests would be here soon. He imagined their familiar forms: his sister with her sunlit halo of hair, Seth, with his reassuring height and his arm around her. His father, stooped now, thick butcher's hands at his sides, coming towards him across the edgelands.

He went out onto the wooden veranda. The evening was still close, the marshes lustrous and pea-green, the only sound the birds in conversation. Stephen inhaled the living air of the place, and was infused with it: this new feeling. A kind of exquisite contentment. It felt as if everything he had ever lost was coming back to him in that moment, all of it, coming home.

Acknowledgements

The writing of this book has been an epic journey. (Feeling not unlike a swift's migration over deserts and rough seas, at times!) I could not be happier that it's finally touched down and I can share it with you. Heartfelt thanks for it getting here go first to Sam Humphreys. Sam, you took this novel with all its flaws and weaknesses and helped me make it into something I'm really proud of. I want you to know how much I appreciate the talent and vision it takes to do that, and how grateful I am. Also, for your unwavering patience and sticking by me!

Same goes for Lizzy Kremer. Lizzy, your support, love and creative input means so much and helps me to continue doing what I love, which is to write and – lucky, lucky me – be published. I don't take any of it for granted.

I want to thank everyone at Mantle and David Higham for being so brilliant at their jobs. In no particular order: Rosie Friis, Samantha Fletcher, Alice Gray, Becky Lusher, Kaynat Begum, Lorraine Green, Christina Maria Webb. I hope I haven't left anyone out.

Huge thanks to Amanda Bergeron and all the wonderful team at Berkley. Also, to Grainne Fox. I'm so lucky to have so many amazing, creative women on my side.

Writing a novel about a homeless man who loves bird-watching when I knew nothing of both was ambitious – some may say foolish! All mistakes are of course my own, but I am indebted to the following for helping me to honour both experiences to the best of my ability: everyone at DENS, Hemel Hempstead, in particular, Ruth, Matt and Darren for being so generous in telling me their stories. Thanks also to Jonathan Brown, Toria Buzza, David Claydon, Janet Hardwick, Olly King, Esther Thompson and Colin Wiley for informing me on aspects of housing, politics and the law.

One of the unexpected gifts of writing this book has been a new appreciation for the genius and beauty of birds. I am very grateful to the following for their ornithological expertise and passion: Roger Busfield, Edward Mayer and John Smart from the wonderful Swift Conservation organization; Justin Quail; and Emma Norrington. Extra special thanks go to Vicky – what a gift to have you take the time to read this book and fact-check the birdy stuff. I am so grateful and in awe of your knowledge.

Thanks to all those who have read parts of this book and commented, listened to me talk about it (for several years) or helped in any way. It has been so long in the writing that I worry I have left people out, but huge gratitude to: Suzanne Cowie, Helen Nesbitt, my mum, dad and family, Louis Quail and our son Fergus, always, for their love and support. A special thank you goes to Jonathan Brown for his unwavering encouragement and invaluable input with this book, our hours of stimulating conversation about it, and for pushing me to do my very best, even when I'd run out of steam!

If you enjoyed *How To Find Your Way Home*,
why not try Katy Regan's previous novel, *Little Big Love*

Liam Jones is the love of Juliet's life. He was her brother's best friend first, then hers, then the father of her son. In those shining weeks after Zac was born, she'd never been happier, and neither had Liam.

Until the night he disappeared without a trace.

Zac is now ten, and collects facts: octopuses have three hearts; the world's heaviest man weighed over 100 stone; only three species of animal have a blue tongue. The one piece of information he really wants, though, is the truth about why his father left.

His family refuse to talk about that night, but when Juliet inadvertently admits to Zac that Liam is the only man she's ever loved, Zac decides to find him and give his mum a second chance at a happy ever after.

After all, nothing can stand in the way of true love . . . Or can it?

Turn the page to read an extract

New Year's Eve 2015

Dear Liam (maybe one day I will call you Dad but not yet),

This is your son, Zac. I am writing this letter to give you an opportunity. I know you did a runner just before I was born and weren't interested in being my dad but how could you decide if we'd never met? I didn't know I wanted to be Teagan's friend until she moved onto the same estate as me. Luckily she was nice but she could have been really annoying.

I don't want to be offensive but I have been really angry with you since the day my mum and me went on the promenade train in Cleethorpes when I was three and my mum told me you existed. I don't know why you didn't want to see me or even phone me if I was your child. You have never even sent me a birthday card. (In case you don't know, my birthday is 25 May.) What kind of dad doesn't send their kid a birthday card?

So I am giving you the opportunity to come to my party when I'm eleven. It's five months away so lots of time to organize it. If you have any more children, you could bring them, as long as they like Toby Carvery because that's where I'm going.

BE WARNED: my mum is really mad with you and my nan says you make her sick, but I am willing to give you a chance.

My grandad says, 'Don't knock it till you've tried it,' and I agree. For example, I never used to like mushrooms but now I would have them on my death row dinner. I think if you met me you'd change your mind too.

Please write back.
From Zac

PS Just so you know, you can only get two slices of meat at Toby Carvery but you can have as many vegetables and Yorkshire puddings as you want.

Chapter One

Zac

Fact: There are only three animals in the world that have a blue tongue: a chow-chow dog, a blue-tongued lizard and a black bear.

So I'd already written to my dad on New Year's Eve, bu deciding to look for him only started, really, the night of my mum's Date from Hell. She kicked everything off that spring she made everything start happening that would change ou lives for the better and make them brilliant. She says it wa me that did it, but it wasn't, it was her. (Even though sh was drunk, it was still her.) That's the only good thing abou wine, I suppose. It can sometimes help you to tell the truth

Grimsby, early February 2016

Sam Bale's dad was walking across our estate in the snow It was just him with his big furry hood up. He could hav been trekking across the North Pole.

'How many points would you give him, then?' I said.

'What, Sam's dad?' said Teagan. 'None. No way. He's been in prison for fighting people, he has.'

'He's rich, though,' I said.

'How do you know?'

'He's got a bath that's a jacuzzi – and he's got a gold car. Imagine how much that would cost. A gold car!'

Me and Teagan were high up, leaning out of her bedroom window playing the dad game. Teagan's my best friend. She lives on our estate but in one of the high blocks on the seventh floor where you can see the whole of Grimsby, even to the sea. We live in a boring old maisonette with only two floors, but it's nicer than Teagan's inside because my mum can work, whereas Teagan's mum's got this disease where she's tired all the time, so if you weigh everything up, it comes out equal.

I was round at hers for a sleepover because my mum was on a date. I don't usually go round to people's houses for sleepovers on a school night, but then my mum doesn't usually go on dates. This was her first in a year and a half. Before that, she was going out with Jason but they split up because there was no chemistry.

The dad game is something me and Teagan made up after Teagan's dad left her mum – and Teagan, and her sister Tia – for Gayle from Ladbrokes. Since then, she hasn't seen her dad much. Teagan's dead angry with her dad and thinks she'll have to get a new one eventually.

My dad did a runner just before I was born, but Mum always said we had a lucky escape because he was waste of space. So I'd like to get a proper dad too some day, and me and Teagan thought it would be good t work out what sort of dad would be best.

Our game's called Top Trumps for Dads. It's just lik normal Top Trumps, except we give scores based on hov good a dad we think someone would be: how kind, stric or funny they are; if they're rich and could take us o adventures; if they'd be able to stick up for us in a figh – and not a fight like Sam Bale's dad's been in, but proper one, where you're fighting for something wort it, not just for the sake of it.

Teagan writes down scores for the dads in our speci file. So far, Jacob Wilmore's dad scores the highest. He got a six-pack and a Porsche and he's just a really nic man. He used to play football professionally and now h sometimes coaches the under-elevens. I wish I was goo at football, just so I could see him more. We've finishe doing all the dads at school now, though, so we're scor ing others we know like Sam Bale's.

'He might be rich, Zac, but he's still been in prison said Teagan. 'There's no point having a dad in prison a the time, you'd never get to see him.'

'Yeah, and when you went to visit him, you wouldn be able to touch him and you'd have to be careful becaus he might be in with all the murderers.'

'And he'd have to wear an orange suit,' said Teagan. 'I've seen it on *Coronation Street*.'

As well as living on the Harlequin Estate with me, Teagan's at the same school as me but in a different class, so on Mondays and Thursdays, when I'm not at Nan and Grandad's, we sometimes play together after tea. We like playing 'The Olympics', where Teagan does her gymnastics on The Bars (three metal bars, basically, all of different heights, in the middle of our estate) and I do the commentary. *This is Teagan O'Brien on the bars, for the United Kingdom*. When it's cold or rainy, though, we like leaning out of her bedroom window and looking at all of Grimsby like we own it. Our estate is at the edge of the town near the sea (it's not actually the sea, it's the Humber estuary, but it goes into the North Sea). But don't go thinking there's a beach like there is at Cleethorpes – it's not like that. If you look at where the sea meets the town in Grimsby, from high up here in Teagan's flat, you can just see loads of cranes and boat masts, with the Dock Tower in the middle, poking out like a red rocket. The line where the water meets the town goes in and out where all the different trawlers have their parking spots. Our town is a fishing port. It used to be the greatest fishing port in the world back when my great-grandad was a fisherman, in the glory days. But then there were the Cod Wars where Iceland and our country rowed about who was allowed to fish where, and that ruined everything basically.

'Hey, if you squint your eyes and look at all the snow, I said, closing one eye, the way Mr Singh from Costcutte does when you go in there and he pretends to be asleep 'you could be in Canada.'

'Jacob Wilmore's been to Canada. He told me it wa boring,' said Teagan.

'I bet it's not, I bet it's amazing.' The snow was amaz ing here too, if you looked closely. It wasn't white, it wa loads of different colours. That's because it's actually frozen droplets of water reflecting the light. I told Teagan this. 'It's the same for polar bears,' I said. 'Their fur's no white either, it's transparent, it just reflects the light s it looks all dazzling. Underneath, their skin is black and under that are eleven centimetres of fat.'

'No way. *Eleven* centimetres?'

'Well, you'd need eleven centimetres of fat if you lived in the Arctic.'

'It's like living in the Arctic in this house,' said Teagan 'And where's my eleven centimetres?'

She leant further out of the window. She makes me nervous when she does that, because she's so light, she could flutter away like a crisp packet. Teagan might be the smallest in our year but she's not scared of anything ever. I'm scared most of the time. Sometimes it feels like our bodies have been swapped around.

I leant a little bit further out too. The cold was lovely, t crept right through your clothes, and the moon was range with this sad, kind face.

'I wonder what my mum's doing now,' I said.

'Why, where is she?' asked Teagan, flicking her hair ound. Teagan's hair is her best feature, like mine is my yes. It's chocolate-coloured and wavy.

'On a date,' I said.

'What, with a man?'

'No, a chimpanzee,' I said and Teagan laughed. She's ot this mad, crazy laugh; you can't help joining in. I adn't said anything to Teagan because I didn't want to inx it, but I was really worried about my mum's date. I vanted it to go well so badly that I'd prayed on *Factblaster* efore I came out. Grandad always gets me a present just rom him at Christmas, and last Christmas it was a book alled *Factblaster*. *Every fact you've ever wanted to know, nswered!* it says on the front. It's totally awesome. I hink it's got lucky powers. I love my facts like I love my ooking. Out of my class, I'm probably second best at acts after Jacob, who knows literally everything but hat's because his dad works on the rigs so can afford to ake him all over.

My mum's date was with a man called Dom. He knows ny aunty Laura (she's not my real aunty, she's my mum's est friend – I just call her Aunty) and he's got a sports ar. My mum really needs a boyfriend. She loves me to

bits but we need a man in the house and, also, I liked
better when she was going out with Jason. I kind of mi
him. Maybe I even loved him.

Teagan sighed. 'Rather her than me,' she said.

'What do you mean?'

'I mean, rather your mum than me going on a date. I'
not going on any dates when I'm older. I'm not going
have a husband or even a boyfriend.'

'Why not?' I said.

''Cause men are stupid idiots, that's why. You won't b
obviously. But that's because you're different.'